SIFTING THROUGH CLUES

A COOKBOOK NOOK MYSTERY

SIFTING THROUGH CLUES

DARYL WOOD GERBER

WHEELER PUBLISHING
A part of Gale, a Cengage Company

Wheeler Publishing Large Print Softcover Cozy Mysteries.
The text of this Large Print edition is unabridged.
Other aspects of the book may vary from the original edition.
Set in 16 pt. Plantin.

LIBRARY OF CONGRESS CIP DATA ON FILE.
CATALOGUING IN PUBLICATION FOR THIS BOOK
IS AVAILABLE FROM THE LIBRARY OF CONGRESS.

ISBN-13: 978-1-4328-9081-0 (softcover alk. paper)

Published in 2021 by arrangement with Beyond the Page, LLC.

Printed in the United States of America
1 2 3 4 5   25 24 23 22 21

*Thank you from the bottom of my heart
to my dear sweet friend Jori,
who has been there for me
through thick and thin.*

ACKNOWLEDGMENTS

"Life is not easy for any of us. But what of that? We must have perseverance and, above all, confidence in ourselves. We must believe that we are gifted for something, and that this thing, at whatever cost, must be obtained."

~ Marie Curie

I have been truly blessed to have the support and input of so many as I pursue my creative journey.

Thank you to my family and friends for all your encouragement. Thank you to my talented author friends, Krista Davis and Hannah Dennison, for your words of wisdom. Thank you to my Plothatcher pals: Janet (Ginger Bolton), Kaye George, Marilyn Levinson (Allison Brook), Peg Cochran, Janet Koch (Laura Alden), and Krista Davis. It's hard to keep all your aliases straight, but you are a wonderful pool of talent and a terrific wealth of ideas, jokes, stories, and fun! I adore you. Thanks to my blog mates on Mystery Lovers Kitchen: Cleo Coyle, Krista Davis, Leslie Budewitz, Roberta Isleib (Lucy Burdette), Peg Cochran, Linda Wiken (Erika Chase), Denise Swanson, and Sheila Connolly. I love your passion for food as well as for books. Thanks to my Cake and Dagger and Delicious Mystery author pals, Julie Hyzy, Jenn McKinlay, Roberta Isleib, Krista Davis, and Amanda Flower. I love your creative enthusiasm via social media.

Thank you to my online Facebook fan-based groups, Cake and Daggers and Delicious Mysteries. I love how willing you are to read ARCs, post reviews, and help me promote whenever possible. Authors need fans like you. You keep us on our toes.

Thanks to those who have helped make this eighth book in the Cookbook Nook Mystery series come to fruition: my publishers, Bill Harris and Jessica Faust at Beyond the Page; my agent, John Talbot; my cover artist, Dar Albert; and my biggest supporter, Kimberley Greene. Thanks to Madeira James for maintaining constant quality on my website. Thanks to my virtual assistants, Sheridan Stancliff and Marie McNary, for your novel ideas. Honestly, without all of you, I don't know what I would do. Eat too many bonbons, most likely.

Last but not least, thank you librarians, teachers, and readers for sharing the delicious world of a cookbook nook owner in a fictional coastal town in California with your friends. I hope you enjoy this next installment.

~ CAST OF CHARACTERS ~

MAIN CHARACTERS

Jenna Hart, owner of the Cookbook Nook and Nook Café

Bailey Bird Martinez, works at the Cookbook Nook

Cary Hart, Jenna's dad, owns Nuts and Bolts

Cinnamon Pritchett, chief of police

Gran, aka Gracie Goldsmith, regular customer at the shop

Jake Chapman, wealthy friend of Cary's

Katie Casey, executive chef at the Nook Café

Lola Bird, Bailey's mother and owner of Pelican Brief Diner

Marlon Appleby, deputy who is dating Aunt Vera

Pepper Pritchett, owner of Beaders of Paradise, mother to Cinnamon

Rhett Jackson, owner of Bait and Switch Sport Supply, dating Jenna

Tina Gump, works at Cookbook Nook

Tito Martinez, reporter, married to Bailey
Vera Hart, Jenna's aunt, co-owner of the Cookbook Nook and Nook Café
Z. Z. "Zoey" Zeller, mayor of Crystal Cove

OTHERS WHO LIVE AND WORK IN CRYSTAL COVE

Alastair Dukas, clerk at Spellbinder Book Shop

Bucky Winston, fireman now married to Cinnamon

Crusibella Queensberry, owner of Spellbinder Book Shop

Darian Drake, librarian

Eleanor Landry, owner of Taste of Heaven Ice Cream Shoppe

Flora Fairchild, owner of Home Sweet Home

Hank Hemmings, owner of Great Threads Haberdashery

Ivy Beale, owner of Dreamcatcher, a healing stones and crystal store

Keller Landry, ice cream entrepreneur, married to Katie

Oren Michaels, local fishmonger

Reynaldo, head chef at Nook Café

Thad, owner of Play Room Toy Store

Wayne, assistant manager at Vines, a wine bistro

Yung Yi, bank manager of Crystal Cove
bank

"It is perhaps both a blessing and a curse that fictional worlds spring into my mind nearly fully formed, and it takes quite a while to sift through everything to find the story."

~ Erin Morgenstern

CHAPTER 1

"Ow, ow, ow!" Bailey hopped on one foot. I feared if she bounced any more she would drop the baby then and there. She was five weeks from her due date, but the way her belly was pressing against her denim jumper made me think the baby might pop out at any second. "Paper cut! Jenna, do something."

I raced across the Nook Café and helped my pal into a chair by the window. For the past hour, I had been filling newly installed bookshelves with cookbooks that our customers could browse while dining, including a couple of terrific selections that were perfect for tea parties, *The Afternoon Tea Collection* and *Afternoon Tea at Home: Deliciously indulgent recipes for sandwiches, savouries, scones, cakes and other fancies.* My aunt insisted that everyone should know how to serve a proper tea.

To keep me company, Bailey had been as-

17

sembling construction paper cookbooks that children could decorate at the children's table in the Cookbook Nook.

"Don't get blood on the tablecloth," I warned. It was only eight in the morning but fresh white linens had been set out the night before. "Drink in the view while I get a Band-Aid." I hurried to the café kitchen and retrieved the first aid kit.

"Pain," Bailey mumbled, sucking on her finger while staring out the window at the ocean. "Pain, pain, pain."

"If that's painful, wait until childbirth," I teased.

"Not. Looking. Forward. To. It."

"Remember our motto." I pointed to a sign I'd posted on the café's entrance yesterday: *We breathe to live. We live to read.*

She stuck out her tongue. "I'm breathing. I'm also anticipating the birth, the terrible twos, high school prom, and college tuition."

I applied the Band-Aid and rubbed her shoulder. "Why don't you take the day off?"

"Over a paper cut? Get serious." She bounded to her feet. "Let's go. You're done here, right? We have so much to do." She trotted along the enclosed breezeway that connected the café to the Cookbook Nook. Over her shoulder she said, "We need to set out all the culinary-themed fiction we just received, plus we have to tweak the book club display. C'mon. Chop-chop."

"I'm right behind you."

The mayor had designated the last few days in April as Book Club Bonanza. Starting tomorrow, Saturday, the inns and hotels would be filled to the max with book club members from all over the West Coast. Tomorrow night, the Mystery Mavens, one of Crystal Cove's local book clubs, of which I was a member, were putting on a progressive dinner event, meaning its more than twenty members would travel from one house to the next dining on appetizers, tea sandwiches, entrées, and desserts while discussing the culinary cozy mystery we'd agreed to read: *The Diva Serves High Tea*. The selection won out over two others: *Death on the Menu* and *Goodbye Cruller World*. I'd purchased a copy of each. I'd almost finished the first, and I couldn't wait to read the other two.

"Ooh, sugar cookies." Bailey paused by the table where Chef Katie had set out treats for customers. "How cute. They look like little books. Which one should I choose?"

"The red one." The cookies were iced in an assortment of primary colors. "Did you read the *Diva* book?" I asked. My neighbor

Crusibella Queensberry, whom I'd only recently learned owned Spellbinder Book Shop, had made the selection. For some reason, whenever I'd gone into her shop, I'd dealt with one of her assistants and not seen her. Each week during spring, Crusibella planned to feature a different mystery genre at the store. This week: culinary cozies. Right up my alley.

"Absolutely," Bailey said. "I'm not missing the event."

"Don't tell me how it ends. I've got three chapters left to read." I'd belonged to a book club when I'd lived and worked in San Francisco, and invariably one or two members wouldn't have completed the assignment. I refused to be that person.

"Don't worry. The ladies agreed no spoilers."

"After a little wine, someone is bound to reveal the end."

"Well, I'm not drinking wine." She chose a cookie and ate it in two bites. Visibly, the little being inside her belly moved. "Is it just me, or does this kid like sugar a lot more than I do?"

"The doctor told you to abstain from eating salt."

"I miss French fries." She petted her

tummy and cooed words I couldn't make out.

I smiled. Bailey had been reluctant to have a child, but her husband had really wanted one. Minutes after she learned she was pregnant, her fear disappeared. She'd been enjoying the experience ever since. Even if she couldn't eat salty foods.

"Speak of the devil. There's Crusibella." I pointed out the picture window toward the parking lot.

Fisherman's Village, the quaint shopping mall where the Cookbook Nook and the Nook Café were located, consisted of a number of shops as well as Cameo, an art house theater, and Vines, a wine bistro. Crusibella, dressed in a silky blue frock that matched the blue streaks in her hair, was chatting with Pepper Pritchett, who owned Beaders of Paradise, the shop cattycorner from ours.

"Pepper looks peeved," Bailey whispered.

Pepper was an expert craftswoman who gave lessons and made nearly all of her own clothes.

"What do you bet they're arguing about what they're serving at the book club?" I joked. Just the other day, I'd overheard Pepper brag that she was making an exquisite cheese appetizer.

"Uh-oh. Sparks will fly." Bailey giggled.

As she went ahead of me into the shop, I noticed movement outside, beyond the women. Someone in a tan jacket with shaggy brown hair ducked out of sight. Man or woman, I couldn't tell.

"Jenna!" Bailey called. "Come here. I need your help."

I glanced at the parking lot again. I didn't see anyone besides the two women. Maybe whoever it was had dropped a set of car keys. I put the moment from my mind and joined Bailey, who was moving aside the one-foot Plexiglas wall that bordered the window display. Without the wall, children's eager fingers could really mess things up.

Tigger, my ginger cat, dashed to us and swatted his tail against Bailey's leg.

"I don't need *your* help, cat," Bailey chided. "Just your mom's. Go back to sleep."

Tigger slinked to his favorite spot beneath the children's table in the rear corner of the shop and curled into a ball.

"Look at the display." Bailey motioned to it. "What's missing?"

On top of a beautiful lilac-themed table-cloth, I'd set a pair of white three-tiered cake stands and filled them with artfully made porcelain candies and cookies. I'd added lavender cocktail napkins as well as a colorful array of cookie cutters, useful to design tea sandwiches. Two fine-boned china cups and saucers finished the display.

"Cookbooks," I said. "Let's add a few dessert cookbooks, like *Afternoon Tea: Delicious Recipes for Scones, Savories & Sweets.* The beautiful purple-and-rose cover will do nicely with the color scheme. And *Teatime Parties: Afternoon Tea to Commemorate the Milestones of Life.*"

"Oh, I love that one," Bailey said. "The pictures are gorgeous, and it teaches you how to steep tea properly. I had no idea there was a method. I thought . . . *Oof.*" The baby kicked. Bailey flinched. "All right already." She pointed to her stomach. "The little general is telling me to get my rear in gear. Books!" She headed to the storage room.

As I was leafing through the new fiction we'd ordered for the visiting book clubs, I heard a *tap-tap* on the front door. Ivy Beale, a petite forty-something with bobbed platinum blond hair, was peering through the glass, hands framing her elegantly beautiful, aging model's face. Beside her was Oren Michaels, a local fisherman who supplied fish to the Nook Café. Towering over her, he reminded me of the handsome seafarer we'd used in a commercial for Old Spice when I worked as an advertising executive at Taylor & Squibb.

Oren said something to Ivy and grinned. She elbowed him playfully.

"Jenna?" Ivy called. "May I come in? I know it's early. Pretty please?"

Ivy owned Dreamcatcher, a healing stones and crystals store. I'd purchased a few items there for my brother and sister as well as for a few friends. Invariably whenever I went in, Ivy would share a secret she knew about someone in town, like who'd had a face-lift or who'd been in rehab or who'd had an affair. *Quirky* was the word my aunt had used to describe her. I liked quirky. Ivy made me laugh.

I opened the door. "What's up?"

"Oh, bless you." She pressed her hands together in prayer. "I absolutely must find a cookbook so I can make some new goodies for tomorrow. Everything I cook is passé. You must have something." She breezed past me toward the dessert aisle, the flaps of her smoky gray cashmere duster batting me in her wake.

Oren stayed outside and scrolled through messages on his cell phone.

"We're not open yet," I said.

"I won't be a moment. You don't mind,

do you?" She took a book from an end-cap display and recited the title, "*Dessert for Two: Small Batch Cookies, Brownies, Pies, and Cakes.* This looks good."

"Good choice," I said. "The author makes it easy to scale back on tried and true recipes."

She flipped through it. "Mm. Salted caramel macarons, lemon meringue pie cookies, and forgotten cookies. Say, those sound mysterious. You know I love a mystery." She clapped the book closed. "Sold."

"The cash register isn't ready yet."

She whipped two twenty-dollar bills from the pocket of her linen trousers. "Bring me the change tomorrow. I trust you." She blew me an air kiss and left as quickly as she'd arrived. For a moment, I wondered if she'd been the person ducking behind cars when Pepper and Crusibella were going at it. Maybe she had donned a tan jacket and wig as a disguise. Was that how she gleaned so many secrets? Had Oren been hiding with her? Maybe it was a lark for the two of them.

Shaking my head, I went back to my chore.

Soon after, my aunt Vera waltzed into the shop clad in a silver caftan that I couldn't recall having seen before. She habitually wore the billowy garments because she offered her services as a fortune-teller and felt her clients trusted her readings more if she dressed the part. Plus, she liked comfy. She carried her matching turban under one arm.

"Good morning, dear." She raked her red hair off her face, which made the multiple bracelets she wore clang. "Was that Ivy Beale who just drove off?"

"Yes. She absolutely had to buy a new cookbook this instant." I laughed. "She's a bit bossy, don't you think?"

"Ivy gets what Ivy wants. She always has, ever since she stepped foot in this town. It's an attitude that comes from wealth. Too-ra-loo," she crooned. "Gorgeous day, isn't it?" She focused on me. "I detect a lot of yellow energy around you. That means it's going to be a spiritual yet playful day. Have fun."

Recently, I'd found a website that sold T-shirts featuring book slogans. I figured for Book Club Bonanza, I should wear a few. Today's was, yes, *yellow* and read: *Good things come to those who read.*

My aunt sashayed past me toward the storage room. "Don't you look darling and young, by the way. All of twelve."

"Ha!" I was pushing thirty-one, but in jeans and a T-shirt, I looked younger. Maybe twenty-five. Not twelve.

"Have you seen all the tents going up on

Buena Vista Boulevard?" she asked after storing her purse.

BVB was the main drag in Crystal Cove. It ran from the north end of town near the lighthouse to the south end, which was marked by a pier that featured a carousel, carney games, shops, and restaurants. The Pacific Ocean lay to the west.

"There are a variety of them," my aunt went on, "hosted by regional booksellers as well as used booksellers. A few book clubs have put up tents, too, to encourage membership. No cookbook sellers, by the way."

I grinned. "Good thing."

"Crystal Cove Library has knocked it out of the park, by the way. Its tent is situated next to the dolphins." At the center of town where Crystal Cove Road met Buena Vista Boulevard stood a statue of dancing dolphins. "The tent is as colorful as a kaleidoscope. There are all sorts of vendors selling gift items, too. I spotted ornate bookstands, handmade bookmarks, elegant journals, and personalized storybooks for children. And there are bright banners featuring all the books the clubs are reading this week. I noticed some foodie favorites including *Chocolat,* as well as some heavier reading like *Beowulf* and *The Canterbury Tales* for the literary set. It's so invigorating." Her

27

enthusiasm was infectious.

I joined her at the sales counter. "You must have had a good sleep. You're oozing positive vibes."

"Positive is as positive does," she chirped. "What's on the schedule?"

I ticked off the items on my to-do list. Finish displays. Restock shelves. Set up the children's table for a cookbook-making session. Each child would be able to create a little book of recipes woven together with ribbon. Bailey was leading it. We were providing the recipes.

"Where's Tina?" my aunt asked.

Tina Gump was the twenty-something clerk we'd hired last year. She dreamed of becoming a chef and was taking culinary classes at night school. She hoped to do well enough to apply to a full-fledged culinary school within two years.

"I gave her the day off. She has midterms."

"All righty then. What would you like me to do, boss?" Aunt Vera asked.

She was teasing, of course. Tina called me *boss,* but I wasn't my aunt's boss. She and I owned the shop together. That hadn't been our arrangement at first, when I'd given up my advertising job in the city, a local term for San Francisco, and moved home to help her open the store and café. However, after a year or so, when she realized she couldn't have made a success of the shop without my help, she decided to spread the wealth and made me part owner. She'd made a ton of money during the seventies, having invested well in the stock market. Recently, she'd added Bailey and Chef Katie as limited partners. Both were my lifelong friends, and I was thrilled that she'd thought to include them.

"How about straightening up the aprons and kitchen items?" I suggested.

The Cookbook Nook was a culinary bookshop. Primarily, we sold cookbooks and food-related fiction, but we also sold a variety of fun kitchen items, including saltshakers and peppermills, aprons, cookie jars, and more. For this week, I'd ordered things I thought book club members might like: literary-themed serving trays and literary coffee mugs. My favorite saying engraved on a tray was: *There is no friend as loyal as a book.* And on one of the mugs: *I'm a book dragon, not a worm.* Too cute. Before I'd even pulled them from the storage room, Bailey had set aside one of the trays for her mother, who was an avid reader.

"Jenna?" Pepper pushed through the front door. "Too early to come in?"

"No, it's fine," I replied. Ivy had already

descended upon us. What was one more? Besides, a fellow shopkeeper was always welcome. "New haircut?" Her silver hair was feathered around her face. She usually wore it in a boxier cut.

She primped. "Do you like it?"

"It takes years off."

She blushed crimson with delight.

"I like your knit dress, too. Very slimming." It was blue and white with vertical stripes. As ever, she'd added extensive beading around the neckline. "Did you make it?"

She adjusted her teensy cross-body purse. "Of course." I had expected her to say as much. She was a whiz at every craft. "Do you have any coffee? My machine is on the fritz. I'm desperately in need of caffeine."

"In the breezeway."

"Lifesaver!" She ran off to fetch a cup of coffee.

When Pepper and I had first met, she'd assailed me. At the time, I had no idea that she'd held a long-standing beef against my father. Years earlier, she'd been in love with him. When she lost him to my mother, she was heartbroken. Soon after, she met someone else and bore a daughter, Cinnamon — our current chief of police — but she'd held a grudge.

Pepper returned with a to-go cup in hand.

"I can't wait for tomorrow," she said. "Four houses. Four meals. Four delicious chats about the mystery. I loved the book, by the way. Did you?"

I nodded. Far be it from me to tell her I hadn't quite finished. I would tonight. No *ifs, ands,* or *buts.* "Pepper, what were you and Crusibella, um, *talking* about a bit ago?"

"It was nothing." She took a sip of her coffee. "We were coordinating tomorrow's events. You know the order we're going in, right? We're starting at Flora's, then on to Z.Z.'s."

Flora Fairchild owned Home Sweet Home. Zoey Zeller, whom everyone called Z.Z., was our mayor.

"Then we're moving on to Gran's."

Gran — a.k.a. Gracie Goldsmith — was one of our best customers. She owned an extensive set of cookbooks that any collector would covet.

"Last up will be Ivy Beale's place."

Aunt Vera joined us, a couple of freshly pressed aprons featuring a stack of library books in hand. "I can't wait to see Ivy's house. I hear it's quite something."

Pepper said, "Just between us, Ivy isn't much of a cook, so we're crossing our fingers."

31

"She buys a lot of cookbooks," I countered.

"To read." Pepper sniggered. "Hopefully, she'll purchase everything for the dessert leg of the evening from the local bakery."

We had a number of great candy stores and bakeries in town.

I said, "I'm baking my contribution tonight. Chocolate coffee cupcakes."

"Those sound yummy," Aunt Vera said. "I love coffee in anything."

"Pepper, back to you and Crusibella . . ." I signaled for her to continue. I didn't believe for a second her story about them coordinating the event.

"Honestly, it was nothing," she said. "I'd agreed to bring a cheese appetizer, and guess what she wanted to bring? A cheese platter." She grumbled. "How much cheese can we eat? Flora approved my offering."

"Don't worry," I assured her. "Everyone loves cheese."

Pepper grumbled. "Crusibella can be so stubborn. She thinks that chakra thing she has going always makes her right."

Crusibella was very spiritual. She could talk nonstop about inner peace and keeping oneself in balance. Nothing horrible ever went into or *onto* her body. Foods or body products had to be pure and organic.

"These are pretty." Pepper moved to one of the displays of tiered cake servers and picked up a pair of scrolled tongs. "They're perfect for a tea party. Wherever did you find them, Jenna?"

"Through our distributor. I thought it would be nice to have a few party items in stock."

"Wish I'd seen them before Cinnamon tied the knot."

Her daughter married an adorable fireman on Valentine's Day. In a barn. On the top of a hill with a 360-degree view. I'd been her matron of honor. The event was magical.

Pepper's cell phone jangled. She pulled it from her purse and stared at the screen. "Are you kidding me?" Her voice skated upward. "Are. You. Kidding. Me!"

"What's wrong?" my aunt asked.

"Ivy Beale, how dare you!" Pepper tapped what appeared to be a text message.

"What'd she do?" I asked. "Bow out of the progressive dinner?"

Pepper waggled her cell phone. "According to Flora, Ivy was flirting with my fiancé."

I gasped. "Hank asked you to marry him?"

"Not yet. But he will." More text tapping.

Trying to ease the tension, I said, "Pepper, c'mon. You know Flora can be quite the gossip and often mistaken. Besides, flirting is harmless. And Hank is quite charming."

Hank Hemmings owned Great Threads, a haberdashery shop. He always had a twinkle in his eye, and he could tell the greatest stories, the kind that reeled you in.

"I'm sure lots of women flirt with him," Aunt Vera agreed. "Young and old."

Like my aunt, Pepper and Hank were in their sixties.

"Even if flirting is harmless, that's not the point," Pepper said, nostrils flared. "Ivy has her own boyfriend. That fisherman. You know him."

"Oren Michaels."

"That's the one. Your fiancé equips him, even though he's the competition."

My fiancé, Rhett Jackson, owned Bait and Switch Fishing Supply and Sport Store on the Pier. When not running his shop, he often fished and sold whatever he caught to local restaurants. Selling fish wasn't his primary business; he did it because he enjoyed it.

"Plus," Pepper went on, "the guy who works for Ivy is head over heels for her. He's an Adonis and very young."

"He's almost my age," I said.

"I rest my case." Pepper flapped a hand. "She's got *two* men in love with her. Both are gorgeous. Why does she need to flirt with my guy?"

I put a hand on her shoulder. "Relax. Hank is head over heels for you, too. He won't abandon you."

Pepper winced, making me immediately regret my choice of words. Her first husband, Cinnamon's father, had split the day Cinnamon was born.

"Ivy always gets what she wants. Always. Ooh!" Pepper wielded the tongs and lunged as if in a duel. "How I'd like to run her through."

CHAPTER 2

After work, Rhett had come over to help me make the chocolate coffee cupcakes — my contribution to the book club progressive dinner.

As I was sifting the flour into the bowl, a billow of it *poofed* upward and dusted my face.

Rhett leaned forward. "Don't you look cute. Like a snowman." He buffed my nose.

"Stop," I begged.

He reached toward the mixing bowl. "Can I taste?"

"Uh-uh," I warned. "Not before it's mixed. And definitely not before I take a taste." I tapped the back of an ice cream scooper on his hand.

"Spoilsport," he said.

"Always."

He nuzzled my cheek with his hint of a five o'clock shadow, which sent a swizzle of desire down to my toes. I pressed him away and gazed at him. Broad shoulders, strong chin, stunning eyes. Would I ever tire of being with him?

"Try this if you want something sweet." I dipped a spoon into the chocolate coffee buttercream icing I'd made and touched it to his lips.

"More," he begged.

"Later." I tossed the spoon into the sink, added the wet ingredients to the dry, and mixed until combined. "Please set the cupcake baking tray next to the sink." I hitched my chin.

He did so. I'd fitted the tray with pretty silver cupcake liners.

"Do I get to insert the stickers after you ice?" he asked.

"Absolutely." I'd found book-themed cupcake toppers on Etsy. The artist had fashioned them after covers of cozy mystery titles. Adorable. "Give me elbow room or I'll make a mess." My kitchen was small, in keeping with the dimensions of my little cottage. The eating nook was barely big enough for a modest table and chairs.

Laughing, he moved to the refrigerator. "Glass of wine?"

"Definitely." We'd eaten a light dinner of chicken, salad, and sparkling water. A glass of chardonnay would be a nice finish.

"You look pretty tonight," he said.

I'd replaced my T-shirt with a loose-fitting white shirt.

"I like the new haircut, too," he added.

I had straight brown hair that usually fell to my shoulders. I'd allowed my stylist to cut off two inches.

"You don't look so bad yourself." I still remembered the moment I'd set eyes on him. He looked very similar to the way he did now: fisherman's sweater, jeans that fit just right, tousled brown hair. And that dazzling smile. "Though you look a tad tired."

"Inventory." He moaned. "Every one of my staff hates doing it, which makes for a major case of the grumps. We're starting fresh tomorrow morning at four."

"You should get going then." He and I were living in our own places until we got married. We weren't old-fashioned; we just didn't want to be crowding each other. Our places were both small. Two months ago, we'd tried to purchase a house, not on the beach like mine and not in the mountains like his. A fixer-upper in town near Azure Park. It sold at auction. We lost. We were still looking, but to date, nothing had caught our eye.

"I'm not leaving until I score a cupcake." Rhett handed me a wineglass and tapped his glass to the rim. "Cheers."

I took a sip and resumed filling the cupcake liners. Katie had suggested I use an ice cream scooper. She said it created the perfect portion.

Rhett swiveled a chair at the kitchen table so he could face me. In seconds, Tigger was in his lap. "I have an idea," he said, scratching the cat's chin. "For the wedding. Something we haven't thought of."

We were engaged but had yet to set the date. For months, we'd been pondering possibilities. Eloping was out. He'd done that the first time, and my marriage to my now-deceased husband had been, well, a sham. Both of us liked the idea of a late summer or early fall event. Agreeing on a venue was turning out to be the biggest challenge. I wanted simple — maybe a beach wedding with a few friends. Rhett felt we should do something bigger.

"Speak!" I said. "Don't keep me on pins and needles."

"Napa."

"Not at your parents' restaurant." His folks owned a well-known French bistro called Intime. It was charming but nearly as teensy as my cottage. "Not that it wouldn't be lovely," I rushed to add, "but if you want a wedding with all of our family and friends, we'll never fit."

"Not there and not at their house, either." Their beautiful ranch-style home overlooked the valley. "Mom heard of a great place in Nouvelle Vie. That's an enclave between Yountville and St. Helena."

"We can't get married at a winery. Bailey did that. I don't want to steal her thunder."

"I'm not a moron," Rhett said. "It's a bed-and-breakfast called Maison Rousseau. Done in the style of Giverny. Lots of gardens. I think we should scout it out. When's your next free weekend?"

I pictured my calendar. "Three weeks." After Book Club Bonanza, Crystal Cove was promoting Spring Fling. That always attracted a huge crowd.

"Perfect. I'm reserving a room."

For the next half hour, we chatted about things we'd like to do in Napa Valley on our visit. Go ballooning. Wine tasting. Maybe take the wine train. When the cupcakes were done and frosted, I packaged up four and accompanied him to his Ford F-250, a handsome truck that was up to every task.

Across the street, a yapping dog drew my attention.

Crusibella was standing in the living room of her Cape Cod–style home, the drapes wide open, the windows, too. A slight breeze made her hair and silk blouse flutter. All the lights were on. She was facing Ivy Beale, who, dressed in lime green pants and forest green sweater, reminded me of an elf. Crusibella's toy poodle was standing on the arm of the sofa barking at the top of its lungs.

"What did you call me?" Crusibella screamed at Ivy and brandished something. A piece of paper? A handkerchief? It was flimsy and hard to tell from this distance.

"You heard me!" Ivy cried. "You're a charlatan. You don't believe in the crystals and stones."

"I do so."

"No, you don't. You're just eager to make a fast buck."

"Liar. You're the one —"

Ivy cut her off, saying something I couldn't make out.

"Renege? You can't renege!" Crusibella cried. "Why, you no-good, double-crossing cheat. We had a deal."

I clutched Rhett's arm. "Uh-oh." So much for sharing a romantic good-night kiss.

"No, we didn't." Ivy planted her hands on her hips and stamped her foot, cementing the elf metaphor.

"I wrote it down. You agreed." Crusibella waved the object again. Apparently, it was something that corroborated her claim

41

about a deal, as one-sided as it might be. "You assert that you're spiritual, Ivy, but there's nothing remotely transcendent about you. And, now, pulling out of our deal —"

"We had no deal." Ivy threw her arms wide. "Are you deaf?"

"Oh, my." Aunt Vera emerged from behind a tree. "This does not bode well."

I startled. "Why were you hiding?"

"Sorry, dear," my aunt sputtered. She smoothed the front of the caftan she'd worn to work. "I didn't want to disturb you and Rhett, in case, you know . . ." She twirled a hand.

My cheeks warmed.

Rhett said, "You've seen us kiss, Vera."

"Of course, but —"

"What are you doing outside?" I asked. My aunt owned my cottage and the charming beach house next to it.

"I was peacefully gazing at the stars until the two of them started going at it. It always does the soul good to drink in the heavens. But not with that clamor." She thrust a hand toward Crusibella's house. "How I wish I'd inserted earplugs. Crusibella thought she had a deal to buy Ivy's shop."

"Dreamcatcher is for sale?" I asked.

"That's just it." My aunt clucked her tongue. "I don't think it is. I'm not sure where Crusibella got the idea. Poor thing."

I gawked. "Poor thing Ivy or poor thing Crusibella?"

Aunt Vera planted her fists on her hips. "Crusibella doesn't think Ivy believes in the crystals that she sells at the shop. Truth be told, she probably doesn't."

"But Ivy is the one who called Crusibella a charlatan," I said.

Lured into the conversation, Rhett said, "Some say Ivy bought Dreamcatcher simply because it was a goldmine, and she desperately wanted to own a business that would be a success."

I arched an eyebrow. "And now she's accusing Crusibella of wanting to do the same thing?"

My aunt nodded. "Exactly."

"The woman who owned Dreamcatcher before Ivy made it the go-to place for all things mystical on the West Coast," Rhett went on. "When she retired to Florida, she received lots of offers. Ivy swept in with all cash."

"What's the big deal with all cash?" I asked. "Why does that secure a deal?"

"No strings attached." Rhett shrugged. "No banks involved."

"There was a rumor that Ivy had something on the previous owner," Aunt Vera offered.

I chuckled. "Well, Ivy is the queen of knowing people's secrets. How did she make enough money to come in with all cash?"

"Her family is extremely wealthy," my aunt said. "They —"

"You're full of baloney!" Crusibella yelled, louder than before. "You don't believe in nature."

"Yes, I do. You've seen how many bonsais I've potted." Ivy sounded whiny. Desperate. She clapped a hand to her chest. "I do it to enhance my soul."

"I'm not talking about the trees," Crusibella scoffed. "I'm talking about the stones. You know nothing about them. What is selenite good for? *Beep.* Time's up. It cleanses and recharges the soul and shields a person from outside influences. How about moonstone?"

"It . . . it . . ." Ivy twisted the hem of her sweater into a knot.

"Buzz!" Crusibella made a razzing sound. "It can open you up to the universe at large."

Ivy stamped her foot so hard that at any moment I expected Tinkerbell and a battalion of fairies to come to her aid. "I'm not

44

required to memorize all these things. I have paperwork to guide me. But I know one thing. If I were you, Crusibella Queensberry, I'd . . . I'd . . ." She shot her hand at her accuser. "I'd wrap my hand around a piece of aventurine and fast. You need calm and balance."

Crusibella growled. "You don't use aventurine for that. You use it to release negativity."

"Give me some credit. I'm trying to learn." Ivy cried. "I've been building my base of knowledge, bit by bit, pebble by pebble. In fact, I recently went on a mining adventure. Why? Because you inspired me to. There's no better way to learn about stones than by getting your hands dirty. Remember saying that to me?" She made the same buzzing sound Crusibella had. "Too late. Time's up! We're through here." She fled through the front door to her silver Mercedes, which was parked on the street.

Crusibella tore after her. "I offered to pay you ten percent more than the asking price, Ivy. You agreed."

"Over a bottle of wine. I was tipsy."

"Your word is your bond." Crusibella raised the flimsy item overhead.

Aha. Perhaps the contract in question had been written on a cocktail napkin.

45

"Read my lips: I'm. Not. Selling. Good night." Ivy climbed into her car, ground it into gear, and zoomed away.

Crusibella spotted us, darted into her house, and slammed the door. The dog yapped at a high pitch and then stopped. The ensuing silence was deafening.

CHAPTER 3

"I love the sound of the surf," Bailey said. "Don't you?"

"Absolutely."

Before opening the Cookbook Nook, she and I had chosen to speed-walk along Buena Vista Boulevard. It was early and traffic was nil, making it easy to hear the ocean.

"And I love sunshine and fresh air, too," Bailey added. "And your cute T-shirt."

"Thanks." Today's was black and featured a colorful grouping of bookish words: *Read, friends, laughter, good times, chat.*

"And I love your studded jeans. And your shoes. Are they Converse? So cute."

Although I preferred flip-flops to shoes, I couldn't take long walks in them. "Boy, are you chipper."

"I'm feeling good." She posed like a vamp. "Do you like my T-shirt?" She had dressed in leggings and a long-sleeved red T-shirt with a bright yellow arrow showing that a baby was inside, as if no one could tell.

"It's to the point."

Bailey needed her exercise, and I was more than happy to keep her company. Tigger had declined the invitation. He hated when I carried him in the cat sling. I think the bobbing up and down upset his tummy. I'd dropped him at the shop and promised I'd be back soon.

"Your aunt was right," Bailey went on. "The town looks so festive with the tents and banners. Book Club Bonanza is a hit."

The tents that the city had allowed along the boulevard were canopy-style, sans walls, so they wouldn't block the view of shops and restaurants. I couldn't believe the variety of colors. Everything from ecru to orange to neon blue. The Blue Hat Book Club owned the latter. Three ladies wearing blue hats were already setting up for the morning.

In addition to banners waving overhead, the shops and restaurants had gotten into the spirit of the theme and were featuring the covers of books in their windows.

When we reached Latte Luck Café, Bailey said, "Look. A cookbook!" She pointed at the display window. "Great choice. *Sally's Cookie Addiction* is one of my favorite sweet treats books."

"Mine, too." The full title was *Sally's Cookie Addiction: Irresistible Cookies, Cookie Bars, Shortbread and More.* I'd made at least five recipes from it so far. I'd only learned to cook a short while ago, but recently I was taking on quite challenging recipes. *Practice makes perfect,* my aunt often reminded me.

In the window of the Pelican Brief Diner was a copy of John Grisham's novel bearing the same name.

"How about getting a coffee at the end of the walk?" Bailey suggested.

"Sure. I'll need something to warm up." The fresh air was invigorating but chilly.

We headed to the north end of the boulevard. The Play Room Toy Store had posted the image of *The Toolbox,* a children's book. As expected, Spellbinder Book Shop was featuring mysteries. Not just one — a bunch of them. My favorite cover was Daphne du Maurier's *Rebecca,* which was bright red and emblazoned with a gigantic capital *R.*

Ivy Beale's store, Dreamcatcher, which was located next to Spellbinder and was part of a six-store complex, each store painted white and faced with brick, had posted the book cover for *Rocks, Minerals, and Gems* on its display window. The display itself featured quartz sculptures, gorgeous candles, a trowel and a sieve, and a handful of eye-catching stones. I spied Ivy inside the shop working alongside her stunning dark-haired clerk. I couldn't remember his name, but he reminded me of the muscle-bound hunk we'd cast in a commercial heralding the Olympics. They were rearranging the centermost glass-and-wood display unit, which held trays of stones. Seashells, candles, geodes, bonsai trees, decorative bookends, and a few metal statues of dragons, chimeras, and gargoyles were wedged between the trays. Seeing Ivy made me think about last night's set-to between her and Crusibella. I hoped they could work out their issue. I liked both of them.

"Who knew there were so many books in the world?" Bailey said.

"I did," I quipped. "Sadly, too many to read in one lifetime."

"If only I'd taken a speed-reading class."

"I doubt that would've helped."

At the north end of town, we crossed the street and headed southward, passing a number of shops, including Great Threads, Sweet Success, Die Hard Fan, Forget Me Not, and Aunt Teek's, each featuring a book title unique to the goods they sold.

We slowed when we neared the library tent, which stood on the sidewalk near the statue of the dancing dolphins. Like my aunt had said, it was colorful. While all the other tents sported solid-colored canopies, the library's canopy was striped. No books were on display this early in the day. All materials had to be removed and stowed each night.

"Oh, gosh." I elbowed Bailey. "Look at that. How cute!" I pointed at the dolphins statue. Each dolphin was wearing huge black-rimmed eyeglasses and carrying a satchel that resembled a library card imprinted with date stamps. Fake books peeked out the tops of the satchels. Even at this early hour, tourists had lined up to pose with the dolphins.

"The woman who runs the Crystal Cove Library has such a great sense of humor," Bailey said. "I plan to take my child to the library every week just to hear her read."

"What a *novel* idea."

Bailey shot me the stink eye.

I shrugged. "I need food. That's my excuse for puns, and I'm sticking to it."

"Latte Luck, here we come."

We waited outside Say Cheese Shoppe for a break in traffic. Showcased in its window was a Cheese Shop Mystery titled *To Brie or*

Not To Brie. On the book's cover was an image of a beautiful wedding pergola in a gardenlike setting, which made me recall my conversation with Rhett. We had to pin down a place and a date. To be honest, I hoped we would love the Napa venue — problem solved.

"Ready?" Bailey asked. "After that white Honda."

"Hey, there's your mom," I said midway across the street. "Want to say hello?"

Bailey's mother, Lola Bird, was standing outside her restaurant, the Pelican Brief Diner, with Oren Michaels. He was tapping something on an electronic tablet while chatting. Lola was smiling, enjoying whatever he was saying. *A fish tale?* I wondered but didn't give voice to the pun. Not after Bailey's earlier reaction.

"Who's that with her?" Bailey asked.

"Don't you know Oren? The fishmonger. He took over his father's flagging business."

Oren had given up his stalled acting career in Los Angeles when his father retired last June at the young age of sixty. Being a man of the sea was not an easy job. Oren had come home to keep the business afloat.

"He delivers fish to the Nook Café," I said.

Bailey nodded. "Aha. He let his curly hair grow long. I didn't recognize him. It suits him. I think he's dating Ivy. I saw them the other day at Dreamcatcher. The chemistry was *ooh-la-la*."

Oren caught sight of us and waved. I waved back. He hoisted a canvas creel bag over his shoulder, tapped the brim of his fisherman's cap to Lola, and sauntered to a red Toyota Tacoma, so new that the license plates weren't even on yet.

"Morning, Lola," I said as we reached her.

"Good morning, girls." Like her daughter, she was petite and sported a pixie cut with long side bangs, though her hair was silver and Bailey's was copperish. Lola slipped her arm through Bailey's and said, "How's my grandbaby doing?"

"As hungry as ever," Bailey replied.

"Are you eating enough?"

Bailey turned in profile. "What does it look like?"

Lola beamed. "Are you two ready for tonight?" She was a member of the book club, too. "I'm making smoked whitefish tea sandwiches."

"I made sinful cupcakes," I said.

"I'm bringing sparkling soda laced with white grape juice," Bailey said, adding, "meh."

Lola released her daughter and eyed me. "By the way, Jenna, speaking of white, I saw the most fabulous all-white buffet for an afternoon wedding." Growing up, Lola had been like my second mother. When my mom passed away a few years ago, Lola had been the first person to console me. Now she was dating my father, and the two couldn't be more in love. "The menu included white tea sandwiches, elegant vanilla pudding, white chocolate desserts, Ramos gin fizzes, and champagne."

I said, "When we get to that point, you can bet I'll come to you for ideas."

"Alert, alert!" Bailey waved her hands. "Mom, they're going to Napa to check out a garden setting for the ceremony. Here's hoping they make a decision." On our walk, I'd told her about our upcoming trip to the wine country. "On the other hand, she's making me look good as a decision maker, right? I didn't lollygag."

"You were the perfect bride." Lola winked.

"Delay, delay, delay." Bailey wiggled fingers in my face. "I need all the brownie points I can muster."

Lola flicked Bailey's arm. "Stop."

Giggling, Bailey said, "We're getting coffee, Mom. Want to join us?"

"Heavens, no. I've got way too much to do if I want to take off this evening for the book club event. Don't forget to pick me up." Lola pivoted and went inside her restaurant. Before the door swung shut, we could hear her giving orders to her staff.

Bailey and I strolled into Latte Luck Café and purchased a couple of decaf cappuccinos to go. Before heading back to the shop, we spent a few moments watching the baker through a viewing window sifting flour onto a marble countertop and rolling out piecrust. Such an art. Someday I hoped I could do the same with ease. Someday.

The morning whizzed by. So did the afternoon. Book club members streamed in throughout the day. Cookbooks flew off the shelves, as did the book club fiction selections. I had created a steady queue of mystery-themed music to bolster the customers' *joie de vivre,* including "Mystery Train" by Bon Jovi and Donna Summer's "Mystery of Love." The Beatles' *Magical Mystery Tour* earned the most lip-synching. We sold two of the stack-of-books porcelain cookie jars, three teapot cookie jars, and four adorable bookworm salt and pepper sets. I was surprised to see that the colorful classic book-themed aprons sold better than the plain white ones sporting clever sayings.

The construction paper cookbooks that Bailey had fashioned were a huge hit with children. Tigger, too. He had a blast trolling beneath the kids' table for ribbon and other craft scraps. Aunt Vera must have given six or seven tarot card readings. Tina, who was a bundle of energy after taking the day off to study, was a blessing to have around, especially when Bailey wilted around three and I ordered her to the storage room to take a nap.

At six, as Bailey was closing out the register and I was dusting shelves, Tina said, "Boss. Bailey. Vera. Go home. Freshen up. Enjoy the book club. I can finish up here."

"Don't you have a date tonight?" I asked. She and her boyfriend invariably went to dinner on Saturday night.

"No." She made a dismissive sound, whipped her long tresses over her shoulders, and shimmied down the hem of her formfitting knit dress. "He's . . ." She rolled her eyes. "He's persona non grata at the moment." She rasped the word *grata*.

Uh-oh. What had he done? Did I want to know? Given her current state of snit, I was surprised how well she'd muscled through the day. Maybe during a lull tomorrow, I would ask for details and offer advice . . . if she wanted it.

"Go!" She shooed us. "I'm fine. Bring me one of your cupcakes tomorrow, Jenna."

Bailey had brought clothes to change into as well as the makings for her beverage contribution, so she drove with me to the cottage. I swapped out my T-shirt and jeans for a chocolate brown silk blouse and matching corduroys, and then grabbed the Tupperware container of cupcakes, deposited Tigger on the kitty condo that my father had made for him, switched on some orchestral music — my cat loved Yo-Yo Ma — and told him not to wait up.

Minutes later, we picked up Lola and headed to Flora Fairchild's place, the first stop on our progressive dinner.

Flora lived in a single-story house in the hills. Like most of the other homes in Crystal Cove, it was white with a red-tile roof, but her garden was a riot of color. A narrow, meandering path lined with white, pink, and red azaleas led to the front door. Myriad pots of vibrant pansies crowded the porch.

At Home Sweet Home, the gift shop Flora owned, she always played music, much like we did at the Cookbook Nook. Tonight was no exception. As we entered her house through the open doorway, I heard the strains of "Funeral March of a Marionette," known best as the theme for *Alfred Hitchcock Presents.* Cute.

Flora noticed us and beckoned us further. "Come this way." She had dressed in a pretty lavender floral dress, her long braid woven with lilac. "I hope you enjoy everything. There's food in the dining room."

Bailey handed her the sparkling water and grape juice. Flora pecked her on the cheek and whispered her thanks.

"Your home is beautiful," I said.

The place was overflowing with handcrafted items. Colorful quilts lay on the couch in the living room. There were lots of chairs, each a different design. An imaginative throw pillow sat on each. Lit candles of all shapes and sizes adorned the mantel above the fireplace. Collections of teddy bears and snow globes for every season stood on a variety of tables.

In the dining room, Flora had laid a bright purple cloth on the table. On top was an appetizer spread fit for royalty: shrimp puffs, mini quiches, melon wrapped in prosciutto, and more. At least a dozen women had shown up for the first leg of our journey, including Pepper and Crusibella. Pepper's pecan-studded cheese appetizer sat on an Italianate serving dish at the far end of the array of food. What I assumed was Crusibella's cheese platter, a robust arrangement of yellow and white cheeses garnished with fresh fruit, laid beyond that.

"Flora, this looks magnificent," I said.

Everyone agreed. A few wondered how they'd have room for the next course.

Flora beamed. "Dig in. Plates are over there. I'll bring beverages to the living room, and then let's have a twenty-minute discussion of the book. I hope you've all read it."

I'd finished last night after Rhett left, and I was glad I did. I had no idea *whodunit* until the climax, although I had winnowed it down to two suspects. Okay, maybe three.

I inched along the buffet following Crusibella, who was eyeing everything but selecting nothing. She couldn't possibly be on a diet. Her sleeveless jumpsuit clung to her slim frame.

"*Psst,* Jenna." Pepper sidled up to me. I hadn't noticed before, but she was a tad disheveled. Her beaded black sweater was uneven at her hips and her hair was mussed. Maybe she'd walked over or perhaps she'd had to park farther down the street. A breeze had kicked up. She hitched her chin in the direction of Crusibella's cheese platter and whispered, "Told you so."

"Don't worry. Your cheese appetizer looks scrumptious." To prove it, I jumped the line to that end of the buffet and added a chunk of the pecan and soft cheese to my plate. I nibbled a corner of it and said to Pepper, "It's yummy. Did you use Stilton?"

"Yes." She preened like a peacock.

"Hello, everyone!" Gran, who lived next door with her daughter-in-law and grandchildren, strolled into the dining room. As always, she looked upscale, clad in hunter green slacks, cream silk blouse, and multicolored Manolo Blahnik sandals. "I won't stay a minute." She picked up a slice of cheddar. "I just wanted to —"

"Compare food?" Flora asked as she waltzed through carrying a tray filled with flutes of champagne or sparkling water.

"No." Gran *tsk*ed. "Don't be paranoid, Flora. I came to assure everyone that the family is out for the evening. We can talk loudly and laugh freely when you come over." She ate the cheese and surveyed the crowd. "Where are Z.Z. and Ivy?"

"Z.Z.'s probably getting one last kiss from Jake," Flora said.

Mayor Zeller and Jake Chapman, one of my father's good friends, had started dating around Christmas. After a few years of being a widower, Jake had been ready for a new relationship. Though he was nearly twenty years Z.Z.'s senior, they had clicked.

"Ivy's probably at the store this minute buying dessert," Crusibella said tartly. She toyed with a loose hair in her chignon and adjusted the strand of crystal beads that were quite fashionable over her silk dress.

I said, "Actually, Ivy bought a new cookbook this morning, just for the occasion."

"Ha!" Crusibella sneered. "I still say she'll buy everything. She's always last minute. In her business. In her life. Heaven forbid she learns how to manage her time."

"What's got you in a twist?" I whispered to her.

Crusibella shot me a look. "Nothing."

Maybe she was dieting.

She sashayed to Flora, grabbed a flute of sparkling water, and led the procession into the living room. "Follow me, ladies."

Bailey leaned into me. "Who made her queen for a day?"

I giggled. "Well, her surname is Queensberry."

Lola clasped Bailey's elbow and followed Crusibella.

My aunt gave me a nudge, but Pepper detained me. "Jenna, do you have a second?"

"Sure, what's —"

Tears sprang into her eyes. She wiped them with her pinky. "I . . . I tried calling Hank on my way here. He didn't answer and he hasn't left me a message. You don't think he and Ivy —"

"Stop, Pepper." I placed a reassuring hand on her arm. "Don't do this to yourself. Ivy is preparing her house for the party. She doesn't have time for a dalliance. And Hank must be busy with . . . inventory," I said, taking a cue from last night's discussion with Rhett. "Spring cleaning is in the air. I don't answer my phone when I'm doing inventory, do you? Now, let's take our minds off real life and chat about the murder mystery."

CHAPTER 4

We stayed at Flora's for a half hour, discussing the setup of the mystery and the imaginative cast of characters that the author had added to give the mystery flavor. When put to a vote, everyone liked the protagonist Sophie the best. Close runner-up was her good friend and premier diva, Natasha.

When a bell chimed, Flora shooed us out. "Up, up, and away, everyone. On to the next house!" she cried. The timer had been Crusibella's idea to keep us on track. "I'll catch up."

We walked to Gran's. From there, we would board a bus to travel to the next two stops — also Crusibella's idea. She didn't want any of us to drive once we'd imbibed a little wine.

I smiled as I strolled into Gran's house. A bit of chaos was to be expected when living with children: toys stuffed into cubbies, stacks of homework papers and school projects on the dining table — the dining room had been converted into an office; Gran's daughter-in-law worked out of the house. The sofa and two easy chairs in the living room looked comfortable and well trampled. The children's artwork hung on every available inch of wall. Like Flora, Gran had set out a number of folding chairs for the event.

"Head for the kitchen first," Gran said, "for food and beverages."

The kitchen was as white as it could get. Bleached flooring. White cabinets. White counters. White country-style table with a bench that was loaded with white pillows decorated with seashells. On the table sat numerous tiered trays. Everything on them was white, too: white shrimp, white asparagus, white cheese, and white tea sandwiches. Did Lola have something to do with the theme? She added her entry to the array.

"We're using paper plates," Gran said, pointing to a stack of white antique scroll plates at the far end of the table. "I hope nobody minds. I hate washing dishes and didn't want my daughter-in-law to think she had to do them."

Lola sidled up to me and said, "All white food has its charm, don't you think?"

"It's quite pretty," I said judiciously. I

loved how enthusiastic my friends were, trying to help me make a decision about the wedding, but I wanted Rhett's input more than anyone else's. I selected one of each tea sandwich — cucumber, chicken with almonds, and whitefish — and found a seat in the living room.

Gran led the discussion. She had found book club questions posed by the author on her website. "A culinary cozy mystery often features snacks and meals," she began. "Many include recipes. Did any of you feel the scenes involving food stopped the story?"

No one did. A few admitted to salivating while reading. To a person, everyone loved Sophie's tips on how to entertain with ease.

"What is your favorite china pattern?" Gran asked for the next question. "Would you recognize shards of it?"

"Wedgwood Hibiscus," Flora chimed. "And I'd definitely recognize a fragment. It's very distinctive. The blue is exquisite."

Lola said, "I'm partial to anything Lenox Marchesa. It's so elegant."

After almost everyone offered an opinion, Gran said, "How did you feel about the ending? Did you figure out who did it, or were you surprised?"

Four claimed they had guessed *who,* but

none had ascertained *why* until Sophie did. The author had buried the clues well.

When the half-hour timer went off, we herded onto the bus and drove to Z.Z.'s house. One woman close to my aunt mooed like a cow. That sent many of us into a fit of giggles.

Our mayor lived a few streets away in a two-bedroom bungalow with a view of the ocean. When I walked in, I felt like I'd entered a spa. Her décor was done in cool blue tones. Sounds of nature played through speakers.

Bailey leaned into me and whispered, "Woo-woo."

I swatted her. "It's lovely. Calming. You would do well to think of these things when having your baby."

"Oh, so now you're the expert?" She smirked.

Dinner items had been set outside on the teak patio table. Chairs for the discussion were also arranged outside. Z.Z. had advised each of us to bring along a shawl or jacket. Luckily, I'd remembered to grab a wheat-colored pashmina on my way out the door.

As promised, Z.Z. offered wine from the local Baldini Vineyards, which was known for its pinot noir. Everyone but Bailey took a glass.

While dining on individual casserole portions of vegetarian lasagna, chicken tostada, or beef ragout, all of which to my surprise my illustrious chef had made — Z.Z. could convince nearly anyone to do her bidding — the discussion homed in on the protagonist's love life. Was her current beau the right man for her? Was a romance necessary in a mystery? These questions drummed up the most controversy of the evening. Half of the club members felt the mystery was the most important thing. The other half thought the character arc and relationships were vital. After all, if they didn't care about a character, why read the mystery? A couple of members said they could do without cute banter, but they were in the minority. Personally, I'd enjoyed it. It made Sophie very relatable.

When many of the group started in on a second glass of wine and the conversation became boisterous, Bailey leaned into me and whispered, "I feel a bit like a bartender watching everyone have fun while I stay sober."

I patted her arm. "It's worth it."

"From your lips . . ."

"And FYI, I'm still nursing my first glass."

"You're a true pal."

"Are you enjoying the food?" I asked.

"Absolutely, although I have to admit I can't wait for dessert. Yours, in particular."

By the time we headed to Ivy's, I was so stuffed I could barely climb the steps onto the bus.

Bailey prodded me. "Hurry up, Jenna. The sooner we're seated, the sooner we get going." She pointed to her belly. "He's craving sugar."

"Maybe that's what gives him a boost."

Crusibella tapped Bailey's shoulder. "Don't eat sugar, sweetie. You'll be putting that baby at risk for gestational diabetes."

"Just a tad," Bailey said. "All things in moderation. I primarily eat protein." Her words came out a bit curt. I guessed she'd had enough *mothers* advising her about this baby — her own, Aunt Vera, and the doctor.

"Good for you." Crusibella gave her the thumbs-up sign. "That's the spirit."

"Speaking of babies, should Sophie have a baby?" Bailey asked, expertly changing the subject back to this evening's book.

I said, "Sophie's in her forties. I think that ship has sailed."

Crusibella said, "Women can have babies well into their forties nowadays. Don't let that myth stop you, Jenna. It's all about your spiritual balance."

Not eager to talk about babies and chakras and such, I settled onto a front row seat.

Bailey sat next to me and whispered, "A second ago, we both referred to my baby as a *he.* Do you think it's a *him*?"

"How would I know?"

"Isn't the wives' tale that if you're carrying him — *it* — all in front, it's a boy?"

"You're asking the wrong wives' tale expert. Can't you find out? Isn't that what the ultrasound is for?" I was clueless.

She scoffed. "Are you kidding? Tito would have my head. It's got to be a surprise. We have lots of names picked out, too."

"Are those a secret?"

"Nope."

All the way to Ivy's place, Bailey regaled me with names that were not in the offing, for example Elinder, Mizely, and Orion. No way, no how. She had put the kibosh on those. I told her Tito was pulling her leg. She said he was dead serious.

"We're here," Crusibella announced. "I hope Ivy is ready for us."

Gran, who had joined us at Z.Z.'s near the end and was sitting in the seat behind me, said, "She sure looks ready. The house is all lit up."

Bailey, with help from the bus driver, disembarked first. I followed, carrying the

Tupperware containing my cupcakes.

"Isn't it dramatic?" I exclaimed as we made our way along the path to the front door.

I'd never been to Ivy's home. It reminded me of a multilevel Italian villa. The plants were gigantic and sumptuous. Exterior lights lit a pair of lofty cypress trees. The neighboring houses on Rhododendron Drive were equally impressive.

I pressed the doorbell.

Bailey nudged me. "Go in already. The door's ajar."

Soft instrumental music was playing through speakers — one of Henry Mancini's themes, if I wasn't mistaken. It wasn't "The Pink Panther" or "Moon River." The name would come to me.

"Hello?" I called from the foyer. "Ivy, we're here!" My voice echoed off the travertine tile.

Ivy didn't answer. Maybe she was upstairs changing. The living room lights were dim. Lit pillar vanilla-scented candles, many of them burned more than halfway, decorated the mantel as well as the grand piano and end tables. A trio of them sat on flat Waterford plates that graced the glass coffee table.

"How pretty it all looks," my aunt said, making her way deeper into the house. "Ivy, dear! Don't let us catch you in a state of undress." She tittered. "She must have lost track of time."

Bailey peered around a corner. "The dining room looks almost ready. Napkins and plates have been set on the table."

Her mother said, "Maybe Ivy ran to the store for a last-minute item."

A cool breeze swept through the opened doors leading to the terrace. A shiver ran down my spine.

"Ivy?" Bailey traipsed through the dining room and peeked into the dark kitchen. "Jenna, I see empty serving trays on the counter but no desserts. Why don't you set your cupcakes on one of them and bring them into the dining room? I need one now." She pressed her hands together in prayer. "Pretty please?"

"Aye aye, captain." I slipped past her and switched on the overhead lights. I hated working in the dark, a habit from my advertising days. Bright light made it easier to see the details of a campaign.

The kitchen was pretty in a Florentine way, done in soft pearl tones with brown accents. All the appliances were high-end stainless steel. The backsplash above the stove was a mosaic of cream-colored glass tiles.

As I rounded the L-shaped island, I stopped short. A scream caught in my throat. Ivy was lying on the floor, faceup. Someone had shoved a rose quartz shard into her chest. Blood stained her white off-the-shoulder dress. Two gold-colored quartz, about the size of half dollars and smoothed to perfection, had been placed over her eyes. Her arms were arranged by her sides. On each palm lay a sparkly green stone. A cypress bonsai tree in a pearl-colored pot sat beside her head. A smattering of its soil dusted the floor.

Lola charged into the kitchen. "Jenna, are you —" She clapped her hand over her mouth.

Bailey scuttled in after her and gasped. "Oh, no! Is she dead?"

I crouched and felt Ivy's pulse even though I knew she would never take another breath.

CHAPTER 5

I rose to my feet. Lola pulled her cell phone from her purse and started speaking to someone at 911. My aunt and the rest of the book club members crowded into the kitchen. Many gasped. Flora sucked back a sob. Z.Z. made a retching sound and fled.

Crusibella peered over Bailey's shoulder and whispered, "Aventurine."

I said, "Everyone, let's go. Out of the kitchen. Don't touch anything. We'll convene in front of the house."

Once on the porch, we tried to make sense of what had happened. Who had wanted Ivy dead? Why stab her with quartz? What was the purpose of the stones on her eyes and in her hands?

My aunt rubbed the phoenix amulet she always wore and shook her head. "Poor Ivy. She didn't deserve this."

"No one does," I murmured.

A few minutes later, a siren blared. Its

sound swelled as an emergency vehicle neared.

Bucky Winston, an EMT and the current poster boy for Crystal Cove's fire department, dashed into the house carrying a medical team kit. His partner, a somber-faced female, followed him.

"In the kitchen," Lola said.

They raced passed us. Lola followed. I trailed her.

Bucky knelt on one side of Ivy, his partner on the other. Soon, they acknowledged what I already knew: Ivy was dead. She had been for at least a few hours. Her body was cold to the touch. That might explain why the candles in her living room had burned so low.

Bucky eyed me and hitched his chin, reminding Lola and me to leave. I took another cursory glance at the crime scene. It was fairly pristine. Very little blood other than at the wound site. No apparent struggle. The way Ivy was posed, on her back with the stones in position, struck me as ritualistic.

Within fifteen minutes, Chief Cinnamon Pritchett and her crew arrived. When I'd first met her, Cinnamon had reminded me of a camp counselor with her blunt haircut and girl-next-door face, but looks could be deceiving. She was as commanding as an army general. She directed her crew to inspect the crime scene. Deputy Marlon Appleby, a giant of a man with a square jaw, tipped his hat as he passed me. At first glance, one might find him intimidating, but down deep, he was as sweet as they came. He and my aunt were in a relationship.

With measured steps, Cinnamon strode toward me while adjusting the brim of her hat and running a hand down the front of her taupe uniform. When off duty, we were friends. "Jenna, fill me in. CliffsNotes style."

"Book club. We had a progressive dinner. Ivy Beale, the deceased, is the owner of Dreamcatcher at the north end of town —"

"I know the shop."

"Her house was the fourth and last on our tour. We were coming for dessert. We started at Flora's and picked up the bus" — I pointed to it — "at Gran's . . . Gracie's. Gracie Goldsmith's. Well, no, not all of us. Ivy wasn't at Flora's. Z.Z. wasn't, either. Her house was the third stop on the tour. Gran lives next door to Flora, so she popped in for a moment and returned home." I realized I was offering needless details but couldn't help myself. "When we got here, the front door was ajar. We entered, thinking Ivy might be upstairs preening. Music was on. Candles lit." I glanced toward the house. "The candles are burned down halfway, which might give an estimated time of death."

"Don't conjecture. That's my job." She twirled a hand for me to continue.

"The table was preset for the buffet. We found her . . ." I swallowed hard. "*I* found her in the kitchen."

"You?"

"Yes, me. *Again.*" Sadly, I'd been first to a crime scene on more than one occasion. "I brought cupcakes. I was going to plate them. I —"

Cinnamon held up a hand and addressed her mother. "Are you all right, Mom?"

Pepper had drawn near and was quaking like an aspen. "I can't believe it. Poor Ivy." She shook her head.

Cinnamon hailed an officer who was heading back to a squad car. "Bring my mother a blanket, please." She refocused on me. "What's your take on this, Jenna?"

I gawked. She'd rarely asked for my opinion until a few months ago when she'd gracefully accepted my help on a case because my father had compelled her to do so. But usually —

"Speak," she commanded.

76

"From the scuttlebutt among the others, I get the feeling Ivy ticked off a lot of people in town. She kept unreliable hours and didn't know her goods. Some didn't like her business practices." I'd overheard Flora reiterate that Ivy had seen Dreamcatcher as a cash cow, nothing more, adding that she hadn't understood the healing side of her business.

"How well did you know Ms. Beale?" Cinnamon asked.

"Not well at all, though I liked her. She bought a few items at the Cookbook Nook, and I'd bought things at hers."

I glanced over my shoulder at the book club group. Crusibella was consoling Z.Z., who was ashen. Lola was hugging Bailey. My aunt was holding hands with Gran. Flora was swaying to and fro. Her mouth was moving. She sang in the choir at church. Maybe she was praying or singing a hymn.

"I heard her parents are wealthy and live in San Francisco," I added.

The officer hurried to Cinnamon with a blanket for Pepper. Cinnamon draped it over her mother's shoulders, and after whispering a few words to her mother, ordered the officer to lead the way to the kitchen. Ten minutes later, she reemerged and approached us.

"Okay, one by one," Cinnamon began, "what did you see? Nothing is insignificant. Mayor Zeller, you first."

The ladies formed a semicircle.

Z.Z. said, "I felt something was off the moment I walked into the house. The music was on a loop, so the same song kept playing over and over."

"It still is," Crusibella said.

"It's a Henry Mancini song," Z.Z. went on.

" 'Love Theme from *Romeo and Juliet*,' " Flora offered.

That was it! Instantly, I wondered why the song hadn't changed. Had the killer activated the infinity loop? Was the killer implying that he . . . or she . . . was Ivy's lover or wannabe lover?

"Mom?" Cinnamon asked. "What about you?"

I glanced at Pepper, who was clutching the edge of the blanket tightly beneath her chin. She was blinking rapidly. She opened her mouth to speak but nothing came out.

"Mom, what's wrong?"

A knot formed at the pit of my stomach. Pepper couldn't have had anything to do with Ivy's death, could she? I recalled the way she'd taken up the tongs at the shop yesterday and thrust them forward like a dueling sword. She'd wanted to impale Ivy.

"Mom?" Cinnamon crossed to her.

I flashed on the moment Pepper had arrived at Flora's. She'd been upset that Hank wasn't answering his cell phone and had worried he might be with Ivy. Did she —

Whoa, Jenna. Backtrack. Pepper had wondered whether Ivy might have skipped the first stop on the book club tour to meet up with Hank. If she had killed Ivy, she would have *known* Ivy was dead, unless she'd groused to me about Ivy to divert suspicion from herself.

A teensy moan escaped my lips.

Cinnamon cut a look in my direction.

I flinched.

Crusibella stepped forward. "I know why Jenna moaned, Chief, but you won't like what I have to say."

"It's not true," Pepper blurted.

"What's not?" Cinnamon swung her gaze from one woman to the other.

"I didn't like Ivy," Pepper cried. "That's true. But I didn't do it."

"Didn't do what?" Cinnamon asked.

"Kill her!"

Crusibella said, "Then why did you arrive late to the book club? Why were you out of breath and disheveled?"

"Because . . . because . . ." Pepper halted.

"Hold it. I'm not the only one with a beef against Ivy. You were angry with her, too. Why do you have a red stain on your sleeve?"

Everyone focused on Crusibella.

She inspected her sleeve then sniffed it. "It's strawberry juice. From my cheese and fruit platter."

"Who slices strawberries for a cheese platter?" Pepper demanded. "They should be served whole." She dropped the blanket and stepped toward Crusibella. "I think you stained it on purpose to cover blood splatter."

"I did no such —"

"Ladies, stop! Be civil." Cinnamon wedged between them. "Mom, why would Crusibella want Ivy dead?"

"I . . . I don't know," Pepper stammered. "I heard —"

"Chief," I jumped in. "Ivy reneged on a deal to sell her business to Crusibella."

"That's a lie!" Crusibella cried.

"You were arguing about it last night when I was saying good night to Rhett. Your poodle barked and . . ." I paused. "What's the significance of aventurine?" She had whispered the name of the stone when she'd seen Ivy's body.

"It's for healing," Crusibella said. "Meant

to erase negative energy. It's resting on her palms."

"Was Ivy sick?"

"No, she wasn't sick. I mean, she had a false scare. Her heart." Crusibella batted the air. "It was why she'd wanted to sell Dreamcatcher."

Suddenly I recalled how Ivy, during the argument with Crusibella, had advised her to grab hold of aventurine to find calm and balance. "Chief, maybe —"

"Hold that thought, Jenna." Cinnamon eyed Crusibella. "Where were you, Ms. Queensberry, before the book club began?"

"At home. Making the cheese platter."

Pepper raised a finger. "I was home, too. Making my appetizer. I was singing along with a Frank Sinatra album."

"Details," Crusibella muttered.

"Details matter," Pepper hissed.

"Did anyone see or *hear* either of you?" Cinnamon gazed from one to the other.

Crusibella shook her head; Pepper waggled hers.

Z.Z. said, "Chief, maybe you should talk to Oren Michaels. He was Ivy's boyfriend. He might know more about who had a beef with her."

"I'm not sure he will," Flora said. "Ivy broke up with him."

"When?" I asked. "They seemed quite into each other when I saw them last."

"This morning. Ivy came into Home Sweet Home to buy a few candles, and we got to chatting." Flora could coax a mime to talk.

"Maybe that upset Oren," Pepper said, looking hopeful. "Maybe he killed her."

"Let's not rule out Hank Hemmings," Z.Z. said. "Pepper, you told me earlier that you wondered whether he was seeing Ivy on the sly. Maybe she jilted him, so he lashed out."

Cinnamon groaned. I did, too. Apparently, Z.Z. didn't realize that Pepper and Hank were an item. If Hank did get involved with Ivy and planned to dump Pepper, then she had just as good a motive as everyone else to want Ivy dead: *jealousy.*

CHAPTER 6

Emotionally drained, I called Rhett the moment I got home. Another murder? What was going on? Until I'd moved to town, Crystal Cove hadn't had a murder in over fifteen years. Was I a magnet for evil?

Over the course of the next hour, Rhett talked me down from the ledge and assured me that crime was up all over the United States. Our town was not the only one suffering. Granted, most of the crimes involved guns, not crystals, but he sloughed that off. He offered to come over, but I told him he didn't need to. Sleep would help me see things more clearly. He asked how Cinnamon was doing. They'd had a relationship years ago, before us. I said she was on edge but would rally when she proved her mother wasn't guilty.

Around seven a.m., after a night filled with frightening dreams featuring quartz knives, swords, and spears, morning sunlight shot through the break in the living room drapes and woke me with a start. I'd fallen asleep on the couch. Tigger butted his head into my stomach. I nudged him to the floor and slogged to the bathroom. In less than fifteen minutes, I took a steaming hot shower, dressed in a tangerine dress with a flare skirt, applied lip gloss, and set off for work.

After setting Tigger on his kitty condo — my sweet father had made a duplicate one for the store — I went to the Nook Café. I was starved. Katie was in the kitchen sifting flour into a huge bowl while giving orders to her staff about specialty items on the lunch menu. Particles of flour billowed into the air.

"Jenna!" Katie cried when she saw me. She set the sifter down and hurried to me. Her hugs could rival a boa constrictor's squeeze. She was as tall as I was but bigger all over.

"Air!" I said.

"Sorry." She held me at arm's length while righting her toque. "How are you doing?" She and I had been friends for years, although during high school we hadn't hung with the same crowd. I had been a budding artist. She had been an aspiring cook. When we were hiring a chef for the café, she'd auditioned for the job and had wowed us with her skills. I loved her to pieces. "I can't believe it. Ivy. Dead. And you found her? She was in just the other day. Ordered her favorite meal. Sent it back, like she often did. She could be so quirky, but she left the staff huge tips."

"Quirky," I repeated. My aunt had used the same word to describe Ivy.

"She came in with Oren. They were holding hands and laughing and obviously in love."

Not any more, if Flora could be believed.

Katie ushered me to the chef's table situated at the rear corner of the kitchen, where she often served elite dinners for up to six. "Hungry?" She smoothed the front of her white chef's coat. "Want a classic egg sandwich?"

"I would —" I stopped short of saying *kill for one.* Wasn't it amazing the phrases we used in everyday life? "I would love one. Thanks."

She laid a place setting in front of me.

I set the napkin on my lap. "Do lots of people buy fish from Oren?"

"Sure. He's tenacious about keeping all the clients his father developed over the years. I'm not sure he has any competition left in town, other than Rhett, of course." Katie fetched an English muffin from a

85

container and split it with a fork. She buttered the muffin and set it to fry in a hot skillet. As she heated the premade sausage and cooked the egg, folding it into thirds, she said, "Early on, Oren tried to sweet-talk me into buying his wares. I didn't bite." She chortled. "*Bite.* Ha! Like I was a fish." She removed the muffins, drizzled them with a honey-flavored hot sauce, topped them with American cheese and slipped them into the oven for a minute. "I made him prove to me his goods were the best. That's what I'd promised you, I told him — only the best — so that's what he had to promise me. It took six months before I gave him ninety percent of our business."

"Do you trust him?"

"Absolutely." When the cheese melted, Katie layered the sandwich together and placed it on a white scalloped plate. "Eat." She set the meal in front of me. "You need your sustenance."

I took a bite and raved about the sauce. "How's it going with the baby hunt?"

"You won't believe how many forms we have to fill out." Katie couldn't have children, but she and her husband, Keller — they'd married a month ago — decided they wanted to adopt. She dabbed her forehead with a clean white cloth. "Bureaucracy. *Pfft.*

One form at a time, I keep telling myself. But we're determined. Boy or girl. Any ethnicity. All we want is a happy, healthy human being."

"Let me know if you need any references."

"You're my employer. I'm sure you'll have a form or two to fill out yourself. *Ahem.*" She planted a fist on her hip. "Promise you'll give me a good review."

"Will do."

Throughout the rest of the day, I worried about Pepper's fate. I'd seen her open her shop, so she wasn't incarcerated. Maybe the police didn't have enough physical evidence to hold her. Or maybe they'd found another suspect. I called the precinct to talk to Cinnamon because I didn't want to ask Pepper about her status, but she wasn't in. I left a message asking her to call me back, and then begged my aunt to check in with Deputy Appleby. She did. He told her there was nothing he could *offer at this time.* How I hated that phrase.

At noon, Z.Z. came in to chat. She felt awful about implicating Pepper. I assured her Pepper was innocent and not to worry, though my insides were in a knot.

Late afternoon, after selling out of every book club title we had in stock, Bailey, Aunt

Vera, and I convened at the vintage kitchen table near the front door. Weekly, we set out a new jigsaw puzzle that customers could assemble. This week's puzzle was book-themed — a bird's-eye view inside a cluttered bookshop. Each of us toyed with pieces as we discussed our thoughts. I took the upper left corner, Bailey the upper right. My aunt liked a challenge and preferred to start at the middle and move outward.

"You don't really believe Pepper is capable of murder, do you?" Bailey asked. "I mean, she's —" The baby's heel pushed against the front of her embroidered shirt. She petted it and continued. "I mean, she's *Pepper*. Sure, she's feisty and she can be prickly and has a temper, but she wouldn't harm a soul."

Aunt Vera nodded. "Of course she didn't do it. But someone did. If we can, let's help the police figure out who."

Bailey nodded. "Crusibella wanted to buy the shop, but Ivy reneged." She fitted two corner pieces. "Maybe killing Ivy was Crusibella's way of making a point."

I winced at the word *point,* remembering the quartz that had pierced Ivy's chest.

"Sorry," Bailey muttered, realizing her gaffe, and then elaborated. "I mean, it was a clear sign that she shouldn't have broken a promise."

"Death makes that certain," Aunt Vera opined.

"The ritualistic way Ivy was killed has to mean something," I said, recalling a scene from one of last night's horrific dreams. I was swimming on my back on a raging river, my eyes covered with tar. "Why put rocks on her eyes?"

"I've been wondering the same thing," Bailey said.

"I think they might have something to do with the underworld." In junior high, I'd loved studying about Roman and Greek gods and goddesses. I'd paid particular attention to the story of Persephone, goddess of the underworld. She was playing in a field when Hades abducted her. Because she ate pomegranate seeds while in hell, Zeus wouldn't let her fully return to earth. Her annual return in the spring brought flowering meadows and fields of grain. Needless to say, being impressionable, I'd been afraid to frolic in a field during high school.

"The underworld," Bailey repeated.

"Yep." I pulled my cell phone from my pocket and opened the Internet browser. In the search bar, I typed: *Stones on eyes for burial.* Up popped a number of sites explaining the purpose of eyestones, many of which were painted with a set of eyes.

"Listen to this." Reading out loud, I said, "According to Greek lore, having one's eyes open after death was a way to help the deceased not fear death. Charon, the ferryman for the god of the underworld — Hades — would collect the stones as payment to transport the dead across the river to its afterlife. If Charon didn't receive payment, then the deceased could be doomed to wander the earth and possibly haunt the living."

"But the stones on Ivy's eyes weren't painted with eyes."

"True."

"Even so," my aunt said, "perhaps the killer was making a loving gesture in an effort to help Ivy cross over."

"A quartz dagger through the heart was hardly loving," I said.

"Maybe" — Bailey let the word hang in the air for a moment — "the killer was ensuring that Ivy wouldn't come back, even in spirit form."

"Why?" The notion jolted me. "Did she know something? See something? What hold might she have had over the killer?"

"Perhaps the literature in Ivy's store could tell us more about the stones," Aunt Vera said.

I scoffed. "As if Cinnamon would let us inside."

My aunt patted my forearm. "Why don't you suggest the eyestone theory to her?"

"And incur her wrath?"

"You helped solve the last murder."

"Because Dad made her listen to me."

"I'm sure she could use a fresh take," Aunt Vera pressed.

"She has a highly qualified staff."

"Who might not understand the significance of the stones." My aunt pursed her lips. "Face it, dear, with her mother as a suspect, Cinnamon is too close to this. You're her friend. Be one. Not to mention, you've been through this yourself. You understand what it means to be suspected unfairly."

CHAPTER 7

On Sunday nights, our family always met for a sit-down dinner, sometimes at my dad's house and other times at my aunt's. I looked forward to hosting one after Rhett and I moved into our new home. I'd already come up with our first menu. Rhett, bless his heart, promised to do the heavy lifting and cook most of it. I would be his sous chef.

My father's house was a beauty of a Mediterranean villa set way up in the hills. My mother had decorated it with an ocean color scheme. I noted a few of Lola's touches in the house: a few extra throw pillows plus additional family photos, including Bailey's wedding photos. From the rear patio, even in the glow of tiki torches, we could see the ocean.

Lola, Bailey, and her husband, Tito, had joined us for dinner. For a laugh, Bailey had brought ice cream and pickles for dessert.

She was seated on the patio divan with Tito on one side of her and Lola on the other. For the past ten minutes, Lola had been cooing about the baby and pressing for names. Tito petted Bailey's hand with regularity. Normally my pal would have acted trapped under such scrutiny, but tonight, she seemed in her element. *Who'd have thunk?*

On the other hand, I couldn't sit still. I chose to lean against the railing, something my father hated. He didn't have acrophobia, but he was afraid the railing, given its age, might break. I assured him it was sturdy and told him to relax, but he couldn't. It didn't matter how many times he, the know-it-all handyman, had checked it out. I asked if he'd like me to don a parachute. That had earned me a wry scowl. Rhett stood next to me, drinking in the view. He didn't seem concerned about me plummeting to my death.

"Wine?" my father asked as he made his way around the patio pouring chardonnay into wineglasses. As always, he looked quite dapper. He was wearing chinos and a light sweater. A thatch of his silver-gray hair dangled on his forehead.

"Sure." I took a glass from him and waited as he filled it halfway. Because the evening breeze was faint but cool, I had changed out of my dress into ecru slacks and boat-neck sweater and was glad I had.

"Your aunt assures me this will go well with dinner," Dad said.

Aunt Vera was busy in the kitchen making her fabulous shrimp curry.

"Don't any of you sneak in there," Lola warned. "Vera swears there's magic in the spice combination she uses. If any of you messes with her concoction, you're toast. She promises the meal will increase your brainpower trifold."

"I could use some brainpower," my father joked.

"Why?" I took a sip of the wine, loving the flavors of melon and vanilla.

"Because Cinnamon called me today."

I silently harrumphed. She hadn't re-turned my call.

"She was quite bereft about her mother's plight and wanted my two cents." My father and Cinnamon went way back. At the behest of my mother, he had reached out to Cinnamon during her teens because she'd been a wild child. Having a father who'd abandoned her had something to do with it. Dad counseled her until she got herself under control. To this day, she was more like a daughter to him than a friend. She sought his advice and listened.

"Dad, I have a theory —"

Lola cleared her throat on purpose. My father cut her a look and received her message: *end of discussion.*

"We'll chat about this another time," Dad said and set the wine bottle aside.

"But —"

"Another time. It's Bailey and Tito's night." He sat on the armchair closest to Lola and swooped the lock of hair off his forehead. "So, mom-to-be, how are you feeling?"

"Good." Bailey beamed. "Thanks for asking."

"Need any help setting up the baby's room? I'd like to get to it before your mother and I go on safari." A few months ago, my father and Lola had taken a cruise on the Danube. Now they were heading to Africa. Pre-baby. Lola wanted one last travel fling before she became a full-fledged grandmother. My parents hadn't traveled much because my father had been devoted to his work at the FBI. An analyst and then consultant, he'd always been on call. When he retired and opened his hardware store, he had time on his hands. Sadly, my mother didn't.

Bailey smiled. "I don't think we need help,

95

Cary, but thanks. Tito hung curtains. To my surprise, he's quite handy with an automatic drill."

Tito smiled. "My grandfather was a carpenter."

"And we've ordered the crib and finally chosen a color scheme," Bailey added.

"Yellow and brown," I chimed.

My father scrunched his nose. "Yellow and brown?"

I said, "Bailey and Tito are designing the baby's bedroom with everything *giraffe*. According to studies, muted colors are soothing for a baby, and giraffes are gentle creatures, which fill the baby's room with positive energy."

They had already repainted dresser drawers to resemble a giraffe's hide and had found wall lights and other little items that reflected the theme. Just last week, I'd purchased a plush giraffe chair as a baby gift.

"I love giraffes," Tito said. "Their long graceful necks. The way they look at you and don't say a word. You know what they're thinking."

Over the past couple of years, Tito had grown on me. I would never forget our first meeting. A reporter for the *Crystal Cove Courier,* he'd barged into the Cookbook

Nook, eager for a story about the murder of my friend — the murder for which I'd been accused. At the time, he'd reminded me of a boxer or bulldog — broad face, broad shoulders, short legs. Now, he just resembled a cuddly puppy, totally smitten with my pal.

Lola said, "I saw the cutest giraffes at Play Room Toy Store."

As she clasped Bailey's hand and started to describe each one, Tito leaned forward, elbows on his thighs. "Jenna," he whispered, "what can you tell me about the murder?"

"*Mi amor,* no," Bailey said. "Not tonight. Please."

"*Pero, novia —*"

She put a finger to his lips. "At least wait until after dinner."

Tito agreed. He couldn't say no to her.

We dined on raita, a shredded cucumber appetizer served with pita triangles, and followed that with Aunt Vera's curry. Every morsel was delectable. The turmeric and other spices in the curry were perfectly balanced. The conversation revolved around decorating the baby's room and the plan should the baby come early. No one thought to ask about Rhett's and my wedding arrangements. I was glad they didn't. We'd know more after we visited Napa.

Following the meal, Bailey and Lola helped in the kitchen. My aunt put me in charge of serving the pear brandy she'd discovered at a distillery near Carmel. She believed the post-dessert beverage would aid digestion, especially after the heavy meal.

The men and I retreated to the patio. I poured the brandy into four Riedel tumbler glasses set on a tray on the coffee table, handed one to Rhett and took one for myself, and settled onto the divan beside him. Dad lifted a glass and resumed his place in his favorite chair. Tito didn't drink. He was too busy pacing.

"Can we talk now, Jenna?" Tito asked.

"About?"

"Don't be coy. The murder."

"Here we go," my father muttered.

"Dad, for Cinnamon and Pepper's sake, we should chat about it. Besides, Cinnamon wanted your input. A discussion might give you something to go on." I eyed Tito. "Tell me what you know so far."

Tito had picked up that Ivy had been stabbed in her kitchen with a quartz shard, but he didn't seem to know about the gold stones on her eyes or the pieces of aventurine in her hands. I told him about those two things but made him promise, on his baby's crib, to keep a lid on it. He absolutely could not write about it. He crossed his heart.

"Who are the suspects?" he asked.

"Pepper Pritchett," Dad said.

"No way." Tito flapped his hand. "She couldn't kill a flea. She's got an edge to her, but she has a decent heart."

I felt the same way.

"Who else?" he asked. "What about Ivy's boyfriend, that clothing store guy?"

"You mean Hank Hemmings?" I asked. "He wasn't her boyfriend."

"I heard he was dating her."

"I think that's a rumor."

Rhett said, "Even if he was seeing her, why kill her?"

I agreed, then said, "Oren Michaels might have a better reason to want her dead. Ivy broke up with him."

Tito pivoted. "A jilted man as a killer is so clichéd."

Dad said, "It happens more often than not."

"Pepper believes Ivy's clerk might have been in love with her." I recalled Pepper ranting about Ivy setting her sights on Hank when she already had two men interested in her. "What if he —"

"Was Ivy that enchanting?" Rhett cut in.

I smirked. "She was smart, good-looking, and wealthy. A pretty attractive package."

Tito harrumphed. "That boy is in his twenties, no? Ivy was more than twice his age."

"Haven't you heard of a cougar?" my father asked.

"I don't see it," Tito said. "No. He did not kill her."

I smirked. Columbo, he was not.

Tito spanked the back of one hand against the palm of the other. "Let's discuss Hank Hemmings. What do we know about him other than he is a traveling salesman?" The way he said the term sounded lewd.

"He is not." I narrowed my gaze.

"Is too." Like a terrier, Tito had sunk his teeth into a theory and wasn't letting go. "I have seen him with regularity at the San Jose airport."

"He travels, of course. He has distributors all over the Western Hemisphere. He sells everything from sewing kits to men's clothing. Hats are his specialty."

Tito said, "Who wears hats around here?"

"Everyone wears sunhats. He sells fedoras, too," I said. "For many of his clientele, Crystal Cove is their second home. A lot of them work and live in the city. Men still wear classic hats there."

"I suppose." Tito didn't sound convinced. "I will keep my eye on him, just in case."

I squeezed Rhett's hand. He squeezed back. Tito was a character.

"Speaking of eyes . . ." My father twirled a hand. "Tell us more about the stones on Ivy's eyes."

I swiveled to face him. "I think they were eyestones."

"Eye what?"

Quickly, I recapped the theory I'd discussed with my aunt and Bailey.

My father said, "I agree that the killer wasn't doing anything loving with those stones. You should tell Cinnamon."

"Me?" I held up both hands. "No way. I'm not going to."

"I bet you two bucks you will." Dad pulled money from his wallet and slapped it on the table. "You won't be able to help yourself."

I nabbed the bills and jammed them back in his hand. "You do it."

"Okay, okay." He cackled. "Now, what's this I heard about you witnessing a fight between Ivy and Crusibella?"

"Rhett and I did. Aunt Vera, too. Late Friday night. Her dog was barking. That's what caught our attention."

My father looked at Rhett, who nodded.

"That Crusibella. *Oy!*" Tito continued to

pace, flailing his hands like an orchestra conductor. "She claims to be spiritual, but she can stir up dust. She comes into the *Courier* at least once a week to complain about something."

"Really?" I didn't know Crusibella well. Until recently, I hadn't even known her name. But she'd always come across as peace and calm personified — other than the night when she and Ivy had gone at it. Whenever she visited Aunt Vera for a reading, she talked about pursuing inner peace and balance. "What does she complain about?"

"The noise. The pollution. You name it."

"She does believe everything should be pure," I said.

Tito aimed a finger at me. "Did you know she wants an ordinance making each item in our local grocery stores organic? No wiggle room."

Rhett said, "She'll have to take that up with the courts."

"She has. Repeatedly." Tito threw his arms into the air.

"Tito, light somewhere." Dad pointed to a chair. "You're driving me crazy."

Sufficiently cowed, Tito sat and tucked his hands between his knees.

"Jenna," my father said, "let's revisit Ivy

and Crusibella's argument."

I explained how Crusibella had intended to buy Dreamcatcher and believed she had a deal with Ivy, but Ivy had reneged.

Rhett said, "Could Crusibella buy it from Ivy's estate?"

"Did Ivy have a will?" my father asked.

"I don't know," I replied. "Her parents live in San Francisco."

Tito popped to his feet. "Siblings? Children? Ex-husband?"

"I don't have a clue."

"I do." Aunt Vera pulled over a chair from the dining table and joined us. "Ivy's father had a prosperous career. After serving in the war, he joined Lockheed Martin. According to Ivy, he was a tough nut. He was all about the bottom line, the dollars and cents, and her mother was colder than an igloo." In order to give a true reading when telling someone's fortune, my aunt did her best to dredge up an exhaustive history from her client. Her brain was a steel trap; she rarely forgot a detail. "Ivy's younger sister died when Ivy was in high school. Heart complications. Ivy blamed her parents for not taking her sister to the doctor when she said her heart hurt. Ivy didn't speak another word to them. When she left for college, her parents gave her a flat sum of cash and washed their hands of her."

"Interesting," my father murmured.

"To add insult to injury, Ivy married, but her husband died a year later. Also heart complications."

"How tragic," I said.

Aunt Vera nodded. "Ivy suffered, but she rallied. She was always trying to better herself as well as prove herself to her parents. That's why she bought Dream-catcher."

I recalled Ivy crowing to Crusibella about how she'd been building her base of knowledge, pebble by pebble.

"Vera, do you know if Ivy had a will?" my father asked.

"If she didn't, I suppose, given that she has no heirs, that her estate will revert to her parents."

Rhett clasped my hand. "What's Crusibella's alibi?"

"She was at home preparing food for the book club," I said. "No one saw her."

"I truly don't see Crusibella as a killer," my aunt said as she wrapped the green shawl she'd brought with her around her shoulders. "She really is spiritual. Living a balanced life means everything to her. What about Ivy's employee?"

Tito fanned a hand. "We discussed this

already. The boy is in his twenties. Too young."

"For murder?" My aunt raised an eyebrow. Tito reddened.

"How about dissatisfied customers?" Aunt Vera asked.

Dad leaned forward, elbows on his knees, and folded his hands. He positioned his chin on top. "Why would a customer do her in?"

"Perhaps one of them believed, as Crusibella did, that Ivy wasn't a devotee of what she sold," my aunt replied. "I've heard tales of Ivy peddling the wrong item or coercing a customer to buy some unnecessary thing."

"Also" — I raised a finger — "Ivy knew about the skeletons in people's closets."

"Lots of people," my aunt added.

"Humbug," my father grumbled.

"Dad, she knew things like who'd had a face-lift and who was in debt."

Rhett laughed. "What did she do, hypnotize them to cough up their secrets?"

Tito said, "Maybe she did believe in the minerals and made potions that would coerce people to spill their guts."

My aunt hooted. "Heavens, no. She was a snoop, pure and simple."

I flashed on the moment I'd glimpsed Ivy and Oren outside the shop. Had they been spying on Crusibella and Pepper in the parking lot to get some dirt?

Tito picked up the last glass of brandy and took a sip. "Maybe Ivy had a personal hit list outlining who she'd blab on next. Her victims would have plenty of motive."

Dad scoffed. "What was she, an aspiring gossip columnist?"

"Money and entitlement equal bored," Tito said.

Rhett shook his head. "Would someone honestly kill to keep a face-lift confidential?"

"I wouldn't think so," I said, "but Ivy is dead, and someone did it."

CHAPTER 8

Rhett spent the night but skipped breakfast Monday morning to hurry to work. I skipped it, too. I had too much to do at the shop. Bad decision. By midmorning, I was starved.

Putting Bailey and Tina in charge of the shop, I made my way to the Nook Café and sat down for a real breakfast — eggs Benedict perfectly plated on two halves of an English muffin. While I ate the first half of my meal, I watched the customers rise from their tables and pluck cookbooks from the new bookshelves, which did my heart proud. I hoped they would wander into the Cookbook Nook and purchase the books they'd browsed.

As I was starting in on the second portion, Katie hurried up to me, her chef's coat splattered with something red. A memory of Ivy lying dead on the floor of her kitchen whizzed through my mind. I set my fork down, appetite quashed.

"How are you holding up?" She plunked into the chair opposite me. "You look healthy. Your eyes are clear. I like that mocha top you're wearing."

The sweater had belonged to my mother, and sometimes when I was feeling off, it cheered me to don something of hers.

"Is your system wonky?" Katie asked. "It must be wonky. Mine would be wonky after what you saw. You know what?" She bounded to her feet. "I'm going to make you a turkey-asparagus sandwich to take with you. Turkey is rich in tryptophan, which will calm your nerves, and asparagus is filled with antioxidants as well as tryptophan so it'll give you a double whammy of good stuff. Plus, I'll throw in a few pumpkin seeds for you to nosh on. They're packed with zinc, which helps the body manage stress."

"Look who's been studying up on nutritional values."

Her cheeks turned pink. "Wait until you taste the dressing I put on it."

"Please don't go to any trouble." I eyed my uneaten food. "I'm not hungry."

"You're going to be sooner or later. I won't take no for an answer. So" — she tapped the table — "I didn't ask the other day. Who do the police think did it?"

"Pepper."

"You're kidding. That explains why Cinnamon was pounding down apple pancakes earlier." Katie stared out the window with the view of Beaders of Paradise. "She must be frantic to prove her mother innocent."

"She ate pancakes?"

"Two helpings."

I gawked. Cinnamon's diet typically consisted of protein and vegetables with an occasional dessert thrown in.

"If I were you, I'd contact her," Katie said. "She could use a friend to talk to. Now, stay put. I'll be right back with your meal."

As she hurried off, I shook my head. What was going on? Was the universe conspiring to pit me against Cinnamon? First, Aunt Vera ordered me to put myself in the line of fire with her and then my father, and now Katie?

Minutes later, Katie came back with my lunch packed in a to-go bag. Before returning to the kitchen, she made me promise to keep her up to date on the murder. I said I would and walked through the breezeway into the shop.

As I was passing the vintage table where Aunt Vera was concluding a tarot card reading for the fretful wife of the Crystal Cove

Bank manager, Tina tore by me, the bow of her pale pink blouse untied and fluttering like wings. She raced out the front door into the parking lot, her cell phone pressed to her ear.

"Uh-oh," I whispered to my aunt when she joined me at the sales counter. "What's up with Tina?"

"Boyfriend troubles." She removed her amber-colored turban and fluffed her short hair.

"He was persona non grata the other day."

"I think he's toast today."

"What happened?" I set my lunch behind the sales counter.

Aunt Vera followed me. "From what I could gather, she caught him with a red-head. Holding hands at Latte Luck Café. He said she was jumping to conclusions, of course." She snorted. "You'd think he'd have been a little more discreet. There are plenty of cafés in towns other than Crystal Cove."

"Poor Tina."

"I had no idea she knew so many colorful words."

Bailey finished arranging items on the buffet table she'd covered with a striped tablecloth and joined us. "Should I give her some advice?"

"No," my aunt and I said in unison. Prior to meeting Tito, Bailey hadn't had the best luck with men.

"Ha-ha. I get the hint. Dear Abby I'm not." Bailey did a teetering pirouette. "How do you like my new smock dress? I've gotten so big, I can only fit into my ultra-stretch maternity leggings."

"It's darling," I said. "The blue goes with your eyes."

"Do I look as big as a house?"

"You look fashionable."

Bailey scoffed. "That was tactful. Hey, I could use some help setting up the shop for this afternoon's event."

Our local librarian, Darian, was going to lead a book club. Yes, whenever I saw her or even thought her name, the lyrics of the charming song from *The Music Man* cycled through my mind: Marian, Madam Librarian. Like the character in the musical, Darian Drake was an attractive, no-nonsense woman. Unlike her fictional counterpart, she preferred to dress simply in slimming suits with her blond hair secured at the nape of her neck. A month ago, she had assigned the book selection *Aftertaste* for today's event. It was a culinary novel about a female chef's fresh start in life and love. All visiting book clubs had been alerted to the choice.

I lifted a stack of aqua blue cookbooks from the rear counter. "Bailey, where would you like me to put these?" To celebrate the event, I had ordered two dozen copies of *The Little Library Cookbook: 100 Recipes from Your Favorite Books,* an enchanting edition featuring recipes like porridge from *The Secret Garden* and crumpets from *Rebecca,* written by a self-proclaimed book lover and book hoarder.

"How about on the buffet, next to the cookies?"

"Ooh, cookies," I said. "Yum." Katie had made an array of cookies, each decorated with a different colored icing and inscribed with an author's name. I snagged the Agatha Christie cookie and set it on a napkin by my purse — for later.

"If you like those," Bailey said, "just wait until you see the other goodies Katie is supplying."

Together, Bailey and I shifted the portable bookshelves to the exterior borders of the shop, and then she and I arranged folding chairs.

When we were halfway done, Tina blazed through the front door. Her face was streaked with tears. She said, "I'll be right there. I just want to freshen up." Seconds later, she emerged from the stockroom with her makeup reapplied and the bow of her blouse retied. "Men," she muttered as she whipped open a folding chair. "Can't trust them as far as you can throw them."

"Yes, you can," Bailey said.

"No, no, no."

I hated to see Tina disillusioned at such a young age, but better to go into a relationship with eyes wide open. I hadn't been wise to my deceased husband David's antics. I'd paid the price.

"Where should I put this?" Tina held out the gift basket we were presenting to one attendee. It was filled with items from the shop: two cookbooks, an apron, a spatula, and more.

"Set it beside the roll of raffle tickets on the sales counter," I said. "Next to the sign Bailey made." Each attendee could purchase up to five raffle tickets. Proceeds would go to the library.

For the next hour or so, I tidied the shop, all the while pondering whether I would call Cinnamon, as Katie had suggested. Ultimately, I gave in. Like before, she wasn't available, so I left a message. Rather than say I was worried about her and her mother, I asked if my father had talked to her. After all, she'd wanted his input. Thanks to last night's discussion, he had quite a lot to impart.

Around two thirty, Katie brought in a service cart filled with platters of snacks: cinnamon madeleines, muffins, bite-sized cakes, and mini fruit tarts. She set the platters on the buffet table and said, "I'll be right back with the coffee and tea services."

"Bailey, you weren't kidding about the array of goodies," I whispered.

"Told you." She winked at me. "I've got my eye set on one of those madeleines."

"Don't eat them until the party starts," Katie warned and bustled off, whistling along with the latest tune that had come up in the queue, "Love's a Mystery" by the Pretenders. Luckily, Tina, in her given state of snit, wasn't paying attention to the mushy lyrics. If she were, she might have burst into tears.

Minutes later, Darian, dressed in a chic tan suit and broad-brimmed sunhat, strolled in. She shifted her hefty briefcase from one shoulder to the other.

I crossed to her. "Welcome. Thank you for doing this."

"My pleasure." She removed her sunhat and fluffed her hair. "Silly things, hats. But we have to keep our faces covered nowadays, don't we?"

"Yes, indeed. By the way, I love the library's book tent on the boulevard. The dolphins with the glasses are hysterical."

Darian grinned. "Our adorable mayor suggested it. She's got such a great sense of humor."

"Yes, she does." Z.Z.'s sense of humor was even sharper now that she was dating Jake.

"Oh, I see some of my patrons. Give me a moment." Darian joined a couple of book club attendees who were browsing the front display table and chatted for a moment before crossing to Katie, who was setting out white china teacups. "Nicely done, Katie." She gave her a friendly hug. "So pretty. Exactly what I'd hoped for. You and I are kindred spirits." She hailed me. "Jenna, where do you want me?"

I ushered her to the children's corner. We'd set up a lectern in case she needed it. "Would you like some water?"

"Sure."

As she pulled all sorts of handouts from her briefcase, I fetched a glass of ice water for her. Then I moved to the antique kitchen table to break apart the jigsaw puzzle, just in case any of our customers wanted to toy with it.

At a quarter to three, Pepper and Hank strolled into the shop. He smoothed the front of his tweed suit and took off his fedora, revealing a thick head of silver hair.

"This way, sweetheart," he murmured and held out his hand to Pepper.

Even though she was wearing what she referred to as her power dress — a blue sheath beaded masterfully at the neck and hem — she appeared nervous. She was chewing her lower lip. Was she still a suspect? Had her daughter made any headway in the investigation? I waved to her. She responded listlessly. Hank whispered in her ear and guided her to a folding chair. She sat, pulled a book from her tote bag, and started thumbing through it.

Darian approached them and extended her hand to Hank. "Nice to see men attend a book club event."

"Wouldn't have missed it for the world," he said.

Pepper gazed up at Darian, and a moment of annoyance crossed her face. Was she worried that our local librarian was flirting with Hank? She needn't be. Darian was married to a well-respected professor at UC Santa Cruz.

Sensing her gaze, Darian said, "Pepper, lovely to see you, too. I'm so sorry about, well, you know, everything." She twirled a hand. "You can't possibly be a suspect despite what everyone is saying."

Pepper opened her mouth but no words came out.

Darian cut a look to the right. "Excuse me. Another gentleman is joining us."

I wondered if I should comfort Pepper but changed my mind when Hank sat beside her and took hold of her hand.

"Welcome," Darian said as she greeted the handsome clerk who worked at Dreamcatcher. It's so nice of you to come."

Sunlight streamed in behind him and highlighted his lean physique. Women in the shop discreetly peeked in his direction. A couple of them gawped. Again, I pictured him in one of my Olympic commercials, maybe a javelin thrower or a high jumper.

"What's your name?" Darian asked.

"Alastair Dukas."

Alastair. Of course. Now I remembered. He'd asked Aunt Vera to tell his fortune a couple of weeks ago. He'd left quite pleased.

Darian said something more and gestured to the chairs. Alastair nodded but proceeded to browse the store.

Bailey scurried to me. "Why is he here?"

"To join the book discussion, I presume." I pointed out the copy of *Aftertaste* tucked under his arm.

"He doesn't look like a reader."

"What exactly does a reader look like?" I asked.

Bailey glowered at me. "Have the police delved into his history? Ivy rebuffed him. Maybe he killed her," she said and reiterated a theory we'd raised at my father's. "He relocated here a year ago. Maybe he followed Ivy from the city. What if he was stalking her?"

I put a hand on my pal's shoulder. "Calm down. What's got you in a tizzy?"

"That guy waltzes into town and gets a job at her shop, and a year later she's dead. Don't you find that suspicious?"

"Not until now."

"You need to tell Cinnamon."

Okay, now I was certain the universe was conspiring against me. I said, "She isn't returning my calls."

"You should track her down. Buy her a coffee. Console her. Give her a shoulder to cry on." Bailey screwed up her face. "Maybe not cry. I doubt she cries. Ever. But perhaps you could offer a receptive ear and then —"

"Whoa." I planted a fist on my hip. "Did Katie and Aunt Vera put you up to this?"

"To what?"

"All of you, including my father, want me to confront Cinnamon."

"I didn't say confront. I said *console*.

There's a huge difference in those two words. First of all, one's seven letters and the other is eight, and there are lots of different letters."

I snorted.

"C'mon," Bailey coaxed. "It must be hard for Cinnamon being the only woman in the department."

"There are a number of other women."

"Not her equal."

"I'm not her equal, either."

"But you're her friend. Reach out to her. Her mother's innocence is at stake, and a murderer is at large."

"Jenna!" Crusibella swept into the shop, the ruffled collar of her chiffon jumpsuit wafting. "Thank heaven you're here. You're just the person I wanted to see."

"About the event?"

"About last Friday night. No matter what you heard going on between Ivy and me, we were friends. True friends. I didn't do it. I didn't kill her."

She had claimed to be innocent at the crime scene, too. Was guilt making her feel the need to repeat herself?

CHAPTER 9

"Vera!" Crusibella rushed past me and plopped into a chair at the vintage table. "Thank you for making time for me." She tapped her nails on the top. "I'm ready for my reading."

I blinked. Apparently, I wasn't the only person she'd wanted to see.

Aunt Vera joined her and patted her hand. "Breathe, dear. We can't start until the book club concludes. I told you to come in around five. Patience is a virtue."

"But the early bird gets the worm," Crusibella sassed.

"Good afternoon, everyone," Darian said from behind the lectern. "Let's get started."

The shop had filled with regular patrons and a number of new faces. I stood at the back of the room with Bailey. She whispered to me, "That exchange with Crusibella was weird."

"I'll say."

"Do you think she protest-eth too much?"

"I was wondering the same thing."

"Okay." Darian raised a copy of the book selection. "Who loved it?" Half the hands shot up. "Did anybody hate it?" One hand. "Why do you think that was? I'm curious."

The blowsy woman who'd disliked it — not someone I recognized — said, "It took too long to get into."

"But once you were into it, did you enjoy it?" Darian asked.

"Sort of."

"The book claims to be a novel in five courses," Darian said. "Let's find out why, shall we?" She handed out the materials she'd brought in her briefcase and resumed her place at the lectern.

For the next hour, she led the audience through the questions included at the back of the novel. Z.Z. and Gran, who had come in just before the meeting started, seemed to have the most opinions. Hank chimed in occasionally. Pepper rarely looked up. Alastair, surprisingly, was well versed on certain aspects of the book, particularly how the food and its preparation were a stand-in for emotions. Even Crusibella, despite her eagerness to have my aunt tell her fortune, entered into the discussion; she had read the book when it had debuted.

After the book club disbanded, the activity in the shop was incredible. Tina and I worked nonstop at the sales counter, ringing up sales and packing books into gift bags. I noticed Aunt Vera dove right in with Crusibella.

By the time the tarot reading concluded, I was dying to know whether the reading for Crusibella had hinted at signs of innocence or guilt. Unfortunately, I was too embroiled with a customer to break free. And then when I was chatting with a book club member from Texas about the copies of *Texas Eats: The New Lone Star Heritage Cookbook* that they'd preordered — a deeply personal cookbook filled with anecdotes and recipes from all over the state — Aunt Vera left for the evening.

"Rats," I muttered to Bailey as we were closing the shop.

"Relax. You'll find out what she gleaned tomorrow. In the meantime, contact Cinnamon." She pecked me on the cheek and, cradling her baby bump, hurried off to meet her husband for dinner.

As I was locking up, Katie sent me a text saying she absolutely had to see me.

I said to Tigger, "I'll be right back, buddy."

When I entered the café, I was pleased to see it was packed with diners. Lit candles at the centers of the tables provided a warm glow. Chatter was muted but steady. I spotted Hank and Pepper sitting by the window and paused. Uneasily, she fussed with the collar of her dress and pulled at the seams around her torso. A waitress delivered two entrées to the table and left. Hank took a sip of his white wine. Pepper idly ran a finger up and down the stem of her glass.

I approached them and eyed their food. They had ordered the same dish but hadn't taken a bite. "Is everything all right with your meal?"

"It just arrived," Hank said, his voice upbeat. "Looks delicious."

"Good choice," I said. "Halibut with lemon citrus *beurre blanc* sauce is one of Chef Katie's specialties."

"Have you eaten?" he asked. "Sit with us."

"I have a meeting in the kitchen. Katie summoned me."

"You look quite pretty in that color," he went on. "It really brings out your eyes. I have the perfect hat to go with that outfit. Provence-style in nougat."

"Thanks, but I only wear hats when I'm riding my bicycle or walking on the beach."

"We all need to keep our faces covered nowadays," he warned. "The sun is so damaging. You wouldn't want your gorgeous skin to suffer, would you?"

Was he flirting with me? Did Pepper have a right to be worried? No, of course he wasn't. He was twice my age. I was reading more into his charming delivery than necessary. "Are you feeling all right?" I asked Pepper. She appeared to be lost in thought, not paying attention to our conversation.

"Mm-hm. I just wish . . ." Her voice drifted off.

Just wished *what*? Wished she could curl into a ball until the murder was solved? Wished she could turn back the hands of time and Ivy would still be alive?

"You're innocent," I said. "Your daughter knows that."

"I'm not so sure about that." Pepper nudged her wineglass aside. "Just in case, I've retained a lawyer."

"Really?"

"Per my daughter, I have a solid motive and a flimsy alibi."

"But you're her mother."

"*Pfft.* The law comes first." Pepper clicked her tongue. "At least she hasn't slapped me in jail yet."

"Do you want my advice?" I asked. When I'd first met Cinnamon, I was the main target on her radar. She thought I'd killed a celebrity chef who had been my college roommate. Over the course of her investigation, she realized I could never have done what she'd accused me of. "Stay low. Don't rile her. And let her do her job. The truth will out."

"The truth." Pepper slapped the table with her palm. "Cinnamon should believe me one hundred percent, but does she? No. She says she has to weigh all the evidence."

"Does she have any evidence that points to you?"

Hank said, "If she did, she'd arrest Pepper, wouldn't she?"

"I think so." I addressed Pepper. "Impartiality makes Cinnamon good at what she does."

"I know," she murmured.

"I don't think she believes you're guilty," I went on, "but she is worried about you. She's —" I stopped short of saying she was pounding down pancakes.

"She should be," Hank said, his voice sharp. "People are shunning Pepper. It's horrid. Her business has decreased at least twenty-five percent since the murder, even though all these book clubs have come to town. Do you want to know where they're going? To Home Sweet Home. Can you believe it?"

Pepper sucked back a sob. "Oh, Jenna,

this . . . this . . . ostracism is crushing me."

"Ostracism," Hank repeated. "Great word."

I cut a look at him. Now was not the time for a vocabulary pat on the back. He blanched under my gaze and sipped his wine.

Pepper pursed her lips. "Look, Jenna, I've told Hank and I'll tell you. It's common knowledge that I didn't like Ivy. She wasn't a nice woman, to me anyway, and I did believe she was homing in on Hank —"

He clasped her hand. "I told you, darling —"

"I know you said you weren't interested in her, but that doesn't mean she didn't have her stealth tracking system aimed at you." Pepper gazed at me. "I'm sorry she's dead, but I didn't do this. Please help Cinnamon solve this, Jenna. She's too close to it. She'll listen to you."

I barked out a laugh. My aunt, my father, Katie, Bailey, and now Pepper . . . all with the same opinion.

"She will," Pepper said.

"More likely, she'd cut off my head so I couldn't speak."

Hank snorted.

Pepper pulled her hand free of his and clasped my wrist. Hard. "Please, Jenna.

126

Help me."

I pried her fingers loose — man, she had a grip — and patted her shoulder. "I'll see what I can do."

"Bless you."

A tear slipped from her eye. Seeing her so vulnerable jolted me to the core.

Minutes later, I joined Katie in the kitchen. She steered me to the far corner and peered over my shoulder. No one was near us. The staff, helmed by the attractive head chef Reynaldo, who was now a keeper as far as Katie was concerned, was turning out dish after dish. The aroma of baked apples hung in the air.

"Pie," I murmured as my salivary glands kicked into high gear.

"Open-faced apple pie," Katie said. "One of my best recipes."

"Must have a slice. Now."

"In a sec. First we have to talk about Hank Hemmings."

I glanced toward the door I'd just passed through.

"I overheard him earlier," Katie said. "During the library event. He'd gone out-side. He was standing at the top of the access." The access was a public stairway between Beaders of Paradise and the café that led to the beach. "He was on his cell phone speaking to someone he called *honey*."

"Okay."

"Something niggled at me, so I checked to see if Pepper was on her phone. She wasn't. She was chatting with Darian."

"Maybe it was Hank's child or grandchild?"

Katie shook her head. "The way he said *honey* sounded much more intimate."

"Maybe it was his ex."

"I've never heard a man coo to an ex, have you?"

The alley door to the kitchen opened and Oren Michaels strode in wearing a fisherman's cap, denim jacket, white T-shirt, and fashionably torn jeans. "Katie, Katie, married lady," he sang at the top of his lungs, riffing on the song from *Funny Girl.* His canvas creel hung over a shoulder.

Reynaldo joined him and patted him on the arm. So did the sous chef. They called him *bro* and asked what had brought him to our neck of the woods.

Katie muttered, "I'll be right back. Oren usually peddles fish in the morning. Hope we don't have a problem about tomorrow's delivery." She weaved around her staff to greet him.

I trailed her.

As we neared, Oren said, "What kind of music should you listen to while fishing?" He waited a beat. All eyes were on him. "Something catchy."

"Ha-ha," Reynaldo said.

"I've got another. Why do fish swim in schools?"

The freckle-faced sous chef said, "Because they can't walk."

Oren shot her a mock-sour look and waggled two thumbs at himself. "Hey, who's telling the jokes here?"

The sous chef toyed with her ponytail and blushed.

Oren grinned. "Relax. You're new. I'll cut you some slack. You didn't know. Okay, last one. How do you communicate with a fish?" He mimed casting a spinning rod. "Drop it a line."

"Ba-dum-dum," Reynaldo said.

Oren scratched his chin. "Though I guess you'd have to send an email nowadays. Nobody writes letters anymore."

"Guess you'll have to work on that joke," Reynaldo said.

Katie clapped her hands. "Okay, everyone, back to work. The floor show is over." She approached Oren. "What's up? Have we got an issue?"

"Hey, Katie. Hi, Jenna. Nope. No issues."

"Did you lose your sense of day and night?" Katie asked. "You're not due until tomorrow morning."

"You know me. I like shortcuts. Why fish for more than I need to?" He pulled out his cell phone and tapped an icon on the screen. "Do you want me to add a large striped bass to your regular order? I've been catching a lot of it lately. One, two?" His finger hovered over the phone app.

"Two."

"Great." He typed in the order and pocketed the phone.

"Oren" — Katie drew closer — "are you okay?"

In an instant, his jokester persona vanished, and he sagged like he was dog-tired. His eyes were red-rimmed. Had he been crying? "Yeah. Sure. It's just . . ."

"Ivy," Katie said and nodded.

"Yeah. She's gone. Like that." His shoulders heaved. "She was the one, Katie." He swiped a tear off his cheek. "The. One."

She clutched his shoulder. "Do you have someone to talk to?"

"Like a therapist?"

"Like a friend."

He bobbed his head. "I've got my dad. He's a good listener."

"Oren," I said, "I'm sorry for your loss."

He nodded thanks. "I can't believe the way she died. People said she was stabbed. With quartz or something. And stones painted like eyes were on her —" He indicated his own eyes.

"Who told you about the crime scene?" I asked. The Mystery Mavens were advised not to talk about it.

"Can't remember."

Someone had blabbed. Cinnamon would not be pleased.

I said, "It must be hard knowing you can't make up with Ivy. I felt that way when my husband died, wishing I could have said what was really in my heart."

"Make up?" He shook his head, perplexed. "What do you mean?"

"I heard she broke up with you."

"That's not true. We were going to get married." He gazed between Katie and me. "You don't think I killed her, do you? I didn't. I couldn't have. I was on my boat at the time of the murder." The creel started to slip off his shoulder. He lugged it into place. "I'm practicing night runs so I can expand my business to include overnight events during the summer. People will pay big bucks to sleep on a boat in a cove packed with fish."

"But your boat is so small," Katie said. "It

can't accommodate guests."

"I've got my eye on purchasing a specialty boat. We'll fish for croker and salmon. If the summer pays off like I hope, I can take people whale watching in the winter. That was Ivy's suggestion." He swallowed hard, as if it hurt to say her name.

"How long did the trip take you, Oren?" I asked.

"I left at dusk, traveled two hours north up the coast, waited for two hours in the cove, and then made the trip home."

"Six hours," I said, doing the math. "That's a haul."

"You're telling me. Well, I have to be going. I've got to contact the rest of my customers about the bass. Hate to land any I can't sell. See you in the morning." He tapped the brim of his cap and hurried off.

As he said goodbye to a few of the staff, I wondered about his alibi. Could anyone confirm it? What if, under the cloak of darkness, he'd veered back, stolen to Ivy's, murdered her, and returned to his boat to establish the final leg of his alibi?

CHAPTER 10

Because Crystal Cove was driven by tourism and tourists often enjoyed three-day weekends, we took Tuesdays rather than Mondays off at the shop. Sometimes on our days off we played catch-up and did inventory, but this week we didn't need to. I awoke eager to spend a day free of thoughts about business or murder.

After feeding Tigger, I dressed in yellow capris, a light cream sweater, and sandals — I didn't need anything warmer; there wasn't a hint of a breeze — and then I donned sunblock and a broad-brimmed sunhat and rode my bicycle to the Pier. A cup of coffee was in order. Rhett couldn't play hooky and spend the day with me because, thanks to flu season, he was one sales clerk short. Even though he and I were going to meet for dinner, I wanted to see him.

Due to the early morning hour, the parking lot was fairly empty when I arrived. I wheeled my bicycle along the boardwalk to the bakery and purchased two lattes. Then I headed to Bait and Switch Fishing and Sport Supply Store, a huge warehouse-type store. It opened at five a.m. because eager fishermen and sports enthusiasts wanted to get an early start.

As I was strolling up, Oren Michaels and his father were leaving. Oren wasn't carrying his creel. Maybe he'd come in to pick up the pamphlet he was perusing.

"Morning, Jenna." He tapped the brim of his seafarer's cap as he drew near. His father, who was an older version of Oren, gave me a nod, as well.

Out of the blue, the notion that Oren's father might have helped him establish an alibi coursed through my mind. I felt my cheeks flush. Could either of them sense what I was thinking? Oren didn't seem sad about Ivy today. Had he tried to put one over on Katie and me yesterday? No, I couldn't see it. Someone who appreciated silly fish jokes was not a killer.

Oh, really? How naïve are you, Jenna Hart? Clowns can be cruel.

"Good morning, Oren," I replied, my tone even. My high school acting teacher would have been astonished by how well I was covering my jitters. "All done delivering fish?"

"Over an hour ago. Thought I'd take my old man to breakfast."

"I'm not old," his father groused. "I'm seasoned." He winked at me and said, "Say, have you heard this one, Jenna? What do sea monsters eat?"

"I don't know, what?"

"Fish and ships. Get it? *Ships?*" He slapped his thigh.

"Very funny." I jerked a thumb. "Forgive me, gentlemen, but I'm going to give Rhett his coffee before it gets cold."

"Be my guest." Oren swept a hand permitting me to pass, and he and his father left the store laughing.

The store's rich green leather and mahogany décor reminded me of a mountain cabin that had been relocated to the ocean — homey and comfortable. Rhett and two of his staff were reorganizing display tables, which looked like a hurricane had hit them.

"Hey, beautiful," he said. "What a nice surprise."

Holding out the coffee to him, I said, "Did you have a sale yesterday?"

"How could you tell?" He pecked my cheek and accepted the container. "What brings you to my neck of the woods?"

"I missed you."

"I missed you, too." He took a sip of his drink and hummed. "Perfect, as always. Walk with me." He strode toward the front of the store.

"Oren didn't seem bereft about Ivy," I said.

"Men often cover their feelings. You know that better than most."

He was referring to my ex, of course. The ultimate actor.

"Why were Oren and his father here?" I asked.

"He's looking to buy a new boat. Says he wants to increase his business."

"You aren't selling yours, are you?" Not only did Rhett supply fish to some of the local restaurants, but on occasion, he took groups deep-sea fishing.

"Are you kidding? Not a chance." He smirked. "Old Jake is ready to divest of *Joy of the Sea.*"

Jake Chapman was one of the wealthiest men in town. Way back when, my grandfather, in a show of thanks to Jake for saving my father from drowning, had taught him to invest.

"He's selling his beautiful red boat?" I exclaimed. "It's fabulous."

"An Avenger. Top of its class."

Jake had offered to take me for a ride. I hadn't found the time. I said, "Oren's business must be pretty good if he can afford that plus a new truck."

"According to him, the season has been quite fruitful." Rhett wrapped an arm around me. "What have you got planned today?"

"Bailey wants to go shopping again."

"Your favorite thing to do." He grinned. *"Not."*

"For her, anything. She's nesting like crazy."

"Speaking of nesting, Z.Z. has a couple more houses to show us." In addition to being our mayor, Zoey Zeller had taken up selling real estate. Her son had gone back to college, and she'd offered to help him with tuition. Any extra income helped. "Can you spare a few hours over the weekend?"

"I'll carve out the time." I kissed him goodbye and headed out.

By midmorning, the sun was blazing down on Bailey and me. With all the stops and starts she insisted on making along Buena Vista Boulevard, we were getting plenty of sun exposure. Good thing she had worn a long-sleeved maternity tunic over stretchy pants as well as a sunhat.

At one of the Book Club Bonanza tents called Book Addicts she purchased an ornate brass bookstand. She refused to give up challenging her mind after having the baby and thought a bookstand might help her read hands-free. At One More Chapter, she bought an animal print journal for Lola to take on her safari trip. At Play Room Toy Store, thanks to her mother's heads-up, she chose a variety of giraffes for the baby's room. After that, we were starved.

As we were polishing off soft fish tacos that we'd purchased to go at the Pelican Brief Diner, Bailey pointed north. "Hey, is that Cinnamon?"

A few doors down, a fit woman in neon blue roller blading gear, including kneepads, sunglasses, and a helmet emblazoned with a gold lightning bolt, was twirling with her leg in arabesque. Definitely Cinnamon. Pepper had taught her to skate. Was she doing so now to work out her aggression or work off those pancakes?

Somewhat peeved that she hadn't returned my calls — after all, I'd contacted her as a friend — I hustled in that direction.

She came to a halt using her toe stop and jammed her hands on her hips. "What?"

"Well, isn't that a fine how-do-you-do?" I

said. "What are you doing?"

"What does it look like? Skating during my lunch hour. I need the exercise. It clears my head."

"I left you a couple of messages."

"I don't owe you a daily report."

"That's not why —"

"Look, Jenna, we will solve the crime."

I scratched the back of my neck. Why did talking to her make me itchy sometimes? "One question. Did my dad talk to you?"

"About?"

"He said you wanted his two cents. I posed a theory to him."

She shook her head. "Sorry. Nope."

I clenched my jaw, slightly ticked at my father. He'd bet me that I wouldn't be able to help myself and I'd blab everything to Cinnamon. *Okay, Dad, so be it. You win.* "It has to do with the stones over Ivy's eyes. I think they might correlate to a Greek myth."

"Like I said, we're on it. See you at dinner." Cinnamon tore away as fast as a speed skater, expertly dodging a few pedestrians.

"Gee whiz, she's maddening," I said to Bailey. "So much for needing consoling."

"Yeah, she can be —" Bailey made an *oof* sound. "Oy, I've got to rest."

"Let's go inside Spellbinder." I jutted a

finger in that direction. "We can sit at the bar."

In addition to a sizeable reading room, which was fitted with a round table, cozy chairs, and a variety of lamps, the mystery bookstore boasted a reading bar, where customers could sit and browse through a book while sipping a nonalcoholic beverage.

I added, "I'll bet Crusibella could use some cheering up." Also, I wanted to follow up on her declaration of innocence yesterday. Why had she come to me? Did she think I could convince the police of her innocence? "Even though the week is about books, books, and more books, I'll bet the street vendors are taking business away from her."

"Lead the way."

A teensy bell jingled overhead as we stepped inside the shop. At the same time, a dog yapped. Crusibella's toy poodle charged us and made an abrupt U-turn, disappearing through a drape at the rear of the store.

Bailey whispered, "Who needs a doorbell with that watchdog around?"

I giggled.

The short, perky clerk I had interacted with on previous occasions greeted us from the sales desk. "Welcome. Feel free to ask me anything."

As predicted, the shop was not overrun with customers. Two men were flipping through books in the noir section. The woman who was perusing the classics repeatedly glanced over her shoulder at two young children — hers, I decided since they sported the same nose and tons of freckles — who were seated at a small table similar to the children's table in the Cookbook Nook. They were poring over books pulled from a set of the Spiderwick Chronicles.

Bailey removed her sunhat and craned an ear. "Do you hear someone crying?"

I hurried down the aisle, past the cascade display filled with culinary cozies to the rear of the store where the dog had disappeared, and peeked through the drapes. Crusibella was pacing in the storage room, her gaze riveted on the floor, her cell phone pressed to her ear.

"Uh-huh. I understand, but —". Someone on the line cut her off. "Yes, but —" She listened some more. Tears trickled down one cheek. "Please. I'll do whatever I have to. I'll get a co-signer. I'll get two. I'll —" Whoever she was talking to interrupted her again. More head bobbing. After a long moment, she hissed, "Thanks for nothing," and ended the call. She shoved her phone into the pocket of her aqua blue jumper and lifted her chin. "Oh!" She stopped short. "Jenna. I . . . I didn't realize you were —"

"I'm sorry we startled you. We came to check on you."

Crusibella blotted the tears with her fingertips.

"Are you all right?" I asked.

"Do I look okay?" she snapped and instantly her cheeks turned crimson. "Sorry. That was rude." She pushed past me into the store.

Bailey joined us. "What's wrong?"

"Nothing." Crusibella edged along the aisle, righting any books that weren't aligned on the shelves.

"Crusibella, c'mon," I said. "You're clearly distraught. Is someone sick?"

"Or in trouble?" Bailey asked.

Crusibella whirled around. "No one is sick. No one is in trouble. Truth? This is ridiculously superficial, but I want to get a loan and the lender dismissed me."

"A loan for what?" Bailey asked.

"To buy Dreamcatcher?" I asked.

Crusibella nodded. "I know it's not for sale yet, but it will be. With Ivy's death . . ." She twirled a hand. "I realize it's crass of me to be thinking ahead, but she doesn't . . . *didn't* . . . have children, and her parents are bound to put it up for sale. She and they were estranged. They didn't give a hoot about her business. I figure they'll sell sooner rather than later. I need to be ready." She shook her head. "If only Ivy hadn't —" She bit her tongue.

"Reneged on your deal," I whispered.

Crusibella placed a hand on her chest. "You must think I'm horrid, talking about a sale when her body isn't even cold. Maybe I am. But I've had my heart set on owning the store for ages. Ever since she hinted that she was ready to bail."

"Do you know why she wanted out?" I asked.

"Like I said, she'd had a heart scare. Plus, I think it was hard to always be excited about something she didn't believe in." Crusibella grabbed a pair of books from the Cupcake Mystery series and brought them to the checkout desk. "Wrap these up for Mrs. Sanders," she told her clerk and then continued on, tweaking, as I often did at the Cookbook Nook, making sure book titles faced out and displays were neat. "By the way, it's not a secret that Ivy didn't believe. I'm not telling tales out of school."

"My aunt said something similar."

"When you're selling items that are supposed to center the soul, you should believe in their powers, don't you think? For heaven's sake, the store is called Dreamcatcher. Not Reality 101."

Bailey bit back a laugh.

"Bad, bad, bad." Crusibella finger-combed her frazzled hair. "I shouldn't speak ill of the dead. She was a good friend."

I smiled supportively. "So you said the other day. Tell me about your friendship."

"We talked daily." Crusibella hitched a thumb. "We'd meet in the alley out back, and she'd have a smoke, and I —"

"Ivy smoked?"

"Two cigarettes a day. She was very disciplined in that regard. We'd catch up on the latest gossip. Boy, that woman had her finger on the pulse of this town, let me tell you."

"If you bought her store, what would you do with Spellbinder?"

"Keep it. I could never sell it. Books are my life's blood. I can't wait to come to work every day." She pointed to the wall adjoining Dreamcatcher. "I plan to cut a door right there so customers can move freely between the two. It's a perfect match when you think about it. Reading stirs the imagination, and the items in Dreamcatcher stir the soul."

Bailey let out a teensy moan.

I gripped her elbow. "Are you okay?"

"I need to sit down. My feet are swollen."

"Let's go to the bar. I'll buy you a sparkling water. Crusibella, come sit with us."

She fanned the air. "I would, but there's so much to do. I have a book club coming in later to use the reading room. They're discussing a very dark tale by Edgar Allan Poe. The room needs a proper dusting, and —"

Boom, clack!

Bailey shrieked.

Something fell next door, then the walls rattled and a man swore. I ordered Bailey to sit and tore out of Spellbinder.

CHAPTER 11

The door to Dreamcatcher was ajar. I dashed in and found Alastair futilely bracing a rack of natural wood shelves against the wall. One of the two-inch support legs had come loose and lay beneath the lowest shelf. If he dared to move, all the items on the shelves, many of them breakable, would crash to the floor.

Crusibella tore in after me. "Oh, my."

"All I did was remove a box," Alastair moaned. "One. Darned. Box." He glared at a toppled carton packed with smaller containers. "The moment I did, everything went haywire. I had to drop it."

"Crusibella, put your hand here." I gestured to a spot midway along the shelving. "I'm going to screw in the support leg." I glanced at Alastair, who didn't look quite as Olympian as usual with perspiration peppering his upper lip. "Why are you here by yourself?" I asked him.

146

"The executor for Ivy's estate wants a complete inventory so her parents can prepare the place for sale. Everything has to come out of its box to ensure nothing is broken. I'm supposed to take pictures and send them to him."

"I told you they'd put it on the market, Jenna," Crusibella said.

Alastair hitched his chin in the direction of the wall. "I think I damaged it."

"It's nothing that a little paint and spackle won't fix." I patted his shoulder. "Now hold still." I knelt to the floor and scrounged beneath the shelves for the support leg. "Got it." I peered up at Alastair. "Can you lift your side a smidge?"

He did.

I probed for the hole that the leg's screw went into. "Steady." I twisted the leg *righty-tighty* as my father had taught me. When it was secure, I said, "Okay, let's see if that holds."

Cautiously, Crusibella released her grip. Then Alastair. Everything remained stable.

"Thank you. Whew!" He dusted his hands on his jeans and smoothed the front of his work shirt. "I had visions of my paycheck covering the damage."

I lifted the box off the floor. "Where do you want this?"

"On the center counter. They're the quartz shards we received Saturday. Ivy intended to —" His voice caught. "She intended to set them out yesterday. She hated when things were left in boxes. 'Can't sell anything people can't see,' " he said in a female tone, making air quotations. "She really knew how to influence customers. She —" He winced. "I can't believe she's dead."

"None of us can." I placed the box on the glass and studied the surrounding trays. Many were beautiful in their own right. Some were ornately carved wood. Others were marble, china, or glass.

Alastair sauntered to the sales counter, peered over his shoulder and bobbed his chin, mentally calculating items. Then he entered the information into a desktop computer.

"Would you like me to help you unwrap the individual boxes?" I asked.

Crusibella said, "I'll help, too."

"Gosh, that would be great. Thanks. I suppose the executor will want me to repack them . . . after he inspects the photos I send him, of course. At some point, he said he'd stop by to take a closer look at those." He motioned to an enclosed glass case filled with loose gemstones and semiprecious stones. "Don't ask me when. It's like waiting for a shoe to drop. Just set whatever you open" — he pointed to a velvet cloth lying between a cypress bonsai and a set of mining tools — "on that. Longest pieces to the left, shorter to the right."

Seeing the tools reminded me of the argument between Ivy and Crusibella and how Ivy had boasted that she'd gone on an adventure to learn about stones, pebble by pebble. Had she been lying to irk her friend? Was Crusibella to be believed about really being friends with Ivy?

Bailey pushed through the front door as I pulled a box from the carton. "Is everything okay in here?"

"Yes." I withdrew a bubble-wrapped item and unfurled it. Inside was a sizeable piece of quartz. "Minor catastrophe averted." I told her what had happened with the shelving. "If you're up to it, help us unpack these."

She joined me, her baby bump pressing against the counter. "He's kicking like crazy."

"Probably because you spooked him with your shriek."

"I didn't shriek. Did I?" She gazed at Crusibella, who nodded. Bailey petted her belly. "Sorry, baby. Mommy didn't mean to scream."

I smiled. She was taking to motherhood like a duck to water.

"Ladies," Alastair joined us and started unpacking a box. "I'm sorry but I've just got to know . . ." He worked his tongue inside his cheek.

"What's up?" Crusibella asked.

"How did Ivy die? I mean, I've read accounts in the newspaper, but they don't say anything other than —" He faltered. His face grew ashen. He wasn't going to puke, was he? If he did, would that mean he was innocent? "All of you were there, right?"

"Ivy was stabbed," Bailey said.

"With rose quartz," Crusibella added.

Alastair dropped the quartz he was holding. It hit the counter with a clatter.

Bailey gasped. So did I.

"Don't worry," Crusibella said. "Quartz won't break. You need a hammer and plenty of brunt force to change the shape."

"Are you sure it was rose quartz?" Alastair asked.

"Guys," I said. "We shouldn't —"

"I'd know it anywhere," Crusibella cut me off. "Why?"

"It's just . . ." Alastair pointed at the piece he'd dropped. "Rose quartz symbolizes unconditional love."

"She was not killed with love," Bailey said.

"No, of course not." Alastair splayed his hands. "All I meant is Oren — Oren Michaels, do you know him? — he understood the meanings of the stones. Ivy schooled him about everything in the store. Maybe he —" The young man stopped short of accusing Oren. "He was madly in love with her but . . ."

"But they broke up," Bailey said.

"Yes."

Crusibella shook her head. "Ivy had limited knowledge, which means Oren probably didn't glean much."

"No, you're wrong," Alastair countered. "Ivy did all right as long as she was reading from pamphlets. She was trying to learn it all. She wanted to be a success."

If that was true, why had she been willing to sell?

"She was teaching him," Alastair went on.

Okay, the guy was definitely trying to implicate Oren. Why? To divert suspicion from himself? What would he gain by killing Ivy?

Bailey whispered to me, "I'm with him. Oren is a good suspect."

I pictured Oren joking with his father and again wondered whether he could be a killer. Maybe the killer didn't have a clue about the meanings of the stones. On the other hand, why pose Ivy's body and why put the stones on her eyes and in her hands?

"Polished gold quartz were placed on her eyes," Bailey said, as if channeling my thoughts.

I threw her a disgruntled look. She mouthed *What?* and shot an accusatory look at Crusibella, as if giving Alastair more details was her fault.

Alastair shuddered. "That's creepy. It reminds me of a myth my Greek grandfather used to tell me —"

"About the stones being meant as payment to transport the body across the River Styx," Bailey said.

"Exactly," Alastair said. "Were there eyes drawn on the stones?"

Bailey shook her head. "I don't know. Jenna?"

I folded my arms.

"It matters," Alastair said. "If there were eyes on them and the eyes faced downward, the deceased's soul would be left behind and might wander the River Styx for hundreds of years as a restless spirit. If the eyes were turned upward, the soul could find safe passage."

Did not knowing about the stones' presence at the crime scene as well as not knowing which way they were placed on Ivy's eyes exonerate Alastair? Or did his knowledge of the myth incriminate him? Maybe the killer had deduced Alastair was Greek and had planted the stones to implicate *him*. But why? What was his motive?

Uncomfortable with any further discussion, I said, "Really, guys. I don't think we should reveal anything else."

Crusibella flapped her hand. "Details are bound to come out, sweetie. Why, just yesterday, I overheard Pepper telling someone about the aventurine the killer put in Ivy's hands."

"Aventurine," Alastair echoed. "What color?"

"It comes in colors?" Bailey asked.

"A lot of them. Brown, orange —"

"These stones were green," Crusibella said. "Aventurine is a healing stone meant to erase negative energy in the lungs, liver, and sinuses."

Bailey said, "Was Ivy sick?"

"Not as far as I know, but she was as bitter as —" Crusibella swatted her leg. "Bite your tongue, woman. What is wrong with you?" Mumbling to herself, she left us and orbited the shop, touching stones and admiring the plants.

Alastair whispered, "Aventurine can also erase negativity in the heart. Some people

153

believe it's a love stone."

"You mean it works like a love potion?" Bailey asked.

He shrugged. "Some think it might."

I recalled Pepper saying Alastair was head over heels for Ivy. Had she returned the sentiment? I couldn't outright ask him. Instead I said, "Alastair, you relocated here a year ago, is that right?"

He picked up the rose quartz he'd dropped and polished it with the tail of his work shirt. "Yep. I was born and raised in San Jose, but I moved because I couldn't stand it there. I had a good IT job at Apple. That's information technology, if you didn't know."

I did.

"But the traffic and the rat race started to get to me. Not to mention living with my dad. He was a drunk." He hesitated. "*Is* not *was.* He's not a mean one, just a sad one. I worried that if I stayed with him, I would never live a fulfilling life. I remembered, as a teenager, visiting here with my mom and loving it. I didn't know what I was going to do for a living, but I knew Crystal Cove was where I belonged. When I saw Dream-catcher was hiring" — he scanned the shop — "it seemed a natural fit. I studied rocks as a kid."

"Being a clerk in a little shop must have been a step down," I said. "Financially as well as ego-wise, from your previous job."

"I didn't mind. Money isn't my thing. Never was." His voice drifted to a whisper. "I don't know what I'm going to do without Ivy."

"What do you mean?" I asked. Was he admitting he loved her?

"You know, when Dreamcatcher is sold. I'll have to find another job here. I'm not moving back to San Jose."

"You'll have one if someone buys the store and keeps it open," Crusibella said from across the shop.

Bailey dragged her finger along the counter's edge. "Alastair . . ." Her voice rose to that flirty pitch she often used to get her way with Tito. What was she up to? "I heard a little rumor that you were in love with Ivy."

"What? No. I mean . . ." He fiddled with the collar of his shirt. "Okay, sure, I liked her. And I told her so. But she said I was too young and she had no interest."

"None?" Bailey asked.

He sighed. "She said she really appreciated me as a clerk and didn't want to jeopardize our relationship. She'd fired quite a few clerks before me. In the long run, I knew she was right. A huge age difference can be divisive. We didn't even like the same songs. I'm into heavy metal. She liked the Rolling Stones."

"Speaking of stones, you didn't give her any aventurine to, like, win her heart, did you?"

He gasped and gawked at my pal. And then me. "No. No way. I didn't . . ." He swallowed hard. "I didn't kill her."

Bailey tilted her head, mulling that over. Did she believe him? Did I?

"I've got to take a load off," Bailey said.

"Sit for a second," I said. "We'll just stay another minute." I pointed at a stool near where Crusibella was browsing books and refocused on Alastair. "Have the police questioned you? Did they ask where you were the night it happened?"

"Yeah, some young cop came in. Can't remember his name. I told him I was here Saturday night. Doing our weekly inventory."

Crusibella rejoined us. "That's sort of a feeble alibi, don't you think?"

About as feeble as being home alone making a cheese platter, I mused.

"We did it every Saturday at the end of business," Alastair replied. "But that night, because Ivy wanted to go home early to prepare for the book club gig, I offered to do it myself."

Ivy wasn't around to dispute him. Was he lying? He had easy access to the quartz and aventurine, and he knew the significance of the eyestones. He lowered his gaze to focus on removing more items from the carton.

"Do you know if Ivy was interested in Hank Hemmings?" I asked, cutting him a little slack by changing the subject.

"Hank." Alastair scoffed. "He reminds me of a guy I worked with at Apple. As phony as a two-dollar bill. No depth and a bit sneaky, if you ask me. But I'm not female. I suppose he has his appeal. Why?"

"Were he and Ivy dating?"

Alastair's teeth gritted for an instant, but then his face grew placid. "I don't think so. On the other hand, maybe that's why Ivy dumped Oren."

And didn't pick you, I noted.

He jerked a thumb. "If you'll excuse me, I've got a bunch of stuff to attend to. Thanks again for your help."

We hadn't nearly finished, but he obviously wanted us to leave, so we did. Crusibella glanced wistfully over her shoulder as she passed through the doorway and headed to her shop. Bailey and I followed her and stopped on the sidewalk.

"Wow, did you detect how much animosity Alastair exuded toward Hank?" Bailey whistled.

"Hank is older and financially set. He has more to offer a woman."

"Alastair seemed to be okay with Ivy's rejection of him, though, don't you think?"

"That could be a ruse. He sure tried to implicate Oren in her murder."

"I agree." Bailey's stomach growled. "I need something sweet to snack on. Where should we go?"

The beauty of living in a tourism-driven town was the plethora of dessert shops.

"How about Sweet Success?" The shop was directly across the street and boasted some of the best chocolates.

"Perfect."

Wind kicked up as we stepped into the crosswalk. I clapped a hand on my sunhat so it wouldn't blow away. Bailey pinned down hers, as well. A woman by the tent named Books, Books, Books wasn't as quick. While trying to grasp the string of her child's balloon, she was struck by a gust of wind. Off flew her hat. I hurried to help, but the hat, like the child's balloon, soared out of reach. The woman hissed out a frustrated breath.

I said, "If you're interested, you can replace it at Great Threads." I pointed to the haberdashery, which was located next to Sweet Success.

"Thanks," she said and then continued her transaction with the book vendor.

"You know, I need a new hat," Bailey said slyly and hitched her chin. "Hank is inside looking quite elegant in his navy suit. Maybe he could pick one out for me."

"You said you were hungry."

"It can wait. Don't you want to get the scoop on Hank and Ivy? C'mon."

"You're incorrigible."

"That's why you love me." She looped her hand around my elbow and steered me into the shop.

Whenever I walked into Great Threads, I felt like I'd entered another era. The shop had a nineteenth-century feel. All the shelving and cabinets were made of oak. The left wall of the shop was filled with wood-framed photographs of Hank with celebrities who'd traveled to Crystal Cove. A bicycle made for two stood next to the display alcove. The warm glow from a half dozen antique Tiffany lamps gave the store a homey feel.

"Need a boater?" Bailey flourished a hand. "Take your pick."

The wall behind the antique sales counter held a variety of hats, including the kind of straw hats that members in a barbershop quartet would wear. Recently, they'd become quite popular with the younger crowd. The lyrics to the Peter Allen song "Everything Old Is New Again" cycled through my mind.

"Be right with you." Hank was ringing up a purchase for an elderly gentleman.

I noticed there was one up-to-date item in the shop, a laptop computer. I spied a sales program that we used, known as Salesforce, on the screen. It was quite helpful in customer relationship management.

Bailey and I headed to a rack of women's sunhats. I spotted the hat Hank thought would be perfect for me — Provence-style in nougat — and decided to try it on. It did look good. As Hank had promised, the color complimented my skin tone.

"How can I help you, ladies?" Hank joined us. "I told you that would look lovely on you, Jenna."

"You were right." I removed it and smoothed my hair.

"How's business this week for you?" he asked. "I have to say, thanks to sunny skies, mine has been stellar. Everyone touring the tents on the boulevard needs a hat."

"We're doing quite well," I said. "The library event was a hit."

"Darian knows her stuff." He peeked out the window and sighed. "What a shame about Ivy."

"It's tragic."

"I see the young man is doing inventory at Dreamcatcher."

"The business might go up for sale," I said.

Bailey poked me in the ribs and hitched her head. Apparently, she wanted me to do the heavy lifting.

"Hank, the other night at the café . . ." I paused. How could I phrase it properly? "Pepper was worried that you were interested in Ivy."

"And I assured her she needn't have been." He hesitated. "Honestly? I did get together with Ivy two weeks ago, but it wasn't a date. She came to dinner at my place."

Bailey said, "Sounds like a date."

"Not a real date. She'd been working so hard. I can't tell you how many nights I saw her poring over her books and eating from a carton of takeout food. Frankly, I think she was realizing how daunting running a business could be."

Maybe the heart scare or the difficulty of learning about her wares wasn't the reason Ivy had wanted to sell. Maybe she'd wanted to get out from under growing debt.

"I figured she might enjoy a home-cooked meal. I make a mean rack of lamb. It's all about the herbs." He adjusted a few hats on the racks. "Anyway, halfway through the meal, she got huffy. She confessed that she'd been hoping I'd ask her out, but she'd expected to go to a restaurant. She called me cheap."

"Wow," Bailey said. "That had to sting."

"Nothing more than a flesh wound. To tell the truth" — he opened his hands — "I've been mocked many times in my life. For my business. For my looks —"

"Your looks?" I gawked.

"See this nose?" He offered a quick profile. "It's taken a few hits. I was an amateur boxer during college. Some say my nose gives me character."

"Did Ivy stick around that evening?" I asked.

"Nope. She skipped dessert and ran off posthaste. I did the dishes alone." He scratched the back of his neck. "All these questions. You don't think I had anything to do with Ivy's death, do you? I'm not a suspect. I have no cause."

No, he didn't have a concrete motive as far as I could tell unless he, like Alastair, had loved Ivy from afar and her rebuke had

162

sent him over the edge.

"She blew you off," Bailey said, giving voice to my thought. Was pregnancy imbuing her with psychic abilities?

"As have many women," Hank replied. "They're all alive and well."

"Ivy loved gossip," Bailey continued.

"Yes, she did."

"Maybe she knew a secret about you."

"Me? Have a secret? Give me a break. My life is an open book." Hank twirled a finger at Bailey's face and winked. "You're teasing me, aren't you, young lady? That baby must be making you feisty."

Bailey's laugh held a sharp edge. I knew the sound. When we'd worked together at Taylor & Squibb, she had loved provoking upper management. What was it about Hank that she didn't trust?

"So where were you that night?" Like a coquette, she batted her eyelashes repeatedly.

"Jenna put you up to this, didn't she?" Hank grinned. "She's the one who's had great success at solving crimes."

"Me?" I squawked.

"Yes, you. Don't hide your light under a bushel. Take credit where credit is due." Hank smirked. "Okay, I'll play along. If you must know, I was hiking along the path east of the Pier. The one that leads to the lake in the mountains."

That was the path near Rhett's cabin. My father hiked that trail.

"I go every Saturday evening," Hank added.

"That's a popular footpath," Bailey said. "You must have encountered a lot of people."

"Not a one. On Saturday evenings, most people stay in town."

CHAPTER 12

On our walk to the south end of town while nibbling fudge that we'd purchased at Sweet Success, Bailey couldn't stop talking about Hank. Was he or wasn't he guilty? He was a charmer, I said, crooked nose or not. And slick, she countered. Really, really slick. In the end, we couldn't come to a conclusion. We didn't have enough information. I kissed her goodbye and told her to have a peaceful evening and to sleep well. We were going to be busy tomorrow.

Later as I dressed for dinner in a stretchy black zipper sheath, I couldn't help thinking about Hank and his tenuous alibi. Granted, my father had a similar iffy alibi when he'd been suspected of murder. Luckily, in the end, someone had seen him where he claimed he'd been, and the police landed the correct killer. Should I tell Cinnamon about Hank's date with Ivy? Being called cheap wasn't much of a motive to kill someone and being a smooth talker wasn't a crime. No, I decided. She obviously didn't want my input. Even still, I worried she wasn't doing enough to exonerate her mother.

Mulling over my options, I made my way to the door. I paused when I spied Tigger attacking a kick-and-scratch toy with zealous vengeance. Apparently, he was feeling as pent-up as I was.

"Sorry, pal," I cooed and lifted him for a hug. "It's my fault you're out of sorts." I set him on his kitty condo and fetched him a calming chewable. "I'll do better tomorrow. Promise."

A half hour later, I was in better sorts. One sip of wine at the Pelican Brief Diner had helped tremendously. I didn't care that Cinnamon and Bucky were late. I was with Rhett at one of our favorite restaurants, drinking in the aroma of fried foods and listening to the comforting chatter of happy patrons.

"Sixty-seven pounds." Rhett was regaling me with a story about the striped bass one of his customers had caught. He stretched his arms to show the length. In a blue sweater that matched his eyes, he looked as handsome as all get-out.

"That's big," I murmured.

Before starting in on the fish tale, he'd filled me in on our upcoming trip to Napa. He'd booked a room overlooking one of the inn's gardens, complete with an in-room continental breakfast. A mini pre-honeymoon, he'd dubbed it. I was still tingling inside, imagining a getaway to plan our future. The trip couldn't come too soon.

Our waitress set down four glasses of water and a basket of freshly baked sourdough bread. Seconds later, Bucky and Cinnamon arrived.

"Traffic," Bucky announced as an apology and offered an easy smile. He pulled out a chair for her. "Sit, babe." His biceps pressed at the seams of his navy Pendleton.

Cinnamon immediately took a piece of bread from the basket, which made me flash on Katie's heads-up about Cinnamon's latest eating habits. Maybe skating was the way she was managing her overeating. In her red wraparound dress, she didn't look like she'd put on a pound, but weight could creep on slowly.

"How was the rest of your afternoon outing?" I asked.

"Swell." Cinnamon glowered at me. "You're not going to grill me about my investigation during dinner, are you?"

"I thought *before* dinner might be better

timing," I retorted.

She shot Bucky a look. "Told you."

"What've you got?" Bucky asked. He never tired of talking shop, maybe because Cinnamon shut him down the same way she shut me down.

Rhett nudged my foot under the table. I ignored the hint.

"Eyestones," I said as a segue.

Cinnamon grumbled. "Let me at least order a drink and an appetizer."

I waited until she'd received her cosmopolitan and a mound of spicy calamari before launching into my theory about the eyestones being payment to assuage the underworld god.

When I concluded, she said, "Well, well, well. That's actually quite helpful."

"It is?" I nabbed a ring of calamari and ate it whole. Lola had included white pepper in the recipe. It added a real zing.

"Yep. The stones *did* have eyes painted on them. They were placed eyes-down. We couldn't make sense of it. Until now. Thanks." She aimed a finger at each of us. "Ahem, that's not for public consumption. Do you all hear me?"

We nodded.

The eyes-down aspect intrigued me. Had the killer placed the stones that way because he or she wanted to doom Ivy to an eternity of traveling the River Styx? Or was placing the stones downward a mistake? If so, maybe the killer had made others.

"Who do you consider a suspect?" I asked.

"Mine to know." She ate three pieces of calamari in succession.

"Hank Hemmings's alibi is thin," I said.

Cinnamon narrowed her gaze. "You asked him for his alibi?"

"No. Of course not. He offered. Out of the blue."

"Uh-huh." Cinnamon cocked her head, clearly not believing me.

Bucky hiccupped a laugh. Rhett chuckled, too.

"Really!" Even though I was telling the truth, I felt my cheeks warm.

"What's Hank's motive?" she asked. "According to him, he and Ms. Beale weren't involved. Yes, I've spoken with him."

Interesting. Hank hadn't mentioned that to Bailey and me. Had he been toying with us?

"Did you believe him?" I asked.

"What's not to believe? He invited Ms. Beale to dinner. They didn't click. What would be his motive?"

"Maybe he has a secret," I said, repeating

169

Bailey's theory. "Ivy was the queen of secrets."

Cinnamon ate another piece of calamari and dabbed her lips with a napkin. "If it will make you happy, I'll do my best to verify his alibi."

His iffy alibi, I mused, but decided not to press the issue.

Bucky pulled the basket of calamari toward him. "Babe, tell her about Ivy's email being hacked."

Cinnamon shot her husband a hard look. "Are you trying to get me to talk so I won't eat the rest of these?" She snatched two more pieces of calamari.

Bucky grinned. "You caught me out." He clasped her hand and tenderly began rubbing her ring finger. "Go on. Tell her."

Cinnamon frowned. "My tech guy scoured Ivy's computer to see who she'd been in contact with lately and discovered her email cache had been wiped."

"Plus she received quite a few wrong number telephone calls recently," Bucky said.

Cinnamon skewered him with a warning glance.

"According to whom?" I asked Bucky.

He deferred to Cinnamon.

Grudgingly, she said, "Ivy and Flora

Fairchild had attended a number of trade shows in recent months and had grown quite close. Flora said Ivy's cell phone rang incessantly at the last one. Always a wrong number."

Odd that Flora hadn't shared that story with my aunt or me. She often dropped into the Cookbook Nook to spill what she knew. Why was she remaining on the sidelines? Perhaps she didn't want to be seen favoring our shop over Pepper's. She was Pepper's friend first and foremost.

"What about Oren Michaels?" I asked.

Rhett shook his head. "I can't see Oren as the killer. I know Ivy broke up with him, but he's a good guy. His father is salt of the earth."

"Oren said he went on a round-trip expedition that night that took six hours," I said.

"How do you know about that?" Cinnamon asked.

"I was chatting with Katie in the Nook kitchen when Oren came in." I added how he loved to chat and tell jokes with Katie and the staff. "He said he spent two hours floating on his boat in a cove north of here. He —"

"Are you talking about Oren?" our waitress asked while handing out menus. "He's, like, so funny. He makes everyone here laugh. Lola included. Did you know he costarred on an episode of *The Big Bang Theory*? He was hoping it would become a recurring role, but —"

"Thank you," Cinnamon said icily. "We'll order in a minute."

The waitress blanched and backed away from the table.

When she was out of earshot, Cinnamon said, "Oren Michaels's alibi checks out. We canvassed the area and found a witness who saw him there."

I leaned forward to keep the conversation confidential. "Saw him or his boat?"

"We have a witness who saw him arrive and leave, and another at the Crystal Cove Marina with the same information. Calculating the mileage and gas usage, he was where he said he was."

"Was anyone on board with him? Would it have been possible to moor the boat in the cove and take a car to town?"

"How would the car have gotten there?" Rhett asked.

"Maybe he dropped it off the day before."

"Or his father gave him a lift," Bucky suggested.

"Or he Ubered back to town," I added.

Cinnamon pushed away from the table. "No, no, no. His father was on a date. No

Uber driver picked him up. Please stop."

I reached for her. "I'm sorry. Sit."

She yanked away.

"Aunt Vera said you need help," I went on. "She said you're too close to this. We're just trying —"

"Tell your aunt to butt out."

"I was the same way when Dad was a suspect."

"And yet you were able to figure out who the killer was, weren't you?" Cinnamon's gaze could have cut crystal. "Give me some credit, Jenna. All of you." She stared at Rhett and Bucky. "I'm good at what I do."

"We know you are, babe," Bucky murmured.

"I don't need every Tom, Dick, and Harriet coming up with theories." She snagged another piece of bread. I eagle-eyed the slice. She dropped it into the basket and jammed her lips together.

"I'm worried about you," I said softly.

"Don't be. Really, Jenna. Don't. Be." She bolted to her feet and jutted a hand at Bucky, who pulled his wallet from his pocket.

Rhett said, "I've got this."

On the drive home — we didn't stay for dinner; Cinnamon's frosty exit squelched our appetites — the wind kicked up something fierce, as if mirroring the emotions swirling inside me. Debris cut across the road. Rhett had to dodge a bunch of loose palm fronds.

As we veered down my street, I swiveled in the passenger seat. "I blew it back there with Cinnamon."

"Yep. You crossed the line. We all did."

"It's Aunt Vera's fault. And Bailey's. And . . . and mine." I groaned. "But everyone has been goading me: 'Take care of Pepper.' 'Be a friend to Cinnamon.' If Pepper weren't the main suspect . . ." I let the sentence hang.

"You care. I get it. So does Cinnamon." He reached for my hand and ran his thumb across my knuckles. "But you have to be cautious with her. If you poke her with a stick, she's liable to attack. She has fangs." He knew better than most. "Please tread lightly, my love."

I promised.

As he pulled in beside my VW, I gasped. My cottage door was standing wide open.

"Tigger!" I raced out of Rhett's truck and flew inside. I breathed easier when I saw my cat at the tippy top of his kitty condo. The way he was sitting, his head hanging over the edge, reminded me of Snoopy on his doghouse pretending to be a vulture. I picked him up and held him close. His heart revved like a motorboat.

Rhett strode past us and made a tour of the place.

"Did I forget to lock the door, Tig-Tig?" I cooed. "Did the wind blow it open?"

Rhett came back and examined the front door, then joined me and slung an arm around my shoulders. "Nobody here. Door doesn't look jimmied."

I'd forgotten to lock my door twice in the past year, both times because I was in a hurry. I needed to be more cautious.

"Does anything seem to be missing or out of place?" Rhett scanned the room.

With Tigger in tow, I checked my Ching cabinet. All my art supplies appeared to be intact. I sifted through my closet and jewelry box. Nothing was awry.

When I ambled back to the kitchen, about to say *no,* I noticed the laptop computer sitting on the kitchen table was closed. When I'd left, the lid was open. After reviewing the significance of aventurine and gold quartz, I had erased the history on my Internet browser as I always did and put the computer to sleep. Who had shut the lid?

I relayed my concern to Rhett.

"Open it," he said, "and see if anything's

been tampered with."

The moment I lifted the lid, the screen illuminated to reveal the Internet browser home page.

"This isn't right," I whispered. "The Internet shouldn't be open." I checked the Internet history. Nothing. Just as I'd left it. Weird.

"Maybe your aunt came over to use it," he suggested. "Call her."

"She's on a date with Appleby and his children." The deputy had grown kids. They adored my aunt. "Rhett, remember how Cinnamon said Ivy's computer had been hacked?"

"Actually, Bucky said it, and Cinnamon confirmed it."

"Is it possible my computer has been tampered with?"

"Why would you assume that? What would someone want off of it?"

"Nothing. That's just it. All the vital information for the Cookbook Nook is on the computer at the shop."

He cocked his head. "Did you make notes about Ivy's murder?"

"What are you suggesting, that the murderer came to check out my theories?"

"No," he said too quickly.

I shivered. A killer had invaded my cottage in the past. Shoot. I did my best to summon up courage. Or pluck, at the very least. "According to Cinnamon, I won't need to make notes."

"You mean she doesn't want you to."

"Don't split hairs." I knuckled him. "Besides, I jot notes on three-by-five cards." When I worked in advertising, I used to storyboard ad campaigns that way.

A dog barked outside. I raced to the front door and caught sight of Crusibella standing on her porch in a filmy nightgown. A halo of light outlined her body. Her poodle squirmed in her arms.

"Rhett," I whispered, "come here. Look."

Crusibella was staring directly at me, or rather, through me. Was she sleepwalking? If I yelled to her, would the sudden sound startle her? The dog settled down, and Crusibella glided into her house. Like a wraith.

As she disappeared, another shiver ran down my spine. Had she stolen into my cottage? If so, why?

CHAPTER 13

Rhett stayed the night. His presence was nice, but it didn't keep me from tossing and turning and dreaming of Crusibella and quartz shards and eyestones. And hats. Lots and lots of hats. Including a striped bass wearing a boater and dancing in the bay.

I awoke in a sweat and took a quick run on the beach to clear my head. When I returned, Rhett fed me a protein-heavy breakfast. Having skipped dinner, I was starved and ate every bite. Before he headed off to work, he calmed me with kisses. How lucky was I?

After dressing in a cheery peach top, white jeans, and seashell-adorned sandals, I felt better. Soon, my wicked dream faded.

As I was setting Tigger in my VW, I spotted Crusibella working in her garden. Her poodle, which was perched on a teensy director's chair, yapped. She hushed him and said loudly, "Trouble is in the air, sweetie. Beware."

Was she warning the dog or me? A vision of her sneaking into my house and tampering with my computer played in my mind. Had she been the culprit? If not her, who?

I started to call Cinnamon to tell her about the possible break-in but thought better of it. I didn't want her to think I was imagining things, despite Rhett's eyewitness account. Instead, I left her a message apologizing for my rude behavior at dinner. Hopefully, that would earn me a few Brownie points.

When I pulled into the parking lot at Fisherman's Village, Pepper was standing outside her shop conversing with a man dressed in a tan jacket, shirt, and slacks. She didn't look happy. Even though all I could see was the man's back, I recognized him as the person who had ducked out of the parking lot the day Pepper and Crusibella had exchanged words about appetizers for the book club. It hadn't been Ivy in disguise. The man's shaggy brown hair was the giveaway.

"Everything okay, Pepper?" I shouted as I climbed out of the car.

She peered around the man, her eyes blinking wildly. Was she trying to send me a message by Morse code? I popped into the

Cookbook Nook, dropped off Tigger, alerted Tina and Bailey I'd be right back, and hurried to Beaders of Paradise. I came alongside the man and jutted out my hand. "Hi, there. I'm Jenna Hart, and you are . . ." I studied his face, trying to memorize every detail in case he chose to flee.

"Jenna," Pepper said, her voice trembling, her hand fiddling with the beaded collar of her lilac sweater. "This is my ex-husband, Noah Pritchett."

I noted the resemblance to Cinnamon. Strong forehead. Strong nose. Full mouth. They didn't have the same eyes. His were narrow and shifty and bracketed with crow's-feet.

"Pleased to meet you." He didn't shake my hand because the cell phone he was holding jangled.

"Are you here for Book Club Bonanza?" I asked.

"No." His cell phone rang again. "Got to answer this, ladies. Excuse me." He edged away from us.

"What does he want?" I put a reassuring hand on Pepper's shoulder.

"He wants to meet Cinnamon." She plucked at the hem of her sweater. "I'm worried sick. What will she say? She's never met him, but she's always hated him."

"She might already sense he's here," I said. "That could explain why she's overeating."

"No, I spoke to Katie, too. My daughter is binge eating because of my predicament. I used to do the same when I was worried. It's a bad habit. Ultimately, I went to therapy to get it under control." She glanced at her ex. "Noah said he heard about the murder and sensed I was in trouble. Supposedly, he wants to lend support. Personally, I think he's hoping to swoop in like a white knight for Cinnamon if I go to jail."

I thought of Crusibella's warning earlier: *Trouble is in the air, sweetie. Beware.* "Pepper, I think you should —"

Noah rejoined us and pocketed his cell phone. "Sorry, business." His mouth was tight. The left corner twitched imperceptibly.

"What kind of business?" Pepper asked, her tone laced with recrimination. "What are you doing nowadays?"

"I manage a garden shop." To me he said, "I owned a nursery before. When I lived here." He turned back to Pepper. "It's an annex of a home improvement store. In the Bay Area. I had some orders that I had to —"

"I don't need details." Pepper rolled her

181

lower lip between her teeth, looking for all intents and purposes like a nervous young woman on a first date. Did she still pine for Noah? She glanced at his left hand and gasped. "You're wearing a wedding ring."

"Yeah." He massaged the back of his neck. "I've, uh, remarried."

"Oho!" Pepper barked out a laugh. "When you left, you said you'd never marry again."

"I was young. Foolish."

"You were a heel."

"Pepper, c'mon." Noah huffed. "You know as well as I do that I would have been a horrible husband to you and a worse father to Cinnamon. I had a temper."

Pepper nodded. "He did. He could fly off the handle at the littlest thing. He said he blamed me for trapping him."

"I did not."

"Yes, you did."

Noah shrugged. "Fine. History always gets rewritten. Look, I needed time to grow up. To get my act together. Which I did more than twenty years ago."

She scowled. "Why didn't you come back then?"

"Because I knew you wouldn't want me. You wouldn't have trusted that I'd changed."

"Liar. You're still gambling, aren't you?"

She turned to me. "He was a notorious gambler. Mainly poker. But given the chance, he'd bet a stranger which way the wind was blowing."

Noah worked his tongue inside his cheek, obviously trying hard not to utter a retort. After a long moment, he muttered, "I didn't deserve you."

"Cinnamon needed a father."

"Not like me."

"Do you have other children?" I asked.

Noah hesitated. He filled his cheeks with air and let it out slowly.

"Well, do you?" Pepper demanded.

"Yes. Two girls. They're young women now." Noah scrolled through photographs on his cell phone and held one up for inspection.

"Do they have college funds?" Pepper asked.

"Both have graduated college, but yes, they had them."

"Unlike your first daughter. Heaven forbid you invest in her."

"Pepper." He grunted.

Her eyes pooled with tears. She turned away to mop them in private.

I glanced at the photographs of his daughters. "They're quite pretty." I wondered how Cinnamon would feel when she learned she had half sisters.

"Their mother is" — Noah hesitated — "nothing like you, Pepper."

She whirled around. "You mean caustic and toxic? That's what he used to say about me. That I was a pox on society."

"I never said —"

"You did. Repeatedly. You didn't like me harping on you about money. Or your career. Or the gambling."

Noah scrunched his nose. "What man would?"

"You're not the only one who's changed, Noah." Pepper jammed her fists against her hips. "I've changed, too. I'm kind and giving, and I'm an excellent beading teacher and a devoted mother. Tell him, Jenna."

I smiled fondly at her. "She is all of those things as well as a loyal friend."

"You saddled me with major trust issues when you left," Pepper said to her ex.

He hung his head. "I'm sorry. What else can I say?"

Drill bits couldn't have done as good a job as Pepper's gaze at searing through flesh. "Out with it! You're hiding something, Noah Pritchett."

"No —"

"You're not here to meet your daughter, are you? You're in town to do something shady. I can feel it."

"You're wrong."

"Are you here to gamble, Noah?" She eyed me. "Do you know of any gambling games in town, Jenna?"

I shook my head. I didn't have a clue.

"I'm no longer gambling," Noah said. "I toe the line."

Pepper was right. He *was* lying. His gaze darted back and forth.

"Look, Pepper . . ." He rolled his head on his neck. His spine cracked with a *pop-pop*. With great deliberation, he removed a business card from his shirt pocket and offered it to Pepper. "I'm staying at the Crystal Cove Inn. If you're open to a chat —"

"How can you afford that place?"

"I'm doing well financially. Everything I do is on the up and up."

Pepper sniffed. "He couldn't afford alimony. He ran off like a thief in the night and left us with nothing. Nothing."

"A house."

"A mortgage." She folded her arms.

Noah drew in another deep breath and let it out, and then sagged as if the exhalation had deflated him. "Like I said, if you're open to a chat — a *civil* chat — call me." He started toward a burnt orange Toyota Celica and paused. After a long moment, he spun on his heel. "I want to meet Cinnamon. Make it happen."

"Make it happen yourself." Pepper hurled his card on the ground and stomped inside her store. When the door slammed, the glass rattled with a vengeance.

CHAPTER 14

I fled into the Cookbook Nook, negative vibes swirling inside me. Poor Pepper. I couldn't imagine what she was feeling. The moment I slipped behind the sales counter, I called Cinnamon again. She wasn't in. Was she ever? I considered leaving her another voice mail but hung up. Let her hear about her father from her mother. Or from him. It wasn't my responsibility to buffer the shock.

Midafternoon, as I was setting out copies of *Let's Have a Tea Party!: Special Celebrations for Little Girls,* an adorable book designed for preteens who wanted to learn how to make tea, design invitations, and have fun, Crusibella swept into the Cookbook Nook. She was dressed in a sheer blue dress with capelets that split into two fluttering scarf-like tails in the back.

"I'm here," she trilled. She bent to kiss Aunt Vera on the cheek and said, "I can't wait for my palm reading." Aunt Vera had read tarot for Crusibella on numerous occasions, but she'd never read her palm. "Once the children are gone, of course."

How many fortunes did she need to hear in a week? I'd forgotten to ask my aunt what she had foreseen the other day.

"Where will I be doing my presentation?" Crusibella asked.

A couple of weeks ago, she had invited middle-grade children to form a book club. To cross-promote, she suggested we order the book and host the club. Next month, we would do a cooking demonstration at her shop. She would sell cookbooks related to the demonstration. It was a win-win, she assured us. Today, she would read from *Legend of the Star Runner,* which she described as a mix between *Indiana Jones* and *Goonies.* Goofy but fun. The story required young readers to use their puzzle-solving skills. After she read the first chapter, she and the children would discuss the book with questions she had designed.

Moving toward the rear of the store, Crusibella said, "Hello-o-o, Jenna. Don't you look adorable?"

She didn't reiterate that trouble was brewing. In fact, she didn't say anything about this morning's exchange. Perhaps I'd overreacted about the computer issue. Maybe

I'd closed my laptop and had forgotten to lock the front door.

"Where's Tina?" Crusibella asked. "Tina! Sweetie. Yoo-hoo!" She peered into the stockroom and then over her shoulder at me. "Hasn't she arrived? She was supposed to print out my book club questions. I emailed it to the shop yesterday."

"I'll do it."

"Crusibella!" Zoey Zeller blazed into the shop struggling with the strap of her briefcase. "A word." She scurried to the rear of the shop and clutched Crusibella's elbow, drawing her into a private conversation.

I moved to the computer by the sales register and scrolled through email.

Bailey stopped straightening books on the shelves and waddled to me, her baby belly pressing at the seams of her stretchy orange dress. "Ahem," she whispered. "Does Crusibella seem unusually perky today?"

"I think she's excited about expanding her audience." We had taped Spellbinder Book Shop posters near the children's table. If one of our customers didn't know about the store, they would after today. "Where is Tina, by the way?"

"Helping Katie with today's treats. Katie downloaded images of the characters in *Star Runner*. Tina wanted to learn how to spray-paint the images on the frosted cookies. I told her it was okay."

"Absolutely." I browsed email and saw the one from Crusibella. I opened it, double-clicked on the attachment, and suddenly the computer emitted a loud beep. "What the heck?"

The email vanished. So did three more. *Zap, zap, zap.* Then another. And another.

I tapped a back arrow trying to stop whatever I'd started. "Bailey, help."

She hurried behind the counter and nudged me out of the way. With a few keystrokes, she stopped the vanishing act, closed email, and then shut down the computer. "What did you do?" she asked, concerned.

"I opened an email."

"From someone you know?"

"From Crusibella." I peeked in her direction; she and Z.Z. were in rapt conversation, unaware that the chairs we'd set out for the event were nearly filled with children and adults. "Bailey" — I drew her close — "is it possible this email from Crusibella was a ruse?"

"A ruse?"

"Were we hacked?"

"You mean by a Trojan horse? No, it's a glitch, that's all. Emails go *poof* all the time.

When you reboot the computer, it'll be fine. Why would you think we were hacked?"

I explained last night's event with my computer.

"If it was Crusibella, how did she get in?" Bailey asked.

"I might have forgotten to lock the front door. It was windy. The door was open when I arrived home." I shared the story about seeing Crusibella standing on her doorstep in a sort of trance. "I think whoever used my computer browsed the Internet."

"Looking for what?"

"I don't know. The history had been cleared."

"Maybe Crusibella's computer was on the fritz and she saw an opportunity," Bailey suggested. "She is looking to buy Dreamcatcher, after all. Maybe she was looking up comps." *Comps* was the abbreviated word for comparables — what realtors used to evaluate property. She nodded toward Crusibella. "I'll bet that's what she and Z.Z. are talking about."

Z.Z. looked quite somber in a black suit, her forehead pinched in concentration. Crusibella was nodding, a slight smile on her face, as if whatever information Z.Z. was imparting was promising.

"You're probably right," I said. "This email snafu was just a coincidence."

Bailey squeezed my shoulder. "I'm going to check on the cookies."

"And send Tina out. Maybe she made a copy of Crusibella's attachment already." I shuffled through papers by the printer but didn't see it.

"Will do."

Crusibella shook hands with Z.Z., after which the mayor flew out of the shop, a woman on a mission.

Signaling the crowd, Crusibella said, "All right, everyone, let's get started." She eyed me. I raised my hands in frustration and mouthed: *Just a minute.* She frowned but quickly replaced it with a smile. "Who loves to solve puzzles?"

Children under the age of twelve made up half the crowd. They cheered. The accompanying adults raised their hands.

"Sorry, Jenna. Sorry!" With spray paint adorning her cheeks and hands and flour dust gracing the front of her red knit dress, Tina rushed behind the counter. "I did print it out. Let me find it." She pulled a sheet of paper from beneath a pile of preorder forms by the cash register. "Here it is. I'll make copies."

As she hurried to the stockroom to complete the task, I breathed easier. Maybe clicking on the email attachment had nothing to do with the hiccup. Our computer probably needed a tune-up. I jotted a note to contact our local geek.

For forty-five minutes, Crusibella enthusiastically led the children in a discussion. Most had read the book. All of them loved the illustrations. When the session ended and the children were devouring cookies and the adults were roaming the shop for purchases, she joined Aunt Vera and me at the vintage table. To calm my nerves, I'd been putting together the upper corner of the bookshop-themed jigsaw puzzle.

"Vera, I'm ready," Crusibella said.

I rose to leave.

"Stay, Jenna." Crusibella clasped my wrist. "Remember how I told you yesterday that the bank won't give me a loan? Well, I'm having Z.Z. approach them on my behalf since she's the one who wanted me to be preapproved before we —"

"Preapproved for what?" Aunt Vera cut in.

"When Dreamcatcher officially goes up for sale, I will be raring to go."

My aunt let out a little moan.

Crusibella petted her forearm. "I'm sorry if I sound heartless, Vera. As I said to Jenna and Bailey yesterday, I know Ivy isn't buried yet. Can you believe her family hasn't pressed the police to release her body? They're the heartless ones." She spanked the table. Jigsaw puzzle pieces popped into the air and fell back down. "Ivy had wanted to repair that relationship. She was always sorry about the estrangement."

"Yes, dear," my aunt murmured, "so you've said. But back to you. Why won't the bank give you a loan?"

"Because Spellbinder is barely breaking even. People aren't buying print books like they used to. Nearly thirty percent of mystery fans use e-readers nowadays. Can you believe it? Booksellers can't make money on e-books. How I wish we could figure out that angle. Libraries have." She squirmed in her chair then fussed with the tails of her capelet. "Anyway, I told Z.Z. to tell the lender that I will sell my house if I have to for seed money."

"But you love that house," Aunt Vera argued.

"I want the store more." Tears pooled in her eyes. She thrust her hand at Aunt Vera and said, "Make my reading good. I'm feeling very negative."

"Crusibella," I said, "before my aunt gets started, could I ask you something?"

"Sure, sweetie, what's up?"

"Last night when I came home, my front door was open."

"It's no wonder. The wind was fierce."

"Yes. Um, did you happen to see if anyone stole inside?"

Crusibella's face went blank.

"My computer . . ." I hesitated. "It wasn't exactly like I left it."

"How so?"

I explained about finding the Internet page open. "You didn't by chance go in to check, say, comparables for your house, did you?"

Crusibella clapped a hand to her chest. "Are you accusing me of sneaking inside your place?"

I blanched. It did sound accusatory. "No, I —"

"I did no such thing." She gulped in air. "I can't believe you'd think I —"

"Breathe," my aunt ordered.

"Breathe," I echoed.

Aunt Vera cut me a stern look: *Quit while you're behind.*

I retreated a step.

"Let's see what we can foretell." My aunt unfurled Crusibella's palm. "Ahh. I have good news."

Crusibella's face lit up. "You do?"

"Indeed. Your fate line and head line are

very strong." My aunt drew her finger along a crease of Crusibella's right palm. "See here? The fate line is heading toward the sun mound, which means you'll be very prosperous. A financial deal is coming your way."

"As in Dreamcatcher?"

"Maybe."

"You're just saying that to make me feel good."

"I never lie."

Aunt Vera winked at me, which sent a chill up my spine. She did lie. She was great at it. Of course, she only did it to make people feel better, but knowing how well she could lie made me wonder about Crusibella and everyone else on my suspect list. How skilled were they at twisting the truth?

CHAPTER 15

"Jenna, dear." Gran sashayed into the shop with Mrs. Landry, Katie's new mother-in-law.

I rose to greet them, putting my concerns about Crusibella on the back burner. Did I really believe she could be a murderer? Did I truly think she had broken into my house and used my computer?

"I'm so glad you're here," Gran went on.

Both women appeared a little windblown. A breeze had kicked up again outside. Gran was dressed to the nines in a Givenchy dress and Prada purse and shoes. Mrs. Landry was wearing her uniform, a pink dress covered by a pink apron. She owned Taste of Heaven Ice Cream Shoppe on Buena Vista Boulevard. Like her son, she was lanky with a wide-toothed grin.

"Did you receive my order yet?" Gran had requested a variety of Louisiana-based cookbooks. She was determined to introduce her grandchildren to spicy Cajun cuisine. Part of her family originated in New Orleans. She treasured its history. One cookbook in particular, *Cooking Up a Storm: Recipes Lost and Found from* The Times-Picayune *of New Orleans,* told the tale of the citizens' attempt to preserve their culinary legacy after Hurricane Katrina.

"They're in the back," I said and signaled my assistant. "Tina, please ask Bailey to bring out Gran's cookbooks." Bailey had gone into the storage room to rest for a spell. I'd suggested she go home, but she had wanted to stay. She needed to complete her task of cutting cardstock for a craft project before tomorrow.

"How are you holding up, dear?" Gran asked.

I tilted my head, not understanding. "Are you confusing me with Bailey?"

"Mercy, no." She lowered her voice. "How are you doing after, you know, seeing another body? I still can't believe I caught a glimpse. Other than my husband, I've never seen anyone dead, and he died of natural causes."

A lump formed in my throat. The image of Ivy lying on the floor zipped through my mind. I nudged it to the back. "I'm okay."

"Any news from the police?"

After the fiasco of our couple's dinner date, I wondered if Cinnamon would ever speak to me again. I said, "The police are doing their best."

"Ha! You know how I feel about their *best.*" Gran clucked her tongue. A drunk driver had killed her son. Authorities never found the perpetrator. "Which is why we're here and not at the precinct. Eleanor wants to tell you something. It might be significant. It might not. She confided in me when I was having a slice of berry pie. I told her we should contact you because the police might pooh-pooh her. You share the police's confidence."

"No, I —"

"Go on, Eleanor." Gran pressed Mrs. Landry forward. "Tell her what you saw. It involves Crusibella."

I glanced at Crusibella, who was still consulting with my aunt. When Gran caught sight of her, she subtly ushered her friend toward the children's corner. I followed.

"Well, it was late Saturday afternoon." Mrs. Landry nudged her wire-rimmed glasses higher on her nose. "I was taking a stroll, as I often do around five when we have a lull. That's when everyone is off at the grocery store or picking up their kids from activities. You know what I mean,

Jenna. The others at the shop can manage a small crowd without me for a bit." Like her son, she had a slight twang. She was raised in the Midwest.

Gran said, "Get to the point."

"Anyway, I was walking on Crystal Cove Road near the aquarium when who do I see?"

"I don't know," I said. "Who?"

"Crusibella," Gran inserted.

"She was sneaking down the alley behind Hog Heaven." Mrs. Landry used two fingers to mime someone running. "You know, the diner."

I nodded. They made ridiculously good pork sandwiches.

"It wasn't raining, but she was carrying a big trench coat." She spread her arms wide. "That's what caught my eye. It was out of the ordinary, you know. Other items were hanging out of the coat. Clothes and such."

"Tell her what kind of clothes," Gran urged.

"I'm getting to it." Mrs. Landry smoothed the bib of her apron. "At first I thought she was taking in dry cleaning. There's a place near there. Not a very good place. I like the outfit on Buena Vista Boulevard better."

"Focus," Gran said.

"But then something fell out of the coat,"

Mrs. Landry went on. "A pair of thick-rimmed glasses and a red wig."

"And a fat suit," Gran chimed.

"I wondered why Crusibella would have those things," Mrs. Landry said. "She's not an actress. She doesn't do the local plays. I know because I see all of them."

On the Pier there was an intimate rustic theater that put on plays as well as other entertainment, including karaoke night.

Mrs. Landry wove her hands in front of her stomach. "Crusibella is such a pretty woman. I thought maybe she'd donned those clothes to hide from someone and then took them off once she'd, you know, passed the test."

Gran said, "Eleanor and I were discussing the murder. People all over town are doing the same. Anyway, I said Crusibella might have killed Ivy because she had that red stain on her sleeve. Pepper pointed it out. Crusibella said it was strawberry juice. Remember?"

I nodded.

"That's when Eleanor recalled seeing Crusibella Saturday afternoon." Gran lasered me with a look. "You see what I'm getting at, don't you, Jenna? Crusibella lied about her alibi. She was not home making that appetizer."

"What time was this, Eleanor?" I asked.

"Around five thirty, I suppose."

The book club's progressive dinner had started at six thirty. Could Crusibella have gone home after whatever adventure she'd been on, put together a cheese platter, and dressed for the evening in that short a time? I could have, if put to the test.

"Crusibella said she was home alone, suggesting that she'd been there for hours," Gran went on. "Why didn't she mention this little foray?"

"Why, indeed?" Mrs. Landry asked, acting like the perfect straight man.

"Because she'd wanted it to remain a secret," Gran said. "I'm thinking she took a sneaky route to Ivy's house. It's not far from the diner. She dressed in a costume to disguise herself so neighbors wouldn't recognize her. I'm sure the police have canvassed the neighborhood."

I glanced at Crusibella, who was still engrossed in the palm reading my aunt was giving. Was she a killer?

Gran tapped my arm. "There must be security cameras at the aquarium and the diner. There are lots of other businesses in the vicinity, too. And I'd wager there are plenty of houses in her neighborhood with security cameras. You should tell the police to check out this theory."

"Me?"

"Maybe the police can pin down Crusibella's movements."

"Ahem." Mrs. Landry gave Gran a snarky look. "You don't believe in the police."

"No, but Jenna does." Gran grinned.

"Oo-o-oh!" Bailey moaned and grabbed her belly. She stumbled into a bookshelf.

I bolted to her and slung an arm around her shoulders. "What's wrong? Is the baby coming?"

"I don't know. Oo-o-oh!"

"I'll call your doctor."

"She's out of town."

"Gran, tell my aunt I'm taking Bailey to Mercy Urgent Care. Mrs. Landry, please contact the police."

"But —"

"Do it. They're good. They solve crimes. Lots of crimes. Just not all crimes."

Mercy Urgent Care was one of two decent-sized clinics in the area. I swung into a parking spot and scurried to the passenger side of my VW. Bailey hobbled out. Like a bad three-legged potato sack team, we trudged into the reception area. A nurse with spiky hair and a sweet smile asked what was wrong.

"It's obvious, isn't it?" Bailey asked between gritted teeth.

"Contractions," I said. "Her ob-gyn is out of town."

"How far apart?"

"She's only had one so far."

"Oh, hon." The nurse stopped taking notes and put down her pen. "If it's the first contraction, you've got days or weeks to go. Get used to them. Braxton-Hicks can be daunting. Believe me, I know. I've had three kids."

"Oo-o-oh," Bailey moaned. "This doesn't feel normal."

"Nothing about pregnancy is normal," the nurse joshed.

I said, "Maybe my friend should see a doctor just to make sure everything's okay."

"Sure, hon." She called to a stocky nurse. "Put them in room 103. Let Dr. Cook know."

The stocky nurse escorted Bailey down the hall into a room fitted with an examination table and a chair. The room smelled Lysol clean. She promised the doctor would be in soon. Bailey perched on the examination table; I sat on the chair.

"Sorry to take you away from the shop," she said. "I saw you getting an earful from Gran and Mrs. Landry. What's up?"

I filled her in.

"Do you really think Crusibella is the murderer?"

"I don't know what to think. She really wants to own Dreamcatcher. She is primed and ready to buy it the moment it goes on the market. She's willing to sell her house to get a loan. Heck, if she had kids and someone would pay her for them, I bet she'd sell them, too."

Bailey laughed. "Oo-o-oh. Don't make me laugh. You know, if she really is selling her home, you and Rhett should take a look."

"A place that close to the ocean will be way out of our price range. Plus, would you want to live in a murderer's house?"

"She's not a murderer," Bailey said, sounding quite certain. "She's just a bit . . . daffy. Who else is on your suspect list?"

"Not Pepper."

"Not Pepper." Tapping her fingertips, she recited, "Oren Michaels. Hank Hemmings."

I nodded.

"Who else? Do you think Alastair Dukas is a suspect?" she asked. "He knew the significance of the eyestones, though he didn't seem to have an inkling that the killer had used those as well as aventurine at the crime scene."

"He could have been playing dumb, but

what would his motive be?"

"Same as Oren's or Hank's, I suppose. Lover's remorse."

I shook my head. We were missing something, but what?

"How did dinner go with Cinnamon last night?" Bailey asked.

"Not well. I tried to console her. She blew a gasket and ordered me and everyone else at the table to butt out."

"Didn't you say you were looking out for her mom?"

"I did." I hadn't always been a fan of Pepper's. We'd locked horns early on. After she came to my aid in a confrontation with a killer, however, I'd seen her in a different light.

A middle-aged doctor sauntered into the room and greeted Bailey. I stepped out. After he assured her that she and the baby were fine, he released her into my custody.

As we waited for Tito to pick her up — he didn't want me to drive her home; he wouldn't take no for an answer — I told her that I'd researched Braxton-Hicks contractions while the doctor had examined her. They were normal even as early as the second trimester. To help with them, she was to drink plenty of water, and if uncomfortable, drink a glass of warm milk or take a warm bath.

Bailey grinned. "You're going to make a great mother yourself someday."

"Ha! Only if I can parent by Google."

CHAPTER 16

Knowing Bailey was safely on her way home, I called Rhett. Last night's flop of a dinner had been unsettling. I wanted a restful, romantic evening with him. He picked me up and we decided to walk along Buena Vista Boulevard doing pretty much what Bailey and I had done the day before, eating fish tacos while browsing the wares at each Book Club Bonanza tent. Everyone in town was out in force. Gran was with her daughter-in-law and grandchildren browsing the goodies at Learn-a-Lot Books. Flora and her twin sister, both in white sweaters and slacks, were particularly interested in Book Addicts, the vendor that was selling ornate bookstands and more. I wondered if Flora was comparing its prices to those in her shop.

As we strolled past a tent called Turn the Page, featuring a wealth of classic novels, I said, "What do you think of an all-white wedding?"

"Are the white tents influencing your idea?"

"Actually, Lola suggested it. Eating this tasty whitefish taco" — I tossed my taco wrapper into a nearby garbage can — "brought her suggestion to mind. White food. White linens."

"What exactly are white foods?" He scrunched his nose, dubious.

"Shrimp, calamari, white cheeses."

"Cauliflower, turnips, white beans," he said grinning, the former chef in him enjoying the challenge.

"Oysters, pita bread, jicama."

"Potatoes, mushrooms, garlic."

"Oh, yeah," I chuckled. "Let's serve plenty of garlic at the wedding. *Not.*"

Rhett put a hand out to block me. "Hold up."

Ahead, two men were in a heated argument. One was Yung Yi, the manager at Crystal Cove Bank. He shook his head vehemently and whacked the hat he was holding against his thigh. The other was standing in profile, one hand gesturing to Yung, the other hand steadying a mountain bike, a helmet looped over his forearm.

"Is that Oren Michaels?" I asked. The man had Oren's distinctive build and curly hair, but from this distance I couldn't be sure.

"Yep, and he doesn't look pleased."

"Maybe he needs a loan for his boat," I said. He'd already purchased a new truck. Buying Jake's boat would require a lot more cash.

"Could be."

"I wonder if he'll get it? The bank seems to be tightening the reins lately. Crusibella was denied a loan."

"You've got to be kidding!" Yung yelled.

People strolling past gawked at the two men.

Yung flashed a cell phone at Oren, who glanced at it and nudged it in Yung's direction. Yung's mouth moved. Since neither were yelling any longer, I couldn't make out the exchange. A minute later, Yung hurled his hat on the ground. Balancing his bike with one hand, Oren retrieved the hat. Chin lowered in a servile manner, he handed it to Yung, who jammed it on his head and turned on his heel, leaving Oren staring after him.

"If he was asking for a loan," Rhett whispered, "I'd say that's a no."

"An emphatic no."

"So much for being able to follow his dream. Poor guy."

As if sensing our pity, Oren glanced in our

direction. Rhett nodded *hello.* Oren responded in kind and then quickly straddled his bike, strapped on his helmet, and tore off, probably embarrassed that we, or anyone, had witnessed the scene.

A short while later, Rhett dropped me at home and checked out the cottage, but he didn't linger; he had to get some shut-eye if he was going to be alert when he hosted his early-morning fishing expedition.

After he left, I sat at the kitchen table and opened my computer to browse cookbook titles. In the coming weeks, Katie was going to teach a class on how to ice cookies. Tina had talked her into it. I would be the first to enroll. Bailey thought it would be smart to stock books the novice icer could take home as a souvenir.

Whenever I did research, Tigger wanted to take part. He pounced on the table and whisked the computer screen with his tail. Occasionally he pawed the USB port, but he didn't dare tiptoe across the keyboard. He knew that I would banish him to the living room.

To access the shop's future purchase list, I located the cloud account that each of us in the shop could use. I started to enter the password and paused. We'd changed it two days ago. What was it? For security reasons,

Bailey had suggested we create a new variation weekly, but I begged her not to. My beleaguered brain could only manage a switch every four weeks. Aunt Vera kept the password stored on her cell phone, just in case. I wish I had. I drummed the table until the correct answer occurred to me.

I logged on and opened the file. Then I scrolled through our supplier's list of cookbook titles, which were sorted by genre. After a few minutes, I discovered a cookbook called *Icing on the Cake: Baking and Decorating Simple, Stunning Desserts at Home* and knew it was the book to order. As a follow-up to the author's well-received *Layered,* it was a deeper dive into cake decorating, packed with tips and hundreds of beautiful photographs.

"Perfect," I whispered.

As I searched for a second title, a message popped onto my screen. My personal mailbox had received a new email. I opened the mailbox and reviewed the incoming correspondence. I didn't recognize the name of the sender, *Goodguy.* The subject line was intriguing: *I saw what you did.*

Because I could preview the beginning of the email without opening it, I continued reading.

I saw what you did, my victim. I have photo-

graphs to prove it. Pay me five thousand dollars in bitcoin by midnight tomorrow night, or dire consequences . . .

Knowing this was a scam and certain I hadn't done anything worthy of a bribe, I deleted the email without opening it.

Tough luck, whoever you are.

However, as I closed the lid of my computer, a chill cut through me. Was the email a fluke or had my computer been hacked? The shop's email had gone *poof.* Was someone targeting me? Should I alert the police?

Get real, Jenna. Welcome to the unavoidable downside of social media.

Knowing Cinnamon would tease me for months if I admitted I was paranoid, I decided to keep the information to myself.

Edgy and unable to go straight to sleep, I opted to read a book. I selected another of the cozy mysteries we'd considered for the book club and nestled on the couch. Tigger joined me. I read until two a.m., when my eyes couldn't stay open any longer.

Needless to say, nightmares laced with computer malware fiascos were only seconds away.

Thursday morning, Bailey came to work acting livelier than she had the day before. When asked, she said the warm milk trick had worked. I mentioned the email issue to her. She confirmed what I'd determined: receiving a nasty blackmail-type email was the norm nowadays. Spam stunk. *Delete, delete, delete.*

Around ten, Bailey was craving a breakfast burrito from Latte Luck Café. As concerned as Tito was about her overdoing it, I offered to make the journey to the restaurant for her.

The place was packed. All of the wooden tables were filled. The brown leather booths were, too. I understood why. The tantalizing aroma of nutmeg and sugar hung in the air. The café's cookies were renowned. I stood in line and, like a tourist, admired the sepia pictures of Crystal Cove in the early nineteenth century hanging on the walls. Our history was rich, filled with pirates, seafarers, and gold seekers.

As I neared the front of the line, I heard a man clear his throat. In a booth to my left sat Deputy Appleby with Cinnamon. Dare I tell her about the threatening email I'd received? *No, no, no* rang out in my head. And I wouldn't tell her about the other computer issue, either. They were not related to Ivy's murder.

"Morning, Jenna," Appleby said.

"Good morning. How's the cheese Danish?" I eyed Cinnamon's plate. "Looks yummy."

"It is." She smiled. "All the white flour and sugar you're not supposed to eat baked in one delicious morsel."

Appleby snorted. "Carrots are tasty, too."

"Don't mock me just because you can control yourself." Cinnamon shot him a look. "I ran six miles this morning. I earned this." She usually ran three. "By the way, Jenna, I received your voice mail. Apology accepted."

I smiled. "Any —"

"New leads?"

"I wish you'd stop cutting me off," I said, recalling our most recent conversation. "That wasn't what I was going to ask."

She twirled a hand. "Sorry. Go on. Any . . . what?"

"Any surprises lately?"

"As a matter of fact, yes. My father has come to town."

Who had spilled the beans? Her mother? Or had her father reached out?

Cinnamon eyeballed me. "Why do I get the feeling you knew that already?"

Warmth crept up my neck.

"How long have you known?" She patted the table. "Why didn't you tell me?"

"Because it was up to your mother."

"My mother." She scoffed. "We aren't talking."

Appleby bit back a smile and excused himself from the table.

Giving up my place in line, I slid into his spot.

"How did you learn about him?" Cinnamon asked.

"I saw him and your mom arguing in the parking lot outside Beaders of Paradise. Thinking she might need backup, I joined them and introduced myself."

"Aren't you bold?"

"Sometimes."

"Don't get cocky."

"Never." I grinned. "I can see the similarities between you two. The forehead, the nose."

Automatically she reached for her nose. She stopped short and rubbed a knuckle beneath it.

"So have you connected with him?" I asked.

"We met for lunch yesterday."

So it was he who had reached out. Not Pepper. "And how did it go?"

"He was nice enough." Cinnamon twirled a saltshaker while toying with her earlobe, moves that I'd bet she'd made as a young girl when discussing an uncomfortable subject. Catching me watching her, she stopped doing both and folded her hands on the table. "I don't want to talk about it."

"Let's see, what can we talk about then? Oh, I know." I snapped my fingers. "Did Mrs. Landry contact you?"

Cinnamon narrowed her gaze. "Are you determined to rile me?"

"It was a simple question. She came into the shop to tell me about —"

"Crusibella Queensberry and a fat costume hidden in a trench coat."

Appleby exited the men's room but didn't move toward us. Instead, he stopped and chatted with a couple at a table. Coward.

"What I want to know is why did Eleanor Landry come to you first?" Cinnamon asked.

"Gracie Goldsmith prompted her. You know what happened with Gracie's son. She thinks the police —"

"Got it." Cinnamon, to her credit, did stay up to date with various individual's histories. "I will speak with Ms. Queensberry and discuss her trek behind Hog Heaven, okay?"

"And see if any security cameras might have —"

Cinnamon exhaled sharply.

I held up a hand, acknowledging she didn't need me to continue. "Between you and me, I don't think Crusibella's motive of wanting to buy Dreamcatcher is strong enough."

"I've run into weaker motives."

"Like your mother's?"

Cinnamon started twirling the saltshaker again.

"Don't you think a man killed Ivy?" I asked. I'd thought about this theory while showering and getting dressed. "I mean, wouldn't it have taken a lot of brunt force to, you know . . ." I didn't want to spell out the gory details.

"I could have done it," she said. "So could you. Ivy was a small woman. Plus —" She stopped short.

"Plus what?"

Cinnamon scanned the room to see if anyone was listening and lowered her voice. "We found a poison in her system. A paralytic called muscimol, as found in Amanita muscaria."

"What's that?"

"A type of mushroom. The paralysis sets in within twenty to thirty minutes. The medical examiner believes the killer inserted it into a cream puff. Only one was eaten off a tray we found in the refrigerator."

"Meaning the killer must have handed it to Ivy. It was someone she knew and trusted."

"Most likely." Cinnamon pushed the saltshaker aside. "As I said the other night, this info is not for public consumption. My theory is the murderer wanted her immobile —"

"So it wouldn't take as much effort to impale her."

Cinnamon nodded. "And in order to provide enough time to set up the ritualistic scenario."

I winced. "This wasn't done out of love."

"Definitely not love."

"Except according to Alastair Dukas, the aventurine —"

"When were you talking to him?" Cinnamon demanded.

I told her that Bailey and I had been next door at Spellbinders when we heard something crash at Dreamcatcher. "I wanted to clue you in the other night, but you —"

"Lost my cool. Got it. Go on. While you were helping him organize his inventory, you chatted about the crime scene? How many times do I have to —"

"Not me. Bailey and Crusibella." It was my turn to cut her off. My turn to defend myself. "Crusibella claimed all sorts of book club members were sharing theories. I tried to clamp down on Bailey and her, but they wouldn't listen to me. If you care, they do not know the eyestones detail you revealed the other night. I won't blab about that or about this poison. Promise." I raised three fingers and pinned the pinky with my thumb. Once a Girl Scout, always a Girl Scout.

Cinnamon sighed. "So according to Mr. Dukas . . ." She signaled for me to continue.

"Aventurine heals the heart, except Ivy's heart issue was a scare. She wasn't sick. Alastair implied that the stone might work like a love potion and that whoever held that stone might be enticed to love the giver."

"Interesting."

"In addition, Alastair said placing the eye-stones on the eyes is a gesture of love. A way to help the deceased make a smooth transition into the underworld, except not if the eyestones are turned downward." I leaned forward on my elbows. "Is it possible —"

"No." She stood up abruptly.

"No what?"

"No more theorizing."

"All I was wondering was —"

"Stop. I mean it." Cinnamon drew in a breath and released it. "I'm allowing you to provide me with details of conversations, but do not theorize. Every time you do, you imply that I'm not —" She inhaled sharply again and then moaned. Sort of like Bailey had.

"Are you all right?"

"I'm fine. Thank you, Jenna, for your input."

"Don't you mean for doing my civic duty?" I snapped, taking umbrage at her curtness.

"Yeah . . . *that.* Have a great day."

I sighed. I wasn't suggesting that she wasn't good at her job, and she knew it.

Cinnamon signaled to Appleby. "Let's go." She turned to leave.

I said, "About your mother —"

Cinnamon shot a scathing look over her shoulder. "What about her?"

"She's upset about your father. She doesn't trust him."

"Let me be the judge —" She grasped the back of the chair. "I don't need you to —" She clamped her lip with her teeth. Definitely in pain. Perspiration beaded on her face.

I scrambled to my feet and gripped her arm. "Cinnamon, what's wrong? Are you having a heart attack?"

"No."

"A panic attack?"

"I don't panic," she hissed. "Let go of me."

I did.

Steeling her back and shoulders, she strode toward the exit.

I raced after her and cried, "For the record, I care!" but my words fell on deaf ears.

CHAPTER 17

After purchasing Bailey's burrito and my nutmeg cookie, I headed back to the shop, worrying about Cinnamon. Had she suffered a panic attack? Sure, she was the chief of police, but she was also my friend. What could I do to help? Granted, she had plenty of police backup to provide her with support as well as alternative theories, but were they doing so? Were they as concerned about exonerating her mother and finding Ivy's killer as I was?

"Whoa!" a man shouted.

I drew up short and said, "Sorry." Thanks to walking with my head down, eyes fixated on the cobblestones, I'd almost creamed into Oren Michaels in the middle of the Fisherman's Village parking lot. "I was lost in thought."

"Is everything okay?" He removed his sailor's cap and tucked it under his arm.

"I should ask you the same thing. Last

night on the street . . ." I twirled a hand. "With Yung Yi. Did he turn you down for a loan?"

His brow furrowed. "No."

"He was upset. He threw his hat on the ground."

"Oh, that." Oren rubbed the back of his neck. "He's been having a little money trouble. I was advising him."

"You were advising *him*?"

Oren grinned. "I know. Talk about turning the tables, right?"

"That might explain why his wife seemed so fretful the other day when she'd visited my aunt for a tarot card reading."

Oren scoffed. "Fortune-telling is hog-wash."

"Some people steer their lives by it."

"Some people are whacko." Oren started toward the stairs leading to the second floor. "Yung and his wife will be fine. Nothing they can't get past. As for me, the bank is giving me a loan, and I've already contacted a guy to make an offer on his boat."

"Jake Chapman's *Joy of the Sea.*"

"Yes. How did you —" His eyes widened. "Aha! Rhett must have told you. You ran into my dad and me at his store."

"Rhett says it's a great boat. Top of its class. Congratulations."

"Thanks. As a matter of fact, I have a meeting with Jake at Vines right now to seal the deal. Sorry to run off." He headed upstairs. Over his shoulder, he said, "Make sure you do something about that mumbling habit. Wouldn't want people to think you're crazy."

"They already do." I smiled.

"Jenna!" Bailey rushed out of the shop. "I'm so glad you're here." She clasped my arm.

"What's wrong? More contractions? Are you in labor?"

"Will you stop with that? I'm fine. The baby isn't due for weeks. It's Tina." She steered me into the shop. "She's sick. Green at the gills. I sent her home. We need you inside. We're swamped with customers."

I gaped when I saw the crowd. The shop was packed. Customers squeezed past others in the aisles. I whispered, "Are we having a sale?"

"No, but the word got out that we just received a shipment of *The Book Club Cookbook.*" The official title was *The Book Club Cookbook, Revised Edition: Recipes and Food for Thought from Your Book Club's Favorite Books and Authors.* The book recommended not only great books to read, like *Water for Elephants* and *Life of Pi,* but also suggested recipes paired with authors' remarks to go with each book. Very clever. "Luckily, we ordered fifty copies."

Aunt Vera was manning the register. I went to assist her. After the crowd ebbed, I joined Bailey at the children's table to help her finish the project she was assembling for an upcoming event — specifically, her baby shower. Her mother had decided to throw a safari-themed tea for her at the Nook Café to compliment the giraffe theme for the baby's room.

Today, thanks to her mother's suggestion, Bailey was wrapping teensy hostess gifts, which were "books" made out of cardstock she'd cut yesterday and Hershey's nuggets. Earlier, she had pasted teensy images of *The Jungle Book* on the cardstock. The nuggets were the guts of the books.

When one of the covers didn't stick with hot glue, Bailey grunted. "Mom found the design for these little gems on Pinterest, but does she have time to make them? No, she does not."

"They're cute."

"Actually, they're adorable." Bailey set aside the glue gun and sighed. "I'm worried about Tina."

Her sharp segue nearly gave me a whiplash. "Why?"

"Men make things so complicated."

"Do you think she's sick because of something her boyfriend did?"

"He had a tryst and tried to slough it off as nothing, and now he's begging her to forgive him. What does he think she is, a yo-yo?"

I cleared my throat. "You reacted the same with you-know-who."

"Don't remind me." Before Tito, my pal had been involved in quite a few ill-fated relationships. She resumed folding cardstock around nuggets. "Speaking of men we can or cannot trust, what do we think about Cinnamon's father?"

"Darling, are you talking about Noah?" Lola swooped onto a stool beside my pal and bussed her on the cheek. My father was accompanying her, but he remained standing. He didn't like sitting on a toddler-sized stool.

"Have you met Noah?" I asked Lola.

"Briefly. At the diner last Friday."

That didn't jibe. Hadn't he told Pepper he'd come into town because he'd heard about the murder, which occurred Saturday?

"I didn't know he was Cinnamon's father at the time." Lola freshened the ruffle of her aqua blouse. "I found out a bit ago. One

227

of our customers was chatting about him. She thought he was quite dishy for an older man."

My father grunted and shoved his hands into his trouser pockets.

"Why was he at the diner?" Bailey asked.

"He was hungry."

"Well, *duh,* of course, but last Friday —"

"Ivy was dining with Oren Michaels. Noah was hovering nearby. I think he wanted to talk to Ivy, but she and Oren were in a heated conversation."

"Talk to her about what?" I asked.

"I haven't a clue. Maybe he ordered something from her shop and it didn't show up? He waved a couple of times to catch her eye, but she ignored him."

"How heated was her discussion with Oren?" I asked.

"*Heated* heated. After a few sailor-savvy words, Ivy told Oren to take a hike."

"So that's when they broke up," Bailey said.

"Except Oren claimed they didn't break up," I countered.

Lola scoffed. "If they didn't, you could have fooled me. Ivy shoved back her chair and hurled her napkin on the table. Oren leaped to his feet and grabbed her in a hug. He whispered something in her ear. She wriggled free and slapped him."

My father bent forward. "You've told the police all of this, I presume."

"Do I look like I fell off a turnip truck, Cary? Of course I went to the precinct." Lola swiveled to face Bailey and me. "Back to Noah. There he was, ready to chat with Ivy, but when Oren and she bolted from the restaurant, he was left high and dry."

"He didn't run after her?"

"Would you approach a woman who'd just slapped a man? I'm sure he wanted to give her a little space. He sat at their table and ordered the fish burger with herb sauce." She peered at the favors Bailey was making, picked one up, and showed it to my father. "Aren't these adorable?"

"Adorable." He moseyed to Tigger, who was playing merrily on his kitty condo.

As Bailey and Lola set to work to finish their project, I moved to the sales counter. Oren had been adamant that he and Ivy hadn't broken up. Why would he lie about it? And why hadn't Noah mentioned his business with Ivy?

CHAPTER 18

Following a late morning onrush of customers — yes, we sold out of *The Book Club Cookbook* as well as every copy of *Tastefully Small Finger Sandwiches: Easy Party Sandwiches for All Occasions* — I needed a breather. Before I took a walk, however, I called Tina at home. She sounded horrible, like she was stuffed up from crying, though she swore she'd contracted a nasty cold. After she assured me that she was drinking tea and would call if she needed anything, even something as minor as one of Katie's sunshine cookies, I set off.

Many of the customers who had flooded the Cookbook Nook earlier were roaming the boulevard. All appeared to be enjoying the mild weather and festivities. I noticed a few food trucks had situated themselves on side streets. On the road leading to Azure Park, one truck called Sweet Pea's Tea Time caught my eye. A huge knot of people waited in line. I understood the lure. An entire "high tea" service stood in front of the truck. I imagined our local tea and coffee shops weren't too happy with the truck's presence, but it would be temporary.

Moving on, I browsed windows all the way to the north end of town. On the return loop, I neared the Crystal Cove Library tent. Darian, dressed in a cream-colored suit with sunglasses balanced atop her head, was listening to Hank tell a story. Animatedly, he whipped his cowboy hat against his thigh. Darian whinnied full throttle. As I ducked under the awning of the tent, I caught the tail end of the story as Hank promised that, no matter what, they would have a rollicking good time. Was he inviting Darian and her husband to a rodeo? A few local events were coming up in June.

"Hi, Jenna," Darian said, catching sight of me.

"Hi, you two."

"Say, which books are on your to-be-read list?" Darian gestured to a stack of what looked like library book rental cards; however, instead of date stamps along the left, each row held a space for the title of a book. On the right was a spot to enter the date the reader finished the book. Darian handed one to me. "I'm giving these to all my patrons. It's yours to fill out. Consider it a wish list."

"What a great idea."

I flipped the card over. The front boasted a beautiful picture of the library with a view of the ocean beyond. In bold yellow letters were the words: *Stop in for a New Adventure.* I brandished the card. "Free swag is so important for promotion nowadays, don't you think?"

"Absolutely. The library doesn't have a large budget, but the mayor vowed that the more readers we lure in, the more she'd find a way to grow the funds."

At the Cookbook Nook, we gave away bookmarks and kitchen magnets, but I pocketed the card thinking a wish list card would be a nice addition to our giveaways. Our customers could write down which cookbooks they coveted and give the card to a loved one who was on the hunt for a gift.

"So what were you two chatting about before I interrupted?" I asked. "I'm guessing a rodeo or a roundup." A few dude ranches liked to offer the latter to their guests.

"Rodeo?" Hank winked. "Nah. We were just horsing around."

"*Horsing* around." Darian clapped him on

the arm. "Stop. You're too funny."

"Hi, everyone." Z.Z. chugged beneath the awning while cooling herself with a book-themed fan. "Isn't it a brilliant day? Look at what I scored at Book Clubs R Us." She shook the fan and hooked a thumb at one of the tents across the street. "The club leader commissioned an artist on Etsy to make them."

Darian inspected it and handed it back. "Nice craftsmanship."

"Are you pleased with the foot traffic?" Z.Z. asked.

"It's been terrific. Over one hundred people have signed up for library cards." Darian patted Z.Z.'s back. "I hope you'll keep your promise about increasing our budget."

"I'll do my best."

"We need more books. Fresh titles. We could even entice new authors to do lectures if we carried their books. Our readers are avid."

"Speaking of avid, Jenna," Z.Z. said, "I hear you're doing all you can to help Pepper. That's admirable, dear."

"It is." Hank nodded. "She's not guilty."

"Who told you I was helping?" I asked. "Certainly not Cinnamon. She wants noth-ing to do with me."

"As a matter of fact, it was." Z.Z. grinned. "Our chief of police might not like your tactics, but she does admire your pluck."

I coughed out a laugh. "Is that what she called it?"

"Her choice of words was a little juicier." Z.Z. winked.

All of us laughed.

"Yoo-hoo! Hank!" Pepper was crossing the street, carrying to-go cups.

Darian said, "Speak of the devil . . ."

After looking both ways so no cars would run her over, Pepper scurried across the street, the skirt of her shirtwaist dress flouncing and the ribbons of her bejeweled sunhat fluttering. "Your assistant said you were strolling, sweetheart. I thought I'd join you." She handed Hank one of the cups. "Here you are. Coffee with one cream, just the way you like it." She looped her hand around his elbow and smiled winningly at him.

Darian took a step backward. Hank shifted feet. When I noticed them exchange a furtive glance, a lump caught in my throat. Was I wrong thinking that the two of them had been joking about a rodeo? Had they been flirting? Had I been mistaken the other day at the Cookbook Nook? Maybe there was more to their relationship than met the eye.

Pepper said, "I want to get a bite to eat. Let's go to Hog Heaven. It's just up the way."

"I only have a few minutes," Hank said.

"Me, too. Let's share some sliders." She pulled him in that direction.

Hank didn't argue. He donned his hat, gave a tip of the brim to Darian, Z.Z., and me, and they were off.

Z.Z. stared at Darian. "Are you okay, dear? Do you need a tissue?"

"No, thanks. Darn wind." Darian dabbed one eye. "It's kicking up dust."

There wasn't a hint of a breeze. Feeling me studying her, she quickly covered her eyes with her sunglasses, cementing my earlier notion. She and Hank *had* been flirting. What about her perfectly wonderful husband? I gazed at Hank's retreating figure. What was his allure? Okay, he wasn't bad-looking for an older guy and he was quite charming, but c'mon.

I flashed on the conversation Katie had overheard Hank having on his cell phone. He'd called someone *honey.* At the time, Katie had seen Pepper talking to Darian, so it couldn't have been either one of them. Did Hank have another woman on the side? It dawned on me that perhaps Ivy had known about Hank's proclivity to attract women and confronted him. Was hiding multiple affairs something a man would kill over?

"Jenna" — Z.Z. lowered her voice — "Pepper seemed a little, um, calmer than the other day, don't you think?"

"After being accused of murder? I should think so."

"I'm not talking about that." Z.Z. shook her hand. "I'm talking about after she bumped into her ex-husband for the first time in years. She was still fuming when I saw her an hour later. It had to have been a shock."

Darian's eyes widened. "Her ex is in town? But didn't he run off thirty years ago?"

"Thirty-six," I said.

"Why return now?" she asked.

"He came to town to meet Cinnamon." At least that was the story Noah was telling. After learning Lola saw him in her restaurant the day before Ivy died, I was beginning to question that account. Pepper had accused him of coming to town to gamble. How did his interaction with Ivy factor in?

"*Shh.*" Z.Z. held a finger to her lips. "Cinnamon is heading our way. It's a sensitive subject."

Cinnamon and Deputy Appleby were moving with purpose toward us. As she neared, she glowered . . . at me. What had I done now?

I rotated my head and neck to remove any tension and smiled broadly. "Hey, Chief. Isn't it a gorgeous day?"

"Your father called me," Cinnamon said.

So much for a preamble.

"And reached me instead," Appleby countered.

I could mess up the game of Telephone with the best of them. What had gotten mixed up in this translation? Had my father, to amuse himself, purposely thrown me under a bus?

"Should I leave?" Z.Z. asked.

"Stay," both officers ordered.

Cinnamon and Appleby flanked me. Did they think I would run? Exactly how far would I get? I was fast, but Appleby had legs for days.

"Let me have it," I said. "Both barrels. What did I do?"

"You didn't *do* anything," Cinnamon said. "That's the point."

"I beg to differ. You said *you* were going to contact Crusibella about the —"

"I'm not talking about Ms. Queensberry," Cinnamon said, cutting me off. "I'm talking about Lola Bird. She came to you with information, is that correct?"

"Yes, but before seeing me, she'd gone to the precinct to give a statement."

"No, she hadn't."

"She told my dad —" I paused and licked my lips. What exactly had Lola said to him? She'd given him a sassy *falling-off-a-turnip-truck* reply and said of course she'd gone to the precinct. Had she left before someone could take her statement, or had someone on the force recorded it but lost it? Not wishing to get anyone in trouble and seeing as I was always in hot water with Cinnamon, I decided to take the hit. "I must have misunderstood her."

"Fill me in."

"Didn't my father tell you the gist?"

"No. He said you would."

I sighed. Good old Dad had set me directly in Cinnamon's crosshairs. I'd bet he was having a jolly laugh at my expense right about now.

"Lola saw your father at the diner last Friday." I explained how Noah had waited to chat with Ivy, but after Ivy and Oren fought and split, he'd cooled his heels. "Why he wanted to meet with Ivy is a conundrum. Lola suggested he might have ordered something online from Dreamcatcher, and it didn't show up. Of course, he didn't have to come to town to deal with that. He could have called her on the phone."

"Don't theorize."

"Right." I'd forgotten her reprimand. "The way Lola told it, he hovered waiting for a break in the conversation. Your mother thinks —"

"I don't care what she thinks," Cinnamon said.

I stared daggers at her. "Your mother thinks your father is up to something shady."

"Does she think he had a hand in Ivy's murder?"

"She didn't say that, but he has a history of . . ." I hesitated.

"Of what?"

I would not gossip. If Pepper wanted to tell her about Noah's gambling history, so be it. "You should ask her."

Cinnamon glanced at Appleby. "Does Dreamcatcher have an online presence?"

"Not sure."

"Check it out," Cinnamon ordered.

"On it, ma'am." He removed his cell phone from his pocket and tapped the Internet icon. After a moment, he said, "What does site under construction mean?"

I explained that *site under construction* often meant a website was being built for the first time while *site under renovation* usually meant what it said, that something that already existed was being refreshed, although newbies might mistakenly use the former when meaning the latter.

"Well, it's under construction," he said.

"Cinnamon, forgive me if I'm overstepping . . ." I worked my tongue inside my mouth, deliberating my next comment.

"Out with it."

"Noah is your father. Why don't you ask him what went down?"

A guarded expression crossed her face. "I would, but he's not answering my calls."

CHAPTER 19

As Cinnamon and Deputy Appleby left, I made a beeline for Dreamcatcher. If Alastair was in the shop doing whatever the estate lawyer demanded to make the place ready for sale, I could nip this query in the bud. Also, Alastair might have met Noah already and would know what business he'd wanted with Ivy.

When I spotted the *Closed* sign hanging on Dreamcatcher's door, I deflated. So much for that idea. I made a U-turn. A few steps later, I paused. Alastair was standing at the sales counter inside Spellbinder holding up a piece of paper for Crusibella's inspection.

I strode in and let the door shut behind me. The store was packed with customers. In the reading room, a dozen or more women in matching neon blue hats were seated at the round table. Each held a copy of Agatha Christie's *Three Act Tragedy.*

"Blackmail my foot," one lady exclaimed and flailed her book. "It was not blackmail."

"Yes, it was," exclaimed another book club member. "Look right here." She whipped open her book with gusto.

I had read a lot of Christie's work but not that one; I didn't have a clue. Moving on, I strolled to the sales counter.

"Do you need every section filled out?" Alastair asked Crusibella. "I've only had two employers. You have spaces for five."

"Are you applying for a job?" I asked as I drew near.

Alastair glanced over his shoulder, and I was shocked to see how drawn he looked. It didn't help that he was wearing a drab gray polo and faded jeans. Had he dressed to match his mood? "I've got to be proactive in case Ivy's parents decide to close Dreamcatcher entirely."

"Is that a possibility?" I gazed at Crusibella, who looked pristine in a pearl white silk blouse and matching trousers. "Don't they know you want to buy the business?"

"Z.Z. has contacted the executor, but she hasn't heard back. I'm sure it will work out fine."

"I'm not." Alastair's tone was lackluster, as if the possibility of losing his job was eating away at him. "The dude called earlier today. I swear, he is possibly the dourest person on the earth. And vague to boot." He set the application on the counter, licked the nib of his pencil, and jotted down more information. "He said Ivy's parents were being sticklers, whatever that means. Sticklers about price? Sticklers about selling? Like he's not a stickler, asking me to photograph every item in the shop? Sheesh."

Crusibella rolled her eyes in my direction and mouthed: *Poor guy.*

"How many places of residence do you need?" Alastair swooped hair off his forehead. "I've only lived in my father's house and now in my apartment."

"Write down both."

"And I don't own a car. I ride my bike everywhere."

"That's fine."

Alastair resumed filling out the rest of the form.

"Jenna" — Crusibella reached out to me, a sparkle in her eyes — "I have to tell you, your aunt's reading for me yesterday was spot on. A steady stream of customers has come into the shop over the last twenty-four hours, all of them buying books."

"I saw the Blue Hat club in the reading room."

"Aren't they a hoot?"

243

"They're certainly vocal," I said.

"For all I care, let them wail, because the club's chairwoman has preordered their books for the entire year."

"Wow!"

"Yes, it's going to be a gold mine." Crusibella winked. "And more clubs are planning to preorder because I'm giving them a discount to rival any online seller. Plus free shipping."

"That's wonderful."

"So, you see, I'm quite positive that I'll be able to buy Dreamcatcher. My fortune said a financial deal was coming my way."

"That could mean all the book clubs and their preorders."

"Or it could mean something bigger. Better."

I wanted to share her enthusiasm, but the notion that she'd killed Ivy in order to buy Ivy's business kept creeping into my mind.

"Done." Alastair set down the pencil and handed Crusibella the application. "I hope you'll give me a job."

"Apply everywhere," Crusibella cautioned him. "Paper the town. That's always the best policy. I don't have an opening right now, but if this keeps up" — she swept a hand to encompass the bustling activity — "I just might, and in the event I purchase Dreamcatcher —" She cleared her throat. "When I purchase Dreamcatcher, you'll be first on my list."

"Thank you, ma'am." Alastair bobbed his head submissively. "I really appreciate that." He backed a few feet toward the exit.

"Alastair, wait," I said. "One question."

He paused.

Blurt it out, Jenna. Chop-chop. "Dreamcatcher's website says it's under construction."

"That's right."

"Meaning you don't sell anything online?"

"No. We do, just not while the site's down." He smiled sadly. "Ivy never could get the term right. See, whenever she tweaked the site to add new product, which she was doing all the time, she'd put up the wrong notice." He chuckled. "Heck, she couldn't even get the password right most of the time, like when she wanted to check activity on the site. I finally made it easy for her — six zeroes and a dollar sign. Can't mess that up, right?"

"Do you have a lot of online buyers?" I asked.

"We have regulars. Why?"

"Did you encounter someone named Noah Pritchett?"

Alastair scratched his neck. "The name

doesn't ring a bell."

"How about anyone with the last name Pritchett?" Perhaps Noah's wife or daughters had ordered something.

"No, ma'am. I don't think so. Is that all?" He jammed his hands into his jeans pockets, once again looking crestfallen.

"Yes, thanks."

"I wish she were here," he whispered so softly as he slogged out of the store that I almost missed it.

Crusibella clicked her tongue. "He's got a bit of growing up to do, but he'll rally." She clipped his application to a group of applications on the pegboard behind the register. "Jenna" — she swung around and scanned the customers, none of whom were standing near the sales counter — "sit with me." She directed me to the reading bar. "We need to talk."

"About?"

"The police were just in. They asked me about a story they heard from Eleanor Landry."

A thrill zinged through me. My words to Cinnamon hadn't fallen on deaf ears after all. Why hadn't she mentioned it when she'd waylaid me at the library tent?

"I know Eleanor Landry spoke to you first." Crusibella fetched a bottle of Pellegrino from a mini refrigerator and popped it open. She poured the contents into a honeycomb-style iced tea glass. "Lime?"

"No, thanks."

She pushed the glass toward me. The air between us grew thick with tension. I took a sip of the sparkling water and set the glass down without breaking eye contact.

"Now that the police know what happened, I think you should hear, too," she said.

"That's not necessary."

"Yes, it is. I —" Crusibella nestled onto the stool next to mine. Tears pressed at the corners of her eyes. She dabbed them with a cocktail napkin. "I'm a compulsive eater. I mean I *was* compulsive. In college. Before I moved to Crystal Cove. I was super fat." She threw her arms wide. "But then I found the light. The spirit. The essence of life. Not in church or anything like that. Oh, sure, I went to Overeaters Anonymous meetings and they advocated for a spiritual rebirth, but where I truly found balance was in nature. In the universe. In the metaphysical."

More tears leaked from her eyes. She blotted them again. "Focusing on the positive helped me control my cravings, and within a year, the weight fell off me. That's why I want to own Dreamcatcher so badly. Yes" — she fanned the air with the napkin — "books are my life. They always have been, but stones and crystals move me. I adore sifting through soil to search for unpolished gems. I love running my fingers over them. I crave their healing power. For over ten years, I have fed myself from within instead of from without." She thumped her chest with her fist. "But after Ivy called me — *me* — a charlatan during our set-to last Friday night, I began to question my motives. Had I duped myself? Was I an impostor? Did I want Dreamcatcher for all the right reasons?"

I took another sip of my drink, waiting for her to continue.

"I'm ashamed to say it" — Crusibella crumpled the napkin and tossed it into a bin behind the reading bar — "but I awoke the next morning eager to find something to fill the void. In other words, *food.* And not just any food. Fatty food. Salty food. Anything to feed the monster." She placed both hands on the counter, palms down. "I fought the urge all day. I moped. I meandered. I meditated. But Saturday afternoon, I couldn't restrain myself any longer." She worked a fingernail along the groove of the wood counter and then tucked her hands beneath her armpits. "I knew if people saw me gorging myself, it would get back to Ivy and she'd throw it in my face. My reputation of being spiritual and calm would be toast. When she was truly ready to sell Dreamcatcher, she would block me from buying it at every turn."

"Why would she do that? She was your friend."

"She could be cruel."

I stiffened. If a friend would say that about Ivy, what would her enemies say?

"To try to curb my cravings, I dressed in a costume." Crusibella released her arms and used her hands to describe her outfit. "A few years ago, I bought a curly red wig and a fat suit and required myself to put it on once a month to remind myself how huge I'd been and that I never wanted to be that again." She rose from the stool and poured herself a glass of Pellegrino. She squeezed a quarter of a lime into her glass, took a long sip, and remained standing. "But putting on the suit didn't deter me from my goal that day. So I stole to Hog Heaven" — she polished off her drink — "and ordered a Pig Pack pork sandwich slathered in barbecue sauce. Nobody at the diner recognized me. I'd donned horrid makeup and the red wig. When I'd stuffed myself to the point of getting sick, I dashed out —"

"And sneaked down an alley."

"Along the way, I clawed the disguise off me. The overcoat and fat suit were hot and heavy."

"That's when Mrs. Landry saw you."

"It must have been. I ran all the way —"

"Home to make a cheese platter," I finished.

"No. To Overeaters Anonymous, where I met with a counselor." She ran her finger down the length of her glass. "For one full hour, we broke down the reasons I'd fallen short. When I felt in control, I told her I needed to go to the book club soiree. She advised me to own up to my problem with a friend, and I would have. To Ivy. But when we found her dead, and when you told the police about our argument, I panicked. If people found out about my weakness, I feared my aspiration of owning Dreamcatcher would be dashed. Ivy would drag me down from the grave."

"Isn't it worse to be suspected of murder?"

Crusibella sighed. "Don't you get it? Who would believe someone like me could guide them in matters of health and healing if . . . if . . ." She gulped in air.

I reached for her hand but she recoiled.

"I gave the police my counselor's name. They're following up." She gazed at me, her eyes moist with tears. "Believe me, Jenna, I would never have hurt Ivy."

On my way back to the Cookbook Nook, I ran through the names of the other possible suspects. Crusibella was innocent, and Pepper wasn't guilty. Did Oren or Alastair kill Ivy because she'd rejected them? Did Hank kill her to keep an affair secret? Or was there another reason someone wanted her dead?

As I was passing the Pelican Brief, my cell phone rang. *Jake Chapman* appeared on the screen.

I answered. "Hi. What's up?"

"Z.Z. needs your help."

"Help with what?"

"The executor for Ivy Beale's estate is putting her house on the market. Z.Z. convinced the guy to use her as the realtor."

"That's a big deal." There was another realtor in Crystal Cove, a real cutthroat negotiator, who picked up most of the listings.

"Yep, but here's the hitch," Jake went on. "She's afraid to go in Ivy's house by herself."

"Afraid?"

251

"Because of the murder and all. She'd like you to accompany her."

"Why me?"

"Your aunt suggested it and your father seconded the idea. We were all having lunch. I thought it was a swell idea."

"Swell," I echoed, unable to hide the snarkiness in my tone.

"You've been inside the house," Jake added, "so you won't get the heebie-jeebies if you take another tour of it."

Says who? I knew what would happen the moment I stepped foot in the kitchen. I would picture Ivy lying there and see the quartz shard in her chest and stones on her eyes and my stomach would churn. Heck, it was churning now. "Jake, I am not the go-to escort for a dead person's home."

"Jenna, you can do this."

"Chief Pritchett will demand my head on a platter."

"She'll thank you for doing your part."

I croaked. "What universe do you live in?"

He roared with laughter.

"Why don't you go with Z.Z.?" I asked.

"Uh-uh," Jake said. "She and I have strict rules. She doesn't mess with my business and I don't mess with hers."

Tag, you're it. Silently cursing my aunt and

father, I said, "When does Z.Z. want to do it?"

"Right now. She's waiting in her car outside the house. Your aunt said she'd cover for you at the store."

Wasn't she accommodating!

"Just so you know," Jake went on, "Vera read your tarot and determined this good deed will help you reap a heap of favor from the spirit world."

Sure, but would I reap enough favor so that I'd never have to see another dead body in my lifetime? A girl could dream.

CHAPTER 20

If I was going to help Z.Z., I needed fortification first. I jaywalked across the boulevard and hurried to Sweet Pea's Tea Time mobile truck. When I made it to the head of the line, I ordered a miniature lemon tea cake and a cup of Earl Grey tea. I opened the cake, which was delivered in a pretty cellophane bag and tied with ribbon, and took a taste. Perfection. When I asked the owner of Sweet Pea if she'd share the recipe, she told me I'd find it on her website.

I finished my treat on the way to the Cookbook Nook, poked my head in to tell my aunt I was going on the mission that she had so kindly created for me, and set off in my VW.

Minutes later, I drove along Rhododendron Drive to Ivy's multilevel Italian villa. Sunlight graced the red roof. Z.Z. stood at the foot of the front path looking very professional in a tailored black suit.

When I joined her, she pecked me on the cheek. "Thank you for coming. I hate to be a sissy, but —"

"Glad to be of help," I lied. I'd never confess to being a tad apprehensive.

"Okay, here we go." Z.Z. pulled her cell phone from her briefcase and pressed the recording app. As she strode along the walkway, she made verbal notes. "Garden needs tweaking. We should stage the front porch. A swing. Potted plants. Entryway needs paint and new hardware." Using a key, she let us into the house. She paused the recording. "Seeing as I'm the realtor, the police gave me the keys and such. FYI, they've cleared away all of their, um, evidentiary materials."

The last time I'd entered the house, "Love Theme from *Romeo and Juliet*" had been playing. Given the loving, healing stones placed on Ivy's hands and eyes, I'd wondered whether the killer had been intentionally pointing a finger at Oren. Now, in the eerie silence, I speculated whether the killer had been laying blame on Alastair or Hank.

"It's so quiet," I whispered.

"Yes. Maybe we should consider adding a waterfall," Z.Z. noted, missing the significance of my comment. "Let's begin with the lower floor and work our way up." She restarted the recording. "Paint looks good in the living room. Neutral colors. No personal photos. Don't have to do much. The bonsai trees are a nice touch. Very soothing. Let's move on to the kitchen." She motioned for me to go first.

Forcing myself to remain calm, I strode ahead of her. The kitchen had been cleaned, the body removed. The empty food trays had also been confiscated or stored. I wondered about the desserts Ivy was supposed to have set out for the event. Cinnamon mentioned a tray of cream puffs. Had there been other foods? Did the killer lace more than one item in the hopes that Ivy would eat one, or did he or she hand-deliver the cream puff personally to Ivy?

"Jenna, what do you think?" Z.Z. asked.

I glanced at her. Had she been talking to me and I'd tuned her out?

"Does it need a fresh coat of paint?"

"I don't think so." As before, I noted the kitchen was pretty in a Florentine way, done in soft pearl tones with brown accents. "It looks very up to date. No chips on the cabinets. The granite is nice, too."

"I agree."

I crossed to the Sub-Zero refrigerator and took a peek. It was filled with the usual: salad dressings and condiments, bottled water, creamers. There were no perishables; nothing in the crisper.

"You'll want to have the refrigerator cleaned and sanitized," I suggested.

Before leaving the room, Z.Z. made a note about adding colorful flowers for the open house, to brighten the mood. I wasn't sure anything could do that once a buyer found out a person had been murdered in the kitchen. By California law, the realtor would have to disclose that tidbit.

We inspected the other rooms on the first floor, which included a workout room, a maid's room, and a guest room, all of which were neutral in tone, almost as if Ivy had prepared the house for sale. Or Ivy had purchased it exactly as it was and hadn't added any personal touches. The warmest of the rooms was the study. Dark mahogany bookshelves lined the walls. A reading chair held the Mystery Mavens' book club selection. A bookmark was slotted about halfway in.

I browsed the titles on the shelves. Mostly classics. "Ivy sure collected a lot of books."

"I own about as many," Z.Z. said, "although I haven't had time to read them lately."

"A lot of romances," I added.

Z.Z. made a note to remove any books

that prospective buyers might consider racy and continued down the hall. When she pushed open the last door on the left, she said, "Interesting," and stepped inside.

I had the same reaction.

The room was devoted to potting bonsai trees. A galvanized steel greenhouse workstation stood against the far wall. Three broom-style and two slanting-style bonsais stood in cream-colored pots on top of the flat counter. To the right, a shallow sink counter was filled with dirt. Bags of fireplace ash as well as akadama, a high-fired inorganic component according to the package, were stored on the shelves below.

"That explains the bonsai plants I've seen in other rooms," Z.Z. said.

"I wonder why she had so many?"

"In a few of my realtor magazines, I've read that in the Eastern art of feng shui bonsai trees are believed to bring good luck and good fortune when displayed in homes."

I shuddered. "Not for Ivy."

"No, sadly."

"Why do you think the killer placed a bonsai next to her head?" I asked.

"What are you talking about?" Z.Z. swiveled to face me. "I didn't see that mentioned in the newspaper article."

"Didn't you see the plant when you came

into the kitchen that night?"

"Heavens, no. I turned green and hurried out."

"Of course. I remember now." Crusibella had consoled Z.Z. on the front porch.

"Maybe the killer set it there like a funeral wreath," she murmured. "In tribute. Or maybe the killer meant it as a warning."

I gazed at her. "A warning?"

"To convey that Ivy's luck had run out." Z.Z. clucked her tongue. "Horrible."

Softly, as if she now considered the room a sanctuary, Z.Z. recorded a note about airing it out, and then she proceeded to the stairs leading to the second story.

"Who will be coming to town to sign off on everything?" I asked. "Ivy's parents or the executor?"

"According to the executor, her parents have no desire to get involved. 'Get rid of everything' " — Z.Z. whipped a hand through the air — "was the command he gave me. He has the parents' power of attorney to manage every detail."

"Wow. No love lost there."

"Not an ounce."

I couldn't imagine being estranged from my family. After my mother died — David had died within months of her — I'd isolated myself, and my father had shut down.

However, in the past few years, Dad and I had reconnected, and I was so glad we had, even if he was currently the bane of my existence, pitting me against Cinnamon as well as suggesting I handle this not-so-entertaining house tour.

Z.Z. paused on the first landing. "Newel is scratched," she said into her cell phone. Despite her misgivings about entering the house, she was acting like a consummate professional in complete control of her emotions. "Floors could use a good polish. Remove personal photographs on walls."

Most of the framed pictures featured Ivy with someone prominent in town. I didn't see any people old enough to be her parents, although I did notice one of her as a teenager with a younger, similar-looking girl. The sister who'd died of heart failure, I assumed.

At the top of the stairs I noticed a series of gold-framed wedding photos sitting on a beautiful Italianate bureau, featuring Ivy with a handsome young man. I had similar pictures with David, all of which were buried in my hope chest. I wondered if Oren, after seeing reminders of Ivy with her husband, had grown jealous. Had Alastair been invited to Ivy's house? If so, how had he felt?

"Oh, my!" Z.Z. exclaimed as she stepped into the master bedroom.

I strode in and gasped. "It's so blue."

"That's an understatement."

Glibly, I wondered whether Vincent van Gogh had a hand in decorating it: blue walls, blue furniture, blue bedspread and linens. Even the broom-style bonsai sitting atop a notepad on the Baroque-period desk by the window was planted in a deep blue pot.

"This room must represent the real Ivy," Z.Z. said and continued recording. "Master bedroom needs an entire makeover: paint, tile, carpet, linens." She clicked Pause. "Given the state of this room, bringing her house up to snuff could take a few weeks. Good thing her shop doesn't need as much work."

"You know Crusibella would buy Dream-catcher in a heartbeat — no changes."

"That's not going to happen. For anyone so it seems. The executor informed me an hour ago that the parents have decided they want cash for inventory, and then they want to back out of the lease."

"But why?"

"I get the feeling they are cruel and spiteful and don't want Ivy to have any kind of legacy."

"Because she held them responsible for her sister's death."

Z.Z. nodded her head. "Family dramas are the hardest to litigate."

"Crusibella is going to be heartbroken. Isn't there something you can do?"

"I will be trying the legal angle. Crusibella did, after all, have a verbal agreement to purchase." Z.Z. shot a finger at me. "Say, you could be our witness. You heard them arguing. You heard Ivy go back on her word."

During the disagreement, Ivy stated that she and Crusibella never had a deal because Ivy had been tipsy when she'd accepted the offer. Would that kind of hearsay stand up in court?

"Say you will," Z.Z. pleaded.

"Of course."

"Bless you." She pointed. "See what's in that desk, would you? If the deed is there, I need to have it in hand."

I crossed to the desk. "Who's going to pack up the house? There's a ton of stuff to move."

"We'll hire a company."

I slid the bonsai off the notepad and set it nearer the window, repositioning the side that had faced away from the window so it could glory in sunshine. "Ivy was a doodler," I said.

"Aren't we all?"

On the topmost pad was a smattering of initials followed by round numbers like *OD 7000, YY 5000, JC 8000,* all smudged due to the ring of dirt left by the bonsai's drain hole.

"I don't see a jewelry box, do you?" Z.Z. asked.

I scanned the room. "Nope. Maybe she kept it in individual bags and hid it with her undergarments."

Z.Z. started opening drawers in the bureau to the right of the closet. "Whoa, nelly! Every one of these is jammed with clothing. Do me a favor. See if there's any jewelry squirreled in the desk. We don't want to leave valuables around for the movers."

I opened the desk drawers one at a time. The left topmost drawer held the usual: a stapler, pens, and paperclips. The bottom drawer on the right held a key chain filled with thumb drives and more notepads with numerical scribbles.

Z.Z. browsed Ivy's closet and then slipped into the bathroom.

"I didn't find any jewelry," I called as I noticed a rectangular outline of dust on the desktop. "Do you think the police took her computer?"

"If it's not there, yes. They're probably browsing her history to see if anyone wrote her a threatening email."

Or looking for the person who had hacked her emails.

A door closed. Another creaked open. "There are no prescriptions," Z.Z. called. "I assume the police took those, too. Oho! Jackpot!" A drawer slammed. "Found her jewelry, like you said, in a series of makeup bags. Beneath the sink. Let's inventory it together."

She strolled out of the bathroom and emptied the jewelry onto the blue comforter. For three minutes, she made verbal notes as I reinserted the silver and gold necklaces, earrings, and bracelets in their respective bags. Two pieces featured opals. None were made with other gems or semi-precious stones, which was interesting given the treasures available in Ivy's shop.

When we finished, Z.Z. said, "I think that about does it. In two weeks, I'll have this baby ready for sale."

My stomach wrenched. How fast the wheels of life were rolling along after Ivy's death. It stunk. I had mourned David for months. Who would mourn her?

CHAPTER 21

When I walked into the Cookbook Nook, I was surprised to see Tina at the sales counter. She was dressed in a lemon yellow long-sleeved blouse over white jeans. Her coloring seemed good, but her forehead was pinched.

I helped her assist customers. After ringing up the last one, I said, "Feeling okay?"

Tina nodded. "I saw a doctor. He said I'm suffering from stress."

"Because of your boyfriend?"

"Mm-hm. Apparently, I can't handle someone who lies."

"Very few people can."

Tina tittered. "The doctor put me on a diet of exercise and meditation. If that doesn't work, he'll prescribe medicine, but I don't like taking pills."

"Me, either, but some drugs really do work." I patted her hand. "In the meantime, talk to Katie about stress-beating foods.

She's becoming an expert."

"Last night, my boyfriend told me to eat more turkey."

"You're still seeing him?" I asked.

"He said he would change. No more lies."

"So he admitted to lying?"

"Mm-hm. I think I can trust him now."

Quite a few women were like Tina and me, hoping that their man would change. David had lied until his dying day.

"By the way, my boyfriend thinks I should go to counseling," Tina added.

"Maybe you both should," I suggested. "That way, you can analyze how differently you approach life. Women and men are so —"

"Oh, he'd never go for that. He talks to his fish. He says they're great listeners."

"Plus, they don't talk back," I teased.

She giggled.

Secretly, I hoped she'd take the advice about seeing a therapist but decided to hold off on a full-court press.

"FYI, we might need to order more of those cookie jars." Tina gestured toward the display, where three women were standing. "Almost every book club organizer came in to ask about them."

A customer set a stack of books on the counter. Tina started ringing her up. Over her shoulder she said, "By the way, boss, Bailey and your aunt are in the storage room trying to come up with which flowers to put in the display window for Spring Fling."

It never ceased to amaze me how quickly one theme ended in Crystal Cove and a new theme was on deck. Following Book Club Bonanza, Mayor Zeller had decided our sweet town should feature flowers. Each shop or restaurant would set out a colorful pot. The city would provide the containers as well as the soil. The establishments could decorate the containers to their hearts' content. When the event was over, the town would relocate the flowerpots to the Pier and various parks. In addition, the mayor was allowing a variety of cart vendors to sell their wares on the sidewalks.

"Will we ever have a week where there isn't a theme?" Tina asked, echoing my inner thoughts.

"Not if Z.Z. has anything to say about it." I made quotation marks in the air. " 'The more themes, the more tourists. The more tourism, the better the economy.' Not to mention each visiting vendor has to pay a street rental fee. *Cha-ching,* as Bailey would say."

"If you want my opinion" — Tina paused

to ask the customer to insert the chip on her credit card into the payment terminal — "I'd say *Cooking with Flowers: Sweet and Savory Recipes with Rose Petals, Lilacs, Lavender, and Other Edible Flowers* should be the main book on the display table. The recipes are creative and the photography is downright gorgeous. There are flowers galore."

I knew the book she was talking about. On the cover was a white *flowerfetti* cake decorated with pansies and petals. Inside, the reader could find recipes like calendula quiche, dandelion muffins, and daylily cheesecake. I'd eaten pansies tossed into a salad, but I'd never tried the others. Daylilies sounded interesting. In addition to the floral-themed cookbooks, I'd ordered floral-covered journals, recipe cards with darling flowers imprinted in the corners, and a wooden bookstand carved with roses. One of each would enrich the display.

Leaving Tina to finish with the customers, I pressed through the drapes to the stockroom. Tigger traipsed after me. I scooped him up and chuffed his chin. "Did you miss me?" He purred his assent. "Good answer." I set him on the floor.

"Jenna," my aunt said, "perfect timing. I'm thinking we should plant pansies in our floral pot." She displayed her iPad to me. On the screen were a dozen pictures of spring flowers. "What do you think?"

"Okay." I paired a slice of manchego cheese and a cracker from the platter Katie had provided. She had a sixth sense about when any of us needed sustenance.

"I think we should do perennials," Bailey said.

Was it just me or had her baby tummy doubled in size in the last few days? Her lilac smock-style blouse billowed forward.

"Maybe we should make a fairy garden," she went on. "I saw one at the Renaissance Fair last year. You know, with a water feature and elves. It was darling. Fairies bring good vibrations to all involved."

"Fairies don't exist," I said.

"Says who?" my aunt chirped.

"We could always use additional good vibrations," Bailey went on, undeterred by my skepticism. "We could start with a miniature gazebo at the center and add a bonsai fir. It'll look like a giant redwood."

The mention of bonsais made me flash on the plants in Ivy's gardening room. Why had she created so many? Had she done so to enhance her soul as she'd claimed to Crusibella during their argument?

"Whatever you two decide is fine with

me," I said judiciously. "In the meantime, I'll check on our orders. Afterward, let's break down the display window. In addition to our floral-themed cookbooks, I'm thinking we should feature a window box filled with silk flowers plus gardening tools and a few of our novelty items."

"And a fairy," Bailey chimed.

"Okay, a fairy, too," I repeated. "Why not?"

An hour later, as I was setting up boxes to hold the book club–themed items that hadn't sold, I glimpsed Cinnamon and her father crossing the parking lot. In her uniform, she came across as all business, while he looked jaunty in a panama and lightweight suit. Even his gait was brisk. They entered the café.

Eager to find out if she had talked with Lola, I hurried along the breezeway to greet them. I whispered to our perky hostess, "If it's okay, I'll seat them."

"Go for it." She pointed to a table on her chart and handed me two menus.

I strode to Cinnamon and her father. "Table for two? Right this way."

Cinnamon gave me an icy look. I ignored it and led them to the designated table.

"Mr. Pritchett, how nice to see you again," I said as he took his seat. "Coming for tea?

We have an extensive selection. I have a fondness for Earl Grey."

"I'm partial to orange pekoe."

"I'm glad you two hooked up." I handed each a menu. "Cinnamon was getting worried about you."

She shot me another surly look.

"My phone died," Noah said. "I forgot to bring my charger. Had to buy a new one." That sounded like a reasonable explanation. To make his point, he tapped the cell phone that he'd set faceup on the table.

"I like your suit, sir," I said. "Is it new, too?"

"Yep. And the hat. I went to the haberdasher at the north end of town."

"Great Threads."

"That's the one. I hadn't bought a suit in the longest time."

Had he ventured into the shop to get a read on Hank? Even though Noah had run out on Pepper and remarried, he might have her best interests at heart.

"My daughter" — he hesitated and licked his lips — "Cinnamon's half sister, is getting married in September. It'll be an informal wedding. This suit will be perfect."

"Will you attend?" I asked Cinnamon, curious about what Pepper's reaction to the news would be.

Noah answered for her. "Of course she will."

A waitress brought two glasses of water. Cinnamon took a sip.

"It'll be fun to have a sister, won't it, Cinnamon?" I asked.

She screwed up her mouth, obviously dubious about meeting two perfect strangers nearly ten years her junior. Was she wondering what they might have in common?

One big happy family, I mused. "Say, Cinnamon," I said as casually as I could, "did you happen to chat with Lola, about your father and Ivy?"

"We'll discuss it later." She whipped open her menu.

"Me and Ivy?" Noah tilted his head.

In for a penny, in for a pound, I decided. "You were at the Pelican Brief Diner. Last Friday."

"No."

"Yes. The owner recognized you. She believed you wanted to talk to Ivy Beale."

"I don't know anybody by that name," Noah said.

"Bobbed blond hair. Pretty features."

"Nope. Doesn't ring a bell."

"She was sitting with —"

"The woman who died, Dad," Cinnamon

272

cut in. "Why did you want to speak with her? Why did you lie and say you came to town days later?"

His cheeks flushed pink. "I was hoping to —" He stopped midsentence.

"Hoping to what?" Cinnamon demanded.

"Nothing."

"C'mon," she coaxed. "Jenna has so kindly brought the subject to the fore." Her sarcasm was not lost on me.

Noah licked his lips. "I was hoping to speak to the guy she was with."

"Oren Michaels," I said.

"Why?" Cinnamon leaned forward on her elbows and casually folded her hands together, a patient and experienced interrogator.

Noah lowered his chin, not making eye contact. "About a business deal."

"What kind of business deal?" she asked. "You run a nursery. He's a fisherman. What business could you two possibly have?"

Noah lifted his glass and guzzled down half the water.

"Dad?" Cinnamon prodded.

"I'm . . . I'm thinking of investing in fish oil fertilizer." He was stammering. Was he making it up on the fly?

"Get real," she countered.

"No kidding. Fish oil's good for nutrients

273

in soil. It's rich in organic matter and breaks down slowly to feed plants and soil microbes over time." He checked his watch. "I have to call my boss." He wiped his mouth with a napkin and started to stand.

Cinnamon clutched his wrist and held on firmly until he sank into his chair. "In a minute." She signaled for me to leave.

I didn't go far. As I busied myself at the tea and coffee station, I overheard them talking about how Noah was trying to impress his new boss with his work ethic. As he talked, he repeatedly eyed his cell phone. He claimed he hadn't spoken with Oren yet — Oren was elusive — but he knew Oren was the kind of man who would appreciate a business proposal.

I returned to the table and said, "So what would you like to order? Orange pekoe for you, Noah." I smiled at Cinnamon. She was not happy that I'd made my way back so soon. "We have delicious scones today as well as lemon-lavender tea cakes."

"I'll take the cheese and fruit plate." Noah pushed aside his menu. "Which reminds me. I do have something important to tell you."

Cinnamon closed her menu without ordering, her gaze fixed on her father.

"It's about your mother," he went on.

"Dad, we don't need to rehash the past."

"This isn't about the past. It's about the present. Well, the recent past, I suppose. Now that I've told you I was in town as of Friday, if it helps, I saw your mother at her house making what I think was an appetizer on Saturday afternoon."

Cinnamon raised an eyebrow. "Did she tell you to say that?"

"Are you kidding me? We haven't spoken. In fact, I didn't say it earlier because she ticked me off the other day." Noah shrugged. "I can hold a grudge."

"She was pretty caustic," I admitted.

"On a side note," Noah went on, "and this will prove I'm not lying, she was singing along with Frank Sinatra. She was playing the album on the turntable I bought for our first Christmas."

"This is wonderful news, Cinnamon," I said. "Remember how your mother said she was singing?"

Skeptically, Cinnamon worked her tongue along the inside of her mouth.

"I wanted to talk to her," Noah went on, "but I didn't have the courage to knock on the door."

"Which song?" she asked.

" 'Spring Is Here.' "

"Her favorite," Cinnamon muttered.

"I thought I might upset her if I showed up all of a sudden." He drummed the table. "I hung around trying to muster up the nerve, but, well" — he leaned back in his chair and wagged his thumbs at his face — "I'm a coward."

"Are you also a peeping Tom?" Cinnamon chided.

Noah winked. "Only the kind who can give her an alibi."

CHAPTER 22

Taking down a display and installing a new one was always time-consuming. It required attention to detail and plenty of patience. So did planting a pot of herbs. Aunt Vera had landed on the brilliant idea of giving our pot a culinary theme. Hearing Simon and Garfunkel crooning "parsley, sage, rosemary, and thyme" had given her the inspiration. She'd affixed stickers with the words of the herbs to the pot and had purchased thirty small containers of herbs to install. No fir tree. No fairies — this time. Bailey had gone home to rest. Yes, I was worried about her, but Tito had taken the day off to tend to her. I was pretty sure ice cream would be involved.

Early afternoon, after nursing my hands back to health with lotion — soil amendments, dirt, and water could wreak havoc on one's skin — I helped Tina with the myriad customers. Spring Fling had brought an entirely new crowd of tourists. One of the books we'd set out, *Wild Cocktails from the Midnight Apothecary: Over 100 recipes using home-grown and foraged fruits, herbs, and edible flowers* was getting a lot of buzz. It was packed with beautiful photographs and tips. There was even a glossary and a wealth of website links. I noticed a couple of ladies tittering about one of the exotic recipes.

Late in the afternoon, Crusibella and Z.Z. rushed in, cornered my aunt, and plunked into chairs at the vintage table. Both women seemed excited, in a good way. While they pieced together the new Herbs for Health jigsaw puzzle we'd laid out, I overheard Z.Z. say that it was time to secure a loan. Had Z.Z. or the executor finally convinced the Beale family to sell Dreamcatcher? For Crusibella's sake, I hoped so.

Unfortunately I was too busy to get the scoop, and then the moment Crusibella and Z.Z. hurried out, my aunt left on a date with the deputy, and Pepper bustled in.

"Jenna. Do you have a minute?" Pepper's beaded necklace was twisted in a knot and all the zippers on her tote bag were un-zipped.

I glanced at Tina, who was dealing with the last few customers. "Sure." I settled onto the chair my aunt had vacated at the vintage table and motioned for Pepper to sit. She did. Tigger leaped into my lap and stared at our visitor. Waiting expectantly. When Pepper didn't speak, I said, "Did you hear your ex-husband provided an alibi for you?"

"He did?"

"Yes. He told me as well as your daughter. Hours ago." Why hadn't Cinnamon called her mother? Leaving her hanging was cruel.

"I . . ." Pepper gripped her necklace and began to twist. "I . . ."

I waited, expecting her to continue. She didn't.

"You're exonerated," I said. "Call your daughter. She'll confirm it."

"I can't." Pepper lowered her gaze. Tears dripped down her cheeks. She swiped them away but didn't look up.

I leaned forward but didn't touch her. I was afraid she might crack. "Pepper, what's wrong?"

"Someone saw me."

"Saw you where?"

"Outside Ivy's. The day she died. I received an email. Whoever sent it said they have a photograph to prove it. They said I have to pay them *or else.*"

I sat taller. Were threatening emails a new

trend? I said, "But you weren't there."

"Yes, I was. I lied." She gazed at me intently. "I went there. In the afternoon. Before I started putting together my cheese appetizer." She drew in a deep breath, as if she couldn't get enough air. "I couldn't handle not knowing where Ivy stood with Hank. We met for about ten minutes. She assured me she wasn't into him. And I swear she was alive when I left."

"Why did you worry about her and Hank later on then?"

She rubbed the underside of her nose. "Because Ivy was known to lie, and I lack confidence when it comes to men. I couldn't believe someone as dapper and charismatic as Hank would be interested in me. When I heard Ivy had set her sights on him . . ." She twirled a hand. "She was so pretty and worldly. She could snare anybody." Pepper stared at her hands, her misery obvious.

"Tell me about the email."

"The blackmailer said he had a picture. One of Ivy's neighbors must have taken it. Or maybe the person on the bicycle."

"Person on the bicycle?"

"There was someone straddling a bicycle down the street."

"Male or female?"

"I don't know. The sunglasses and helmet

made it impossible to tell."

"I'm sure the police have questioned the neighbors," I said. "If a witness came forward with proof of your whereabouts, you'd have been asked about it by now."

"Maybe my daughter found out and intervened."

I shook my head. "She wouldn't do that. She's all about rules." My stomach twisted in a knot. Maybe this was why Cinnamon hadn't told her mother about her ex-husband's corroborating account.

"The extortionist . . ." Pepper toyed with her beads again. "That's what he is, right?"

I nodded.

"He — it could be a she, I suppose — said I need to pay five thousand dollars in bitcoin to obtain the original photograph."

I whistled. That was the same amount my blackmailer had demanded.

Pepper released the beads and bit back a sob. "I've . . . I've never used bitcoin for a transaction," she stammered. "I don't know how."

I tapped her wrist. "Hold on. Did you view the photo the extortionist claimed to have?"

"No. I didn't see an attachment."

"I believe this is a scam. I received the same kind of threatening email."

"Were you caught on camera outside Ivy's?"

"No, that's just it. I didn't do anything wrong. There is no photo. Scammers make vague accusations to bait people into paying them. Do you remember the sender's email address?"

"Good something."

"Goodguy?" I asked.

She nodded. "At vengeance dot something."

"That's the same as mine." I stabbed the table with a fingertip. "The email you received is bogus. Ignore it."

"Except . . ." She shivered. "I. Was. There."

Tigger reached out to Pepper. I allowed him to go to her.

She lifted him beneath his forearms and nestled him in her lap. "Jenna, I have to pay, or else —"

"Don't do it. You know you didn't kill Ivy."

"The police —"

"Think you're innocent. You have an alibi. Your ex-husband heard you singing along with Sinatra."

"How could he have?"

"He was lingering outside your place. He wanted to talk to you, but he couldn't find the courage. He waited a few days before meeting you at your shop."

"You mean accosting me."

I pointed to her tote bag. "Do you still have the email on your cell phone?"

"Yes."

"Let me see it."

She set Tigger on the floor, withdrew her cell phone, opened the email app, and then the email itself. She rotated her phone so I could view it.

I nodded. "The wording is almost identical to the email I received." Although hers was more specific. I scrolled down and gasped.

"What's wrong?" Pepper asked with alarm.

"There is a photograph. Embedded and really small. Too small to make out if it's you. We can't click it. It could be malware."

"Mal-what?"

I explained.

She let out a panicked squeak. "I'm doomed."

Who was this Goodguy? Certainly not a knight in shining armor. Was it the killer? Maybe he or she had been at Ivy's when Pepper showed up and had seen an ideal opportunity to implicate someone else.

Pepper started to hyperventilate.

"Breathe. Do you need a paper bag?" Her skin was pale and her eyes watery.

She shook her head and clapped a hand on her chest. "I'm . . . okay."

"I'm going to put Bailey on the case," I said. "She's a whiz with this stuff."

"You can't tell Cinnamon," Pepper pleaded. "Promise."

Keeping information from the police went against my grain, but I agreed. For now. "Go home. Eat a nice dinner."

"I couldn't possibly."

"Drink tea then. Hug your cat. I'll touch base when I have something."

When she left, I stewed. Bailey could build a website and she'd taken lots of computer classes during college. She'd even been the target of an online phishing scam a couple of years ago. Had she learned how to track down a hacker after that incident? If not, maybe I could hire an expert to follow the leads. Dad had to know someone in the FBI who could do so. On the other hand, he would probably order me to confide in Cinnamon A.S.A.P.

I sent Bailey a text message outlining my plan, added *Call me,* and headed home. I had chores to do. It had been over ten days since I'd focused on my cottage. I hoped doing the mundane would encourage the little gray cells, as Hercule Poirot would say, to work.

While sorting laundry, I listened to Judy Garland croon upbeat tunes. If only I felt so cheery. Who had killed Ivy? If I deduced the motive, could I figure out who the culprit was and help Pepper in the process? I knew Cinnamon and her crew were on the case. Would they uncover the truth? In the meantime, if she found out that her mother had lied . . .

Tigger mewed.

I petted his head. "Yes, you're right. Think outside the box. Who else other than Pepper might have wanted Ivy dead?"

Maybe concentrating on the crime scene would help. I fetched a handful of three-by-five cards. On the first I wrote: *quartz shard.* A kitchen knife would have been much easier to wield. Why use the quartz? I sketched the shard and set the card aside.

On a second card, I wrote: *eyestones.* According to Cinnamon, the painted eyes were facedown on Ivy's eyes. Had the killer done that on purpose or made a mistake? Alastair knew the significance of the stones. So did Crusibella. Oren might have. Did Hank? On the third card, I drew a green stone to represent the aventurine; it ended up looking more like Kryptonite. Sue me. I'd never become a geology artist.

Why had the killer placed the pieces of

aventurine in Ivy's hands? To signify love, accuse a lover, or indicate Ivy needed healing? What if the killer had used it to point out Ivy's inadequate knowledge of the nuances of the stones? I recalled Ivy advising Crusibella to wrap her hand around a piece of it during their argument, and Crusibella chiding Ivy for not knowing the true nature of what aventurine did. Was that significant?

Crusibella had an alibi, if she was to be believed. So did Oren. He had traveled to a bay two hours north of town. Alastair's and Hank's alibis were iffy, although neither Hank nor Alastair had a strong motive to want Ivy dead as far as I could see. So what if Ivy told Alastair he was too young for her, and big deal if she'd called Hank cheap, unless he had a very fragile ego. Now, if Hank had a secret lover and Ivy threatened to expose him . . .

I glanced at my cell phone. No response text from Bailey yet. Not even a peep saying *On it.* Worried that she was suffering, I set aside the three-by-fives and called her. The call rolled into voice mail. Dang. I texted Tito. He didn't respond, either.

Desperate to talk to someone, I dialed Rhett, even though I knew he was occupied entertaining a pair of vintners from Napa Valley who were interested in opening a restaurant in Crystal Cove. Having interacted with Rhett when he'd worked at the Grotto, they now wanted his input on what our town needed. The call also rolled into voice mail. I left a quick message telling him I loved him and added when he had a moment to please touch base.

For the next few minutes, I sifted through my mail, which were mostly offers for new credit cards. After my debacle of a marriage, I paid cash for everything. I tossed the junk in the recycle bin and sat on the floor to play with my cat.

Tigger never tired of the bat-the-knotted-ball-of-yarn game. I hurled it against the wall. It ricocheted and shot under the Ching cabinet. After pawing at it for a bit, Tigger gave in and scuttled beneath the cabinet.

While he was out of sight, I thought about Pepper again. Would the extortionist hang her out to dry? I couldn't let her lose face with her daughter. I had to help her nip the problem in the bud.

Tigger emerged from beneath the cabinet victorious. He dropped the ball of yarn by my side and mewled: *More playtime.*

"Hungry." I mimed feeding myself.

He trotted to where I fed him and peered up at me.

"Yes, you first."

I gave him some tuna and then, craving something savory for myself, made cheddar scones using a recipe Katie had given me the week before. I'd purchased all the ingredients, paying heed to her note about using only the best cheese. I tasted a bite of the Beecher's Flagship Aged Cheddar I'd purchased and knew I'd made an excellent choice.

As I sifted the flour with the white pepper, I thought again about Cinnamon. Had she confirmed Crusibella's alibi with a counselor at Overeaters Anonymous? Did Crusibella's admission that she'd slinked through the alley near Hog Heaven clear her of the crime?

Dang, I hated suspecting people I liked.

While the scones baked, I poured myself a glass of sauvignon blanc and readdressed the three-by-five cards. I made cards for each suspect. On each, I scribbled a possible motive. Then I spread the cards out and glanced from one to the other. What was I missing?

The timer went off signifying the scones were done. I pulled the tray from the oven, placed it on the stovetop, and reset the timer. Given the aroma, it was nearly impossible to wait the obligatory cooling time of twenty minutes. To occupy myself, I dusted the living room and straightened the pillows on the couch as well as the magazines on the coffee table.

As I was putting a concoction together to feed my only live plant — a peace lily Aunt Vera had given me — I thought again about the bonsai at the crime scene. Had the killer placed the plant beside Ivy's head as a warning, as Z.Z. had suggested?

Over the years, I'd sketched many cypress trees, so drawing the miniature tree on a three-by-five card was effortless. When I finished, I stared at the sketch, wondering whether each style of bonsai held a different meaning. Ivy had potted so many. Did the one by her head have a special meaning? I wrote the question on the card and, for inspiration, decided to do some online research. I typed the word *bonsai* into the search bar. Up came numerous images of bonsais, seed kits, and the like. Scrolling down, I found a Wikipedia page as well as sites explaining how to grow bonsais, the value of Zen gardening, and more. Intrigued, I continued my search. A few pages later, I noticed an interesting trend. Apparently, some traders had gone to jail for smuggling exotic foreign bonsai plants into the United States. Some of them were worth millions of dollars.

Ding. The timer went off. Unable to resist any longer, I made a note on the bonsai notecard, closed my search, and headed for the scones.

While nibbling my treat, I studied the cards. Were the police zeroing in on someone who I didn't have on my suspect list? A neighbor? A disgruntled customer? Ivy's parents? A bonsai smuggler? Would the authorities bring the killer in before Pepper succumbed to the extortionist?

Knowing I couldn't solve anything tonight, and with no call or text from Tito, Rhett, or Bailey, I downed another scone and headed to bed.

Needless to say, I slept fitfully. Eating late was never a good idea. I awoke with a major headache. Instead of taking medicine, I applied a cold washcloth to the base of my neck. It helped. So did an egg-and-sausage sandwich and a hot shower. To bolster my mood, I dressed in a pair of ecru capris and my favorite aqua sweater.

While drying my hair, I glanced at my cell phone and noticed two texts. I'd muted the sound on my cell phone and hadn't heard either text come in. One was from Rhett: *Didn't want to wake you. Meeting went late.*

You okay? The other from Bailey: *Sorry, baby moving like crazy all night. Couldn't concentrate. Will do my best today.*

Because I was running late, I decided to respond to both when I got to work. A crisp breeze brushed my face as I stepped outside. Surf pounded the shore with a *boom.* Tigger snuggled into me. He didn't appreciate when big waves crested.

"It's okay, boy," I cooed, hooking him over my shoulder. "Don't —"

I halted. My mother's Schwinn was lying beside my VW. Who had placed it there? I always parked it next to the cottage, kickstand down. I inched closer and yelped. Someone had slashed the tires.

Aunt Vera hurried out her front door. "Jenna, dear, are you okay?"

I gaped at her.

"You screamed. Are you all right?" She hurried down the stairs, the folds of her ocean blue caftan swishing, and skirted the rear of my car. "Why did you —" She gasped. "Oh, my."

My heart chug-a-lugged in my chest.

"You don't think it was personal, do you?" she asked. "Like the last time?" By the *last time* she meant when the killer had hung a black wreath on my door. "Would Crusibella have done this?" My aunt hitched her head toward our neighbor's house.

I spied Crusibella's poodle sitting at the window, nose pressed to the glass. Was he acting as lookout dog? I whispered, "Honestly, I don't know."

"Have you been asking too many questions, incurring the killer's wrath?"

"Aunt Vera, be serious."

"I'm deadly serious."

I checked the pavement for footprints or any kind of clue that might reveal the identity of the culprit. There was nothing. The morning breeze had swept the area clear of debris.

Aunt Vera clucked her tongue. "That's it, young lady. I'm hiring a security guard, and you are going to report this to the police. No argument."

CHAPTER 23

Of course, I argued and suggested a vandal or a wayward teenager, as my sister would say, might have slashed the tires. My aunt huffed. I huffed louder. Truth be told, I didn't want to call the police until I had something more concrete.

The moment I arrived at the Cookbook Nook, I set Tigger on his kitty condo — having picked up on my worry, he was wired and in need of distraction — and then I booted up the computer and searched for sites that carried tires for the Schwinn. Because it was an older model, I had to search for quite a while.

Aunt Vera, clearly perturbed with me for not taking her advice, started dusting shelves. They didn't need it. It was her way of burying her irritation. The noisier, the better. *Swish-swish.*

Tina sashayed in minutes after us, whistling a merry tune.

"You're in a cheery mood," I said.

"The sun is shining. The weather is blissful. And kissing is good for the soul."

Apparently, things were working out well with the boyfriend.

"Morning, Vera," Tina said. "Don't you look nice? I love, love, love the color of your caftan. Great minds think alike." Tina's skater dress was a darker shade of turquoise but close enough.

Aunt Vera grunted.

"Why is she grumpy?" Tina whispered.

"She's mad at me. Give her a wide berth."

"That won't last long. She adores you."

"Not today."

Tina didn't linger. She set to work stocking the cash register and straightening the sales counter.

A half hour later, Bailey waddled in. "Jenna, I'm so sorry I didn't respond to you until . . ." She pressed a hand to her chest. "It was a crazy night. Any time I sat or laid down, the baby kicked. Luckily, Tito was Johnny-on-the-spot." She fussed with the top button of her maternity blouse. "Do you think he . . . she . . . will be this restless all the time?"

"What did you eat?" I asked.

"Tacos."

My aunt *tsk*ed and hung up her feather

duster. "Try something a little less spicy until the baby is born."

"And after," Tina said, "if you intend to breastfeed."

"Thanks for the tips. Jenna" — Bailey displayed her cell phone — "I'll get to this as soon as Tito brings me my laptop. My brain is addled. I left it at home. I don't want to use the shop's computer, just in case. He's running about an hour behind, okay?"

"Sure." What else could I say?

"Now, mind you, I'm not sure I can dredge up the name of the extortionist —"

"Extortionist?" Aunt Vera cried. "Jenna, what is going on?"

She corralled me by the vintage table and demanded to know the whole story. Bailey and Tina joined us.

"Does this have to do with the slashed tires?" my aunt demanded.

Bailey squealed. "Slashed —"

I held up a hand and quickly explained what I knew, which wasn't much. As I spoke, I spied Pepper strolling into Beaders of Paradise and added that she was being blackmailed, too.

"Jenna Starrett Hart, I'm ordering you to tell the police," my aunt rasped.

"I will."

"When?"

"After Bailey takes a crack at solving this."

Aunt Vera clucked her tongue and shuffled away muttering synonyms for stubborn: *obstinate, mulish, pig-headed.* At the latter, I snuffled. She wasn't amused.

Bailey said, "I'll need your password."

"Of course." I strode to the sales counter and found a notepad that Tina must have been using to gauge expenses for her upcoming summer school curriculum. The top note included class names, teachers' names, and lots of digits and dollar signs. I removed it and jotted my log on information on a new piece of paper. "Here you go." I handed it to Bailey.

At the same time, her mother and my father breezed into the store. Both were dressed in white. Lola looked quite fashionable in a broad-brimmed straw hat. Dad had donned a Giants baseball cap.

"Bailey, darling," Lola called. "I'm here! Are you ready?"

I glanced at my pal.

Her cheeks turned crimson. "Oops."

"What did you forget?" I asked.

"We're going bedroom shopping for the baby this morning."

"We've got so much to buy," Lola said. "Linens, bassinet, huggable toys . . ."

"I thought I'd mentioned it to you," Bailey continued sotto voce. "I'll do the *other* thing the moment I get back," she added cryptically. "Tito should show up by then. Are you mad at me?"

I elbowed her. "Not if I get to come along." An hour or two wouldn't make a difference in the big picture, and gazing at baby things might lighten my mood.

"Flora is expecting us in a few minutes." Lola tapped her Apple Watch. "Time is a-wasting." She patted my father's cheek. "Cary has kindly offered to assist as our Sherpa."

Playfully, he flexed his arms. "When I can't bear the load, I'll bring the car around."

After checking with Tina, who said she could hold down the fort, and after assuring my aunt that I would touch base with the police when I returned — I couldn't bear the evil glares she was throwing my way — we headed off.

"Flora has ordered a wide selection of giraffe-themed items," Lola said as we strolled along Buena Vista Boulevard. "Sheets and towels. Wall hangings. You name it. She has such good taste. I can't wait to see everything."

Lola walked into Home Sweet Home first.

The rest of us trailed her.

Like a county clerk, Flora was at the sales counter sifting through a stack of paper: inspect, flip, inspect, flip. Nearby, I spotted Alastair Dukas filling out a form. Apparently, he'd taken Crusibella's suggestion to heart and was applying for a job everywhere. A pair of sunglasses hung from the collar of his mock turtleneck. A bicycle helmet lay on the counter nearby. I gawked at the helmet, recalling that Alastair said he didn't drive; he rode his bike everywhere. Was he the person who had taken a picture of Pepper outside Ivy's place? His former job had been working as an IT guy. He'd know how to hack emails and deal in bitcoin.

"Bailey, I'll be right with you," Flora said. "I've set up everything in the rear corner. Take a peek."

We wove through the aisles, which were filled with spring-themed displays. When we reached what could only be described as Safari Land, Bailey swooned. Not only had Flora stocked up on giraffe items, she had acquired an abundance of elephants, lions, and chimpanzees, as well.

My father picked up the latter. "Eek, eek, eek."

"Put it down, Cary," Lola chided.

"I like this little fella," he teased. "You

know, Bailey, if you have a boy, he's going to be more like a monkey than a giraffe."

Lola seized it from him. "Honestly, darling, focus."

With an impish grin, my dad saluted then left us to check out a display of chess sets. He loved the game.

"Ew." Bailey grasped a set of black-and-white giraffe sheets. "Shorten the necks, and these look like zebras. What was Flora thinking? I want gold and brown giraffes."

"Black and white is very hip," her mother said.

"If you're color blind," Bailey quipped.

"Bailey, how about these?" I held up a crib set featuring baby giraffes with comic faces. "Yellow and brown and darling."

Lola cooed, "I like those."

Flora joined us while pushing up the sleeves of her sweater. "Are you finding everything you need, ladies?"

"Who are you calling ladies?" Lola joked. "Say, Flora, isn't that the young man from Dreamcatcher at the register?" She pointed at Alastair.

"It is. He's applying for a job."

I explained how Ivy's executor might sell off every bit of inventory and close the shop, though I wondered if that were still the case, given Z.Z. and Crusibella's earlier excitement.

"All of her merchandise would sell well here, Flora," Bailey said. "You should consider purchasing it."

"Oh, I couldn't . . ." She blanched and stroked her heavy braid. "No, no, no, that wouldn't be right. Bad karma."

"Poor Alastair." Lola clucked her tongue. "You never realize how many people's lives are affected by the death of another."

Flora said, "It's like that butterfly metaphor, don't you think? The butterfly flaps its wings halfway around the world, yet there could be a consequence right here in Crystal Cove because of the movement it created in the air."

"Alastair might not be such a poor guy, Mom," Bailey whispered. "He might be guilty of murder."

Flora gasped.

"Nonsense." Lola swatted the air. "That sweet young man? He's been in the diner for lunch on numerous occasions. He's always kind and respectful, and he invariably leaves a good tip for the waitress."

"Looks can be deceiving," Bailey said.

"Why would he have killed Ivy?" her mother countered. "Was she a bad boss? Too rigid for her own good?"

"He was in love with her, but she didn't reciprocate his feelings."

"Tosh," Lola said. "A spurned lover doesn't always lash out. Most have a pity party and move on. That's what I did. Does he have an alibi?"

I said, "He was doing inventory at the store."

"Ahem." Flora cleared her throat. "Can we drop this discussion and focus on Bailey?"

Lola tweaked her daughter's cheek. "Of course. You're right, Flora. We'll let you know if we need anything."

As she bustled away, my father leaned in. "Not that I'm eavesdropping, but Alastair was not at Dreamcatcher the night Ivy died."

"How do you know?" Lola asked.

"You were otherwise occupied, so I went walking. The lights were off at the store."

"Maybe he showed up after you passed by," I suggested.

"Nope. Not possible. I made three loops of the boulevard. Took me a couple of hours." A loop was almost three miles long. "The air was the perfect temperature, and you know me." He patted his firm abdomen. "You don't use it, you lose it. Anyway, each time I passed the store, the lights were off. I'd stake my hardware shop on it."

"You have to tell Cinnamon," I said, realizing how hypocritical I sounded. I hadn't contacted her about my bicycle tires yet.

He winked and held up his cell phone. "Already texted her."

After Bailey purchased dozens of items to adorn the baby's room, we decided to go to Latte Luck Café. As we waited on the street for Lola and my father to join us — Lola had insisted we go outside while she paid — I spotted Oren standing outside Play Room Toy Store chatting with the store's owner, Thad, a baby-faced sweetheart of a man, although *chatting* might not have been the right choice of word. More like quarrelling. Thad shook his head and poked Oren's chest. Oren clasped Thad by the shoulders and said something while nodding. After a moment, Thad mimicked Oren's head bobbing, as if agreeing. Oren released him and cuffed him warmly on the arm. Thad's shoulders sagged.

"What's going on over there?" Bailey asked. "Looks fishy."

"Fishy. Ha." I giggled. "Oren's a fisherman."

"I didn't mean it that way. I mean, why would Oren have business with Thad?"

"Who said he does? They look like friends to me."

"What do you think they're talking about?" Bailey whispered.

"I haven't a clue." Maybe Thad had agreed to take a ride on Oren's new boat and was afraid of water. I'd never seen him at the beach. But then I remembered Oren's chance meeting with Yung Yi and a darker notion entered my mind. I replayed the encounter for Bailey and how Oren had shrugged it off, saying Yung was experiencing a little money trouble. "Maybe Yung received an extortion email like me and asked Oren's advice. Maybe Thad is doing the same."

"Did you ask Yung about it?"

"Not my business."

"But you asked Oren."

"Because I plowed into him, literally. We got to talking."

Bailey glanced in their direction again. "What if your assumption is wrong? What if Thad has dirt on Oren or vice versa?"

"You and your conspiracy theories."

"You and your wicked spam email," she countered.

"What kind of dirt?" Lola asked, apparently having overheard our conversation. She was carrying two bags from Home

Sweet Home. My father was carrying five. "Why would either of them have dirt on the other?"

I said, "Ever since Ivy died, your daughter has been obsessed with people hiding secrets."

"Because Ivy knew so many," Bailey contended.

Lola scoffed. "Is everyone in town guilty, darling?"

Bailey replied, "Jenna witnessed Oren having a similar altercation with Yung Yi, the bank manager. Hey" — she gazed at me — "what if Yung and Thad have information that could tie Oren to the murder?"

My father shook his head. "If either men knew anything, they'd have told the police by now. They probably owe Oren money, and he wants them to pay up."

Something niggled at the edges of my mind.

"It's not easy being a fisherman," Lola said. "It's a day-to-day, hand-to-mouth business."

"A real gamble," my father added.

A *gamble*. That was it. "Dad, is there a private poker game in town?" Pepper had accused Noah of coming to town for that reason. "Maybe Oren holds IOUs for these guys."

"I have no idea," my father said.

"Could you find out?"

My father grunted and steered Lola into the café. Was his response a *yes* or a *no*?

As they disappeared, I thought of what Lola had said about fishing being a hand-to-mouth business, and another notion came to me, completely separate from the question of gambling. Smuggling exotic bonsai trees could reap a windfall of cash. Had Ivy hired Oren to transport bonsais across international lines? What if something had gone wrong and endangered Oren, so he'd held Ivy responsible? After killing her, he symbolically placed the bonsai beside her head.

As if Oren sensed I was thinking about him, he glanced my way. At first, his gaze could have bored holes into my forehead, and then he smiled, a disarmingly charming smile.

CHAPTER 24

The moment Bailey and I strolled into the Cookbook Nook, she crossed to the stockroom to call Tito — he had yet to bring her laptop to the shop — and Tigger scampered to me. He butted my leg, begging for attention. As I sat at the children's table and stroked him, my aunt passed by.

"Have you contacted Cinnamon about the bicycle?" she asked.

"Not yet."

"Do it."

"But Dad just texted her about something else. I'm sure she's —"

"She can multitask. Do. It." Aunt Vera trudged away.

When Tigger bounded from my lap to lie beneath the table for a nap, I strode to the sales counter with the intent of calling Cinnamon. However, at the same time, Tito showed up, red-faced for being so tardy. He'd fallen asleep, having tended to Bailey's needs all night. I guided him to the storage room, waited as they exchanged a kiss and she opened her computer, and then I returned to the register to help some customers.

An hour later, as I was rearranging the display table, setting out copies of *The Edible Flower Garden,* its cover so beautiful that anyone would want to display the book on a coffee table, I realized I hadn't contacted Cinnamon. Oops.

Knowing my aunt would have my head if I didn't, I raced toward the telephone and nearly rammed into Bailey, who sailed through the stockroom drapes with her computer in hand.

"Sorry," we both squawked in unison.

"Why are you in such a hurry?" I asked.

"I was able to retrieve the email you dumped. I want to compare it to Pepper's."

"I saw her enter Beaders a bit ago."

"Great. I'll be back." Bailey raced out.

"What email?" Tina asked. "What's going on?"

I patted her on the shoulder. "Relax. It's nothing." Man, I was getting good at lying.

"Bailey is in too much of a rush," Tina carped. "She'd better not stress out the baby."

"She won't." At least I hoped she

wouldn't. "How did we do sales-wise this morning?"

Tina ticked off a list of cookbook titles that we'd sold and recommended we order more of *The Art of Cooking with Lavender.* "It's very popular with the Crystal Cove Flower Society, plus the Blue Hat book club ladies, who are still in town, found it particularly special." She winked. "I think it was the color of the flowers that enticed them."

I liked the book, too. It boasted lots of photos and recipes, one of my favorites being the pot roast with honey barbecue sauce.

"We only have three copies left. Also, I ordered additional floral cookie jars. The hands-down favorite is the one with the *Blessed, Grateful, Happy* slogan on the front. We sold six."

"The one with the matching salt and pepper set?"

"Yep. I already ordered more of those, too. Hope that was okay."

"Of course." I liked how independent she was becoming.

Minutes later, Bailey dashed into the shop and asked to go home.

My stomach did a flip-flop. "Are you feeling okay? Do you need to put your feet up? Is the baby —"

"I'm fine. I simply need complete quiet so

I can concentrate on what I need to do next. I'm going to solve this. I promise. Plus, Tito baked a blueberry pie and it's calling my name. I'll be back in two hours."

"Go." The sooner she could fix the problem the better. When my aunt was done with the tarot card reading, we'd have plenty of hands on deck to take care of customers.

Bailey grinned and scurried out.

"She's a whirlwind today," Tina said. "If I didn't know better, I'd say she was trying to get everything done because she's about to give birth."

"She'd better not." Her mother wasn't prepared. Neither was her husband, I suspected, although baking a blueberry pie and hovering over her all night long suggested he was getting ready. "Speaking of food, has Katie brought in any treats?" I didn't see a tiered tray in the breezeway. Midmorning and midafternoon, Katie provided snacks for the customers.

"Haven't seen her all day."

My stomach did a second flip-flop. Was Katie okay? Not keeping to routine was unlike her. I peeked down the hall. A line of customers was snaking out the entrance to the Nook Café, meaning business was hopping, so I opted to text her.

In an instant, I received a response: *Everything is A-OK. I'll have Reynaldo bring treats. Sorry for the slipup. I'll be in soon for the tea sandwiches demonstration. Okay?*

Given the morning's activity, I'd forgotten about the event. Bad me. We'd decided the demonstration would be a perfect bridge from Book Club Bonanza to Spring Fling. Both of those groups would enjoy learning more about how to prepare a scrumptious high tea.

I responded in the affirmative and set my worries aside. Katie was fine. Phew. I wasn't sure how many more crises — real or imaginary — I could handle.

"Tina," I said, "let's set up for the event. It'll start in an hour."

"On it. Before I forget" — she moved to the floral aprons to rearrange them; thanks to a slew of customers scouring the lot, the collection had wound up in a twist — "Hank Hemmings came in while you were shopping with Bailey. He asked for you."

"What did he want?"

"He didn't say. Before he left, he asked if I'd seen Pepper. I told her she left her shop right after Lola snared Bailey and you for the spree. I suggested he might find her at home, but minutes after he left, Pepper reappeared."

Interesting. Was she avoiding him on purpose? Was she scared of him? Did she think he might be the one who had taken a picture of her outside Ivy's place? She might not have recognized him if he'd been wearing a helmet and sunglasses. On the other hand, maybe Pepper was avoiding him because she'd deduced the seriousness of his relationship with Darian. Perhaps that was why Hank was looking for her. He was worried she would spill the beans to Darian's husband. Once again, I wondered whether Ivy had discovered his secret, and if he'd killed her to keep it quiet. Was Pepper in danger now?

I started for the shop's telephone with the intention of alerting Cinnamon, when it jangled.

Tina scooted around the sales counter and answered. "Jenna, it's for you. It's Rhett."

I hurried to take the receiver from her. "Hey. I've missed you."

"Missed you, too. You haven't been answering your cell phone."

I dug it out of my purse and saw three missed messages from him. "Sorry. I was on a buying spree with Lola and Bailey. How did last night's meeting go?"

"You'll never believe this, but these guys want me to run their restaurant."

My insides flip-flopped for a third time, making me feel a tad woozy. I was never good at gymnastics or diving off a high board. Skydiving was out of the question. "Do you want to do that?" We hadn't talked about him changing careers. Ever. After the arson at the Grotto, he'd locked his chef's knife roll bag in a safe at his cabin. "What about Bait and Switch?"

"I don't know." He sounded on the fence, which made me wonder whether there was more he wasn't telling me.

"Let's discuss it after dinner," I suggested. We'd made plans to dine with my father and Lola. I was pretty sure Lola wanted to pick my brain about what Bailey intended to do career-wise going forward.

"Sounds good." After saying how much he loved and adored me, Rhett signed off.

While I pulled out folding chairs for the guests coming to the high tea demonstration, I thought about Rhett's brief phone call. If he took the job, what would happen to us? Starting a new restaurant took hours of planning, and once it was up and running, it could be a twenty-four/seven operation. Would we have to postpone the wedding? Would we lose precious time getting to know each other better?

Hold it, Jenna. Selfish is as selfish does. I

took a deep breath. If Rhett wanted to take this journey, I'd back him one hundred percent.

Aunt Vera concluded her tarot session and joined me in setting out chairs. "Well? Have you called Cinnamon?"

"I will," I muttered. Before the return of the Ice Age.

Aunt Vera twirled a finger at my face. "Why are you frowning? You're thinking about something life-altering." Her hand flew to her phoenix amulet. "Talk to me." Apparently, her extrasensory powers were in full force. After I filled her in on Rhett's future possibilities, she said, "Let me do a reading for you."

"Later, okay?" Hopefully, it would bring me some calm . . . and get her off my case about contacting Cinnamon.

One of Katie's kitchen staff strolled into the breezeway and set down a tiered tray of tea sandwiches. "Jenna, treats!"

"Perfect. Thanks." I hurried into the breezeway. Having skipped lunch, I was starved. I nabbed three of the inch-wide sandwiches — curried egg, pear and cheese, and tomato basil — and took a bite of each. I nearly swooned. Heaven.

A short while later, after customers had purchased a lot of books and were starting to take their seats, Katie arrived with her mobile cooking cart, ready for action in a floral dress and crisp chef's coat.

"Hello, everyone," she said.

Many of the audience responded in kind, including regulars like Gran, Z.Z., and Flora. After the chairs were filled, Pepper slipped in. She didn't usually join us on Katie's demo days. Was something up? She positioned herself near the display table of floral cookbooks and fixed her gaze on someone. I spotted the object of her attention — Darian, looking angelic in white — and I wondered whether Hank would make an appearance. Did Pepper intend to confront the two of them together?

At precisely three p.m., Katie lit into her presentation with gusto, first describing her cart with its overhead mirror and then enumerating the cookware she had brought along. When she started talking about the various ingredients, many of the audience leaned forward, rapt with attention.

"For light afternoon tea" — Katie flourished her hand like a display model — "figure roughly four little sandwiches per person, two or three varieties, plus two small scones, one with cream and one with jam or honey. In addition, you'll want to serve one to two little cakes or tarts, one rich and the other simple."

Flora said, "Are you kidding me?" She puffed her cheeks like a blowfish.

Katie chuckled. "I know. It sounds like a lot, but when you're chatting for an hour or more, you can get quite hungry. Am I right?"

A few in the crowd said, "Amen."

"There's no secret to making simple cucumber tea sandwiches. First, spread the cream cheese thinly on the bread." Katie demonstrated. "Remember, you want just the right amount of moisture but not too much. Think of it the way you'd think about taking care of your houseplants. Too much moisture will kill them, right?"

Katie's tip made me think of the bonsais at Ivy's house. Who would water them? And why didn't she have any of the other items she sold at the shop on display? No artistic geodes or amethyst bookends. No quartz votive candles or gemstones. I thought of the jewelry Z.Z. and I had discovered at Ivy's house, mostly gold and silver and very few decorative pieces fitted with gems. Was that significant? Had the killer robbed Ivy?

"Also, if you use too much cream cheese, it'll overpower the cucumber," Katie went on. "By the way, I like to use English cucumbers, not the pickling kind." She

315

rinsed one in a silver bowl filled with water. The overhead mirror on the mobile cart allowed the audience to view every step.

"Can you use a regular cucumber?" Gran asked.

"You can, but the English version doesn't have as many seeds and possesses a pleasant, crisp flavor. Now, cut the cucumber thinly." Katie sliced the cucumber on a board as fast as a ginsu chef, held up a slice for viewing, and then set the slices in another silver bowl. "Some people like to remove the skins. I would if it's waxy, but usually I like to leave the skins on." She held up a cruet of vinegar. "Some like to soak the cucumbers in vinegar. It doesn't give them a vinegary taste, but it does soften them up and changes the flavor a tad. Is it worth a taste test? Sure, but we won't be doing that today." She set the cruet aside. "If you would like to do so, use about one teaspoon of white wine vinegar per cucumber."

While Katie finished layering the sandwiches and trimming the crusts, I noticed Pepper twisting and releasing her strand of glittery beads. A pang of concern swept through me. Not only was she a suspect in a murder, and not only had someone sent her a threatening email that might seal her fate, and not only had her ex-husband come to town and thrown a wrench into the works, but she'd also had to contend with the notion that her boyfriend was stepping out on her.

I glanced at the storage room. Had Bailey been able to discover the source of Pepper's and my emails yet? If only she could help us solve that peevish piece of the puzzle.

"In conclusion," Katie said, "one last tip. Remember to cover the sandwiches with a damp cloth or plastic wrap until you're ready to eat them, or they will dry out. That's all. I've had a great time. I hope you have, too." When the applause died down, Katie hoisted a stack of recipe cards. "Don't forget! I've made recipe cards for the cucumber sandwiches as well as for a tuna sandwich and a chicken almond sandwich. I've set samples of all of these on the tasting table in the breezeway. Come on up. Have a sandwich. Take a card."

As a throng of customers surrounded Katie, Bailey nipped my arm and hitched her head, beckoning me. She pressed through the storage room drapes. I followed her but glanced over my shoulder just in time to see Darian slip out of the shop with Pepper at her heels.

Uh-oh. I hoped Pepper wouldn't start a

fracas. That was not the kind of publicity she needed right now.

CHAPTER 25

Bailey weaved through the opened boxes of floral-themed cookbooks and decorative items. Tigger trailed me into the stockroom and made a beeline for his water bowl.

"Take a look at this." Bailey pointed to her laptop, which was open on the desk. She adjusted the waistband of her stretchy leggings and perched on the desk chair. "Sit," she ordered.

I was too antsy to obey.

"Fine. Don't sit." She smacked her hands together. "I dredged up all of your trashed emails and found the one you received from Goodguy. I compared it to Pepper's, and indeed, the emails did come from the same email account." She spun her computer around, so I could see her handiwork. "Same greeting. Same signoff. Same server. However, because I won't send a response, lest it sends me to a site where my personal information might be compromised, I can't cross-check further."

I nodded, fearing that would be the case.

"Instead," she went on, "I searched for similar situations to yours on the Internet. As I told Pepper, there are tons of phishing scams. Typically, the blackmailer obtains a boatload of emails and saturates the market with threats. I found a few scam warnings about someone or some *thing* called Good-rip, Goodcon, and Goodtrick, but I didn't find any for Goodguy."

"So now what?"

"I'll dig deeper, but I think you and Pepper have to wait and see if there's a follow-up email. If there isn't, let it go."

"This guy attached a photo of Pepper outside of Ivy's house."

"I saw that, but without clicking through, you don't know if it's date- or time-stamped. If it's not, it could be from any day and, therefore, not good enough to introduce as evidence." Bailey pointed out the teensy image in Pepper's email. "As far as I can tell, she isn't wearing the outfit she wore that night."

"She went home to make the appetizer. She could have changed at that time. Did you ask her?"

"It's on my to-do list." Bailey flashed a yellow-lined pad filled with notes.

"Do you think I should inform Cinnamon?" I perched on the corner of the desk, clear of the computer. "She might not appreciate my help, but it's my duty to tell her whatever I glean."

"Didn't Pepper swear you to secrecy?"

"Yes, but —"

Katie popped her head between the drapes. "May I come in?" Her cheeks were pink, her eyes gleaming with energy.

I said, "Of course. Great job today, as always."

"Thanks." She bounced on her toes, looking like she was about to burst.

I grinned. "Okay, spill. What's got you keyed up?"

"Are you ready?" She laced her hands together. "We got a baby!" She threw her arms wide. "A girl. A Korean girl. From Korea."

Bailey sniggered. "They usually are."

"Some are born in America," Katie said soberly. "This one wasn't."

"Congratulations." I gave her a hug. Bailey echoed the sentiment.

"I want to celebrate tonight," Katie went on, "but Keller will be busy. He's providing the ice cream desserts at a sixty-year-old's swanky birthday party. Say you'll go with me to Vines after work. Reynaldo will cover the café. Please?"

Her joy was infectious.

"I'm in," Bailey chimed.

"I can go for an hour," I said, "but then I'm meeting Rhett and my father for dinner." I wouldn't share Rhett's big news, yet. I didn't want to dampen Katie's joy. Besides, I didn't know how I felt about his prospects or how it might impact *us*.

Vines was the wine bar located on the second floor of Fisherman's Village, the perfect place for anyone who wanted a nice glass of wine and quiet conversation. The handcrafted tables were set to seat two to four patrons, no more. A few stools stood beneath the curved bar. Tiny LED lights decorated the shelves holding wineglasses behind the bar. Tonight, Mozart's *Jupiter Symphony* was playing softly through the speaker system.

The assistant manager, Wayne, a lanky man in his fifties whose elderly mother was a regular client of Aunt Vera's, hurried to us and set down three cocktail napkins. "Sorry, but you get me tonight. We're short staffed. What'll it be?"

"A bottle of your finest pinot grigio," I said. It was Katie's favorite wine.

"I'll have a glass of Pellegrino with lime,"

Bailey said. When Wayne moved away, she whispered, "I can't wait to imbibe again."

"Soon," Katie said.

"Not soon enough." Bailey sighed. "But it'll be worth it." She petted her belly. "So, c'mon, Katie, show us pictures of your little girl."

Katie swiped her cell phone screen and turned the phone in our direction. A picture of an adorable baby in white swaddling clothes appeared.

"Do you have a name picked out?" I asked.

"Not yet. She's only a month old. Keller wants to hold her before we name her. It's a family tradition." For the next few minutes, she filled us in on the process of adoption and how lucky they'd been to get the opportunity. Not every adoption went through. She already had ideas for the baby room décor, and she knew where the baby was going to go to preschool.

"Yipes," Bailey said. "That's a lot of pre-planning."

"You have to do these things right away. We'll talk." A minute into motherhood and suddenly Katie was the wizened teacher. She patted Bailey's hand.

Bailey gave me a snarky look.

"Run a tab?" Wayne asked as he set down

our beverages.

I pulled out cash to cover the order. "Just the one tonight."

As he left, Bailey whispered, *"Psst."* She hitched her head to her right and mouthed, *Look.*

Oren Michaels was sitting at the bar with a blonde in a tight-fitting sheath. I didn't recognize the woman.

"It sure doesn't look like Oren is missing Ivy," Bailey said.

"Not true," Katie countered. "He misses her like crazy. He mentions her every time he brings in fish."

"Men are different from women," I said. "Women mourn; men move on."

Katie bobbed her head. "Did you ever read that book, *Men Are from Mars, Women Are from Venus*? Keller and I read it cover to cover when we hit a speed bump in our relationship. According to the psychologist who wrote it, women hold on to the past. They dredge it up over and over, while men are fix-it guys. They like to get something working and then" — she mimed wiping her hands — "it's done. Over. *Finito.*"

"Well, Oren sure looks like he's" — Bailey cleared her throat — "*working* on something. Do you think he *fixed* his relationship with Ivy by killing her?"

Katie shook her head vehemently. "No, I'm telling you, he loved her. Jenna, don't you remember how bereft he was the other day? Those weren't fake tears."

I nodded. He had seemed pretty glum and had covered with his jokester persona.

Oren beckoned Wayne, who strode to him. They chatted for a minute. Wayne was one of the most cordial men I knew. Always kind to his mother. Always attentive to customers. However, when Oren gripped Wayne's arm, Wayne tensed up. He glanced over his shoulder like he was worried someone might be listening in on the conversation and quickly wriggled free.

At the same time, Oren peered past Wayne — at us. I feigned an itch at the back of my head and lowered my chin. Heaven forbid he think I was spying on them. After a moment, I stole another peek. Oren said something more to Wayne, laid money on the counter, and rose from his stool. Oren's date, if that's what she was, stood, too.

"Keep the faith, bro," Oren said at full volume.

Wayne nodded drearily. What was up? Why was Oren's presence agitating so many men in town? Was Wayne a target of a blackmail scam, too? Or did Oren hold a bunch of poker IOUs? Even though Rhett said business had been good to Oren, winning at poker might explain how he could afford a new truck and boat.

Wayne approached us and asked, "Is everything all right, ladies?"

I smiled. "I was going to ask you the same thing."

"Me? Couldn't be better. Care for nuts?"

"No, thanks." I beckoned him closer and whispered, "What's going on between you and Oren?"

His face went blank.

"He said something that upset you."

"Nah. Oren? He's a prankster." Wayne grinned and offered a *shaka* sign, the Hawaiian greeting for *hang loose.* "We grew up together. Skateboarded and surfed and basically hung out. He's always joking around. We even did a few plays in high school. Comedies, of course."

I got the feeling Wayne was acting now. On the other hand, maybe I was being too suspicious of Oren.

"Who was the woman with him?" I asked.

"A gal we went to school with. She and her husband are in town for a wedding at the Crystal Cove Inn. Oren and she were catching up on old times."

"She's married?"

"To a millionaire." He raised his eyebrow.

"Wait. You didn't think . . . Oren and her?"
Wayne guffawed. "Ha! No way. Oren holds
a candle for Ivy. He always will."

CHAPTER 26

I fetched Tigger from the shop, dropped him at home, changed into a cream silk blouse and cocoa brown corduroys that hugged my curves — what few I had — refreshed my makeup, and drove back to Fisherman's Village. I parked in the parking lot because finding street parking at night in Crystal Cove was a challenge.

As I strolled to dinner, I took in the various floral pots that businesses had set out today. Outside Home Sweet Home stood a three-pot extravaganza, each pot stacked on the dirt of the lower and each painted with polka dots and emblazoned with the words *Home Sweet Home.* The pot outside Latte Luck Café featured a huge coffee cup with white trailing flowers spilling from it, to signify frothy milk, I assumed. The pot at the entry of the Pelican Brief Diner was decorated with abalone shells and filled with coral-like succulents. Fish-themed garden stakes completed the ocean effect.

When I strolled inside, I learned that I was the first to arrive. After I was seated at our table on the patio overlooking the ocean, I ordered a glass of sparkling water and read Rhett's text; he was running late. Was he talking to the restaurant backers again? Sealing a deal without my input?

Cool it, Jenna. He wouldn't do that. You're a team.

Speaking of teams, I spotted Tina's boyfriend sitting on the porch a few tables down. He was not with Tina. He was with a luscious redhead. Was it the same woman that Tina had caught him with at Latte Luck? Was it my duty to tell Tina he was yet again stepping out on her? Maybe I was jumping to conclusions. Maybe the woman, like Oren's high school friend, was in town for a special event.

"Sorry we're late." Lola hurried to the table.

My father pulled out her chair and then settled onto his. "Where's Rhett?"

"On his way."

Dad folded his arms on the table. "What's new?"

"What's new with you?" I offered a crooked smile as I gazed between them. "Did you set this dinner date hoping to grill

329

me about Bailey?"

"Don't be silly." Lola batted the air. "Of course not." She toyed with a strand of hair by her ear. "Unless there's something you *need* to tell us."

"She's fine. Feeling good. Katie's been giving her a few pointers." I shared Katie's good news. They were thrilled for her. "I don't think Bailey and Tito have to worry about nursery school quite yet, do you?"

"Yes!" Lola said. "That's exactly what we wanted to talk about."

"Not her future employment expectations?"

"Heavens, no. If my daughter wants to work, she'll work." Lola ticked items off on her fingertips. "But nursery school. College. Emergency funds."

My father bobbed his head. "It's never too soon to start investing."

I thought of Pepper accusing Noah of not investing in Cinnamon. Maybe Lola and Dad were right. Bailey and Tito had to address these issues now. And if Rhett and I ever wanted to become parents, we would have to, as well.

I caught sight of a rangy man who reminded me of Wayne, the assistant manager at Vines, and my thoughts made an abrupt U-turn. "Dad, did you find out if there's a gambling game going on in town?"

"So much for talking about my daughter," Lola gibed.

"Grill her yourself," I said and perched an elbow on the table. "Well, Dad?"

"I've been asking around."

"And?"

"My sources didn't come up with anything."

"Your sources?"

"All the guys who come into Nuts and Bolts. Why? Did something more happen?"

"Maybe." I recounted the scene at Vines between Wayne and Oren. "Wayne was reluctant to confide in me."

"Why would he?" Lola asked.

"Because his mother is one of Aunt Vera's best clients. He stops in when she's there. We've chatted a bunch of times."

"Talking about financial issues is a lot different than chatting about the weather and cookbook titles," my father said.

Duh, I wanted to say but didn't.

He ordered drinks as well as a shellfish platter from our waitress and leaned back in his chair. "Why do you care about what's going on between Oren and these guys?"

"Because he's a suspect in Ivy's murder. If he's —"

"She wasn't robbed."

"That's just it. She might have been." I explained about the walk-through with Z.Z. at Ivy's house and added my concerns about the house's lack of decorative items. "Ivy had set bonsai plants everywhere, but there were no gems or geodes like she carried at her store. Doesn't that strike you as odd?"

"It seems a little peculiar," Lola said.

The waitress brought the drinks and said she'd be back soon with our appetizer platter.

"The night before she died," I went on, "I heard Ivy gloating to Crusibella that she was learning her craft, pebble by pebble. She'd even gone on a few adventures to pan for gold and the like. If she was learning to appreciate the stones, why didn't she put any on display? Why only the miniature trees?"

Lola said, "I still don't see how this involves Oren."

I explained my theory of Oren smuggling exotic plants on Ivy's behalf.

"Smuggling?" Lola gasped. "How much does a bonsai go for? Fifty dollars? A hundred?"

"A tree made from a thousand-year-old pine went for a million dollars."

Lola inhaled sharply.

"Oren's boat isn't equipped to go to

Japan," my father said.

"It could reach Mexico," Lola reasoned.

I said, "He's buying Jake's *Joy of the Sea.*"

Dad raised an eyebrow. "That has to cost a pretty penny."

"I know the idea of smuggling is a stretch. Truthfully, I keep going back to the stones and the ritualistic way Ivy was posed. There was something about it that was so cruel."

"Murder is cruel," my father said.

I toyed with my half-eaten piece of bread as another theory struck me. "Noah Pritchett."

"What about him?" Dad sipped his drink.

As Noah's name left my lips, I realized I hadn't contacted Cinnamon yet. I pushed the notion aside. Later. After dinner. "Have you met him?"

"Not yet."

"He owns a garden shop. It's an annex of a big box store. He would know about bonsais."

"Not necessarily," Lola said. "It's a specialized field. Once, I tried to make one and totally botched it. The tree died within a week."

"Why is Noah in town, then?" I asked. "He's very cagey. I don't buy that he came to see Cinnamon or help Pepper." I tapped the table. "By the way, Lola, he said he didn't have business with Ivy on the day he was waiting by her table. He had business with Oren." I stared pointedly at my father. "Before you ask me how I know, it's because he was having lunch with Cinnamon at the café and I happened upon them, and I mentioned Lola's account of having seen him." I did not need to add that I'd specifically seated them to get the skinny. "He claimed he had lingered, hoping for the chance to talk to Oren. Supposedly, Noah wants to invest in fish oil fertilizer and thought Oren would be a good partner. I don't know if that was a cover story, or —"

"Enough speculation." Dad held up a hand, cutting me off. "Can I assume you've brought Cinnamon up to speed with all of your theories?"

I screwed up my mouth.

"No?" His tone was curt.

"I've been meaning to. Life got in the way."

"Noah didn't kill Ivy," Dad said. "According to Cinnamon, he is Pepper's alibi."

I pondered the possibility that Noah killed Ivy and went to Pepper's to establish his own alibi. Or maybe he was the one who had taken a picture of Pepper and was blackmailing her. If he owned up to being Goodguy, her alibi of cooking at home

334

would be toast. Was that his plan?

"Have you told Cinnamon about your slashed bicycle tires yet, Jenna?" Dad asked.

Swell. Apparently, my aunt had reached out to my father. My cheeks burned with embarrassment, making me feel like a thirteen-year-old about to get grounded. Mustering up attitude, I said, "I think the culprit was a teenager on a toot."

Dad blew a raspberry.

Lola rolled her eyes dramatically.

Rhett breezed up to the table and kissed me on the cheek. "What did I miss?"

"Chitchat," I lied and sighed with relief as our waitress set down the platter of shellfish and asked Rhett for his drink order. "Dive in."

The rest of our dinner went smoothly. My father backed off, and Lola pressed Rhett and me for information about wedding plans. Lola was particularly excited that we were taking a trip to Napa Valley to see a venue. She loved the wine country.

After dinner, as my father and I were saying good night, he whispered in my ear. "Touch base with Cinnamon or face your own peril with your aunt."

I squeezed his arm. "Fair warning."

Rhett asked me if I wanted to walk with him so we could talk. Did I ever. I'd been on tenterhooks wondering what the gist of the restaurant offer was and what his plan might be.

Lots of people had the same idea as we did. Many were strolling the boulevard, admiring the flowerpots. Spring Fling signs hung above the street, and cart vendors were out in force. Consistent with the festival's theme, many of the tiered carts featured four-inch indoor plants. My favorite was an ironworks antique flower cart filled with fairy garden items, including miniature fairies and gnomes and their domiciles. I took a photograph to show Bailey; she would be thrilled. If I wasn't mistaken, it was the same vendor who had participated in the Renaissance Fair.

"Please fill me in," I said, clasping Rhett's hand. "I'm all ears."

"As it happens, these are the investors who backed my parents' restaurant."

"Aha. That explains why they sought you out. Your mother and father want you to return to your roots."

He smirked. "They want me to be fulfilled."

"Aren't you?"

"With you by my side, always."

I signaled for him to go on.

"The investors want the restaurant to be

called Intime of Crystal Cove. We don't have a French restaurant in town."

"Lola won't be pleased with more competition."

"Are you kidding? The Pelican Brief Diner will always be the go-to place for fish."

"Don't let Katie hear you say that."

"The go-to place for fried fish," he amended.

I giggled. "Go on."

"It will be a small-scale restaurant. A bistro. They've narrowed it down to one of three locations."

My stomach was in knots. They'd already picked out locations? How long had they been on the hunt? "And you'd be the manager?"

"The executive chef."

I gasped. "The hours —"

"I wouldn't be the only one."

"How can you share that responsibility?"

"I told them that was a deal breaker. I want a life with you, first and foremost." He stopped outside Dreamcatcher, its lights off, and clasped my shoulders. "I adore you and everything about you. I told these guys that I wouldn't do it if it meant losing you."

I smiled. "You couldn't lose me if you tried. Besides, I come with built-in GPS."

He kissed me tenderly. "What we agreed

on was having two managers and two executive chefs. I won't work more than three nightshifts a week. Think about it. After we get married, if I'm around too much, you might grow tired of me. This way you'll get a little alone time. Absence makes the heart grow fonder."

I knuckled his arm and hooked my hand around his elbow. "What about Bait and Switch?"

"As it turns out, my assistant manager is eager to become a partner. He's going to borrow money from his parents to buy his half, and he agrees to be the full-time manager. I'd stay on as a silent partner only."

I couldn't believe how quickly all of this was happening. I felt like I'd jumped onto a warp-speed ride at a theme park.

"So what do you say?" He kissed my cheek. "I have to admit I'm scared."

"Me, too."

"Do we go for it?"

"What's life without a challenge?"

"That's my girl." He threw his arms around me and held me close, his breath warm on my cheek. "By the way, I'm a little rusty in the kitchen. I'll have to bone up on my French cooking. You might have to become my nightly taste tester."

"Poor me." Steak *au poivre,* chicken *à la orange,* éclairs and more? Yum.

He gazed intently at my eyes. "I've already talked to our attorney. I'll have him draw up papers."

That gave me pause, especially given where we'd stopped on the sidewalk. Why hadn't Crusibella insisted upon a formal contract when she'd offered to buy Dreamcatcher? She wasn't naïve enough to think a cocktail-napkin agreement would seal the deal. More importantly, why had Ivy agreed to sell and then reneged? Had she been equally cool and calculating toward Oren? Whether they had been involved in an illegal smuggling business or not, she had ended their relationship, and yet he, if he was to be believed, had convinced himself they'd never broken up and were going to be married.

I sighed. According to Wayne, Oren would always hold a torch for Ivy. Was that honestly the kind of man who could kill another human being?

"Are you okay?" Rhett drew a finger along my arm. "Where did you go?"

I told him about Oren and his emotionally charged discussions with Thad and Wayne.

"Like the one we witnessed with Yung Yi?"

339

I nodded. Then I told him about Hank and Darian hooking up, Crusibella's foray behind Hog Heaven, Alastair's phony alibi, and Noah's dubious reason for being in town.

He stroked my hair. "When were you going to clue me in about your bicycle tires?"

"Dad blabbed?"

"When you and Lola went to the restroom." His voice filled with tenderness. "Promise me you'll track down Cinnamon tomorrow and tell her every theory and clue you have."

"I will."

"And now, back to us. What's your decision?"

CHAPTER 27

"Yes," I said. "Of course, yes, my darling man. You'll be a brilliant chef. It was and *is* your dream. I'm one hundred percent on board."

He kissed me again, and we walked holding hands to Fisherman's Village. He had parked there, as well. To make sure I arrived safely home, he followed me. When we climbed out of our respective vehicles, both of us laughed. True to her word, my aunt had hired a security guard. The bulky man was sitting in a chair on her porch. We introduced ourselves to him and then slipped into my cottage, kissed discreetly, and said good night.

After Rhett drove off, I locked up the cottage and traipsed to bed. Feeling more secure than I had in days, I fell asleep with Tigger nestled at my feet. I didn't awake until the alarm blared.

With a spring in my step, I dressed to

match my cheery mood in yellow capris and cropped sweater. That mood vanished when I strode into the shop with Tigger and found Pepper already there. The unadorned black pantsuit she was wearing did nothing for her ashen color, and her eyes were red-rimmed from crying.

"I let her in," Tina said from behind the sales counter. She, too, looked like she'd been through the wringer. Blotchy cheeks. Puffy eyes. Was heartache in the air? I hadn't told her about seeing her boyfriend at the restaurant. Had someone else?

"Jenna, I need you to do me a favor," Pepper rasped.

"Did you receive another email?" I asked as I set Tigger on the floor and gave his rear end a nudge.

"No. It's H-Hank." Her voice caught. "I . . ." She studied her fingernails. "I'm ashamed to admit it, but I followed him last night." That might explain her covert-looking black getup and frazzled appearance. "He bailed on our date saying he wasn't feeling well, but I didn't believe him." She bit back a sob. "I saw him with Darian. In his car. They were kissing." She smacked her hands together. "I knew it was her. I just knew it. I confronted her yesterday, but she denied it. To my face."

"Oh, my."

"I can't ask my daughter to help me because I don't want her to judge."

"She wouldn't —"

"She would. I love her, but she can be quite critical."

"I'm not sure I'm the right —"

"Please. There's more. My suspicions didn't start with Darian. They began a week ago. Something didn't feel right about Hank. He can be so aloof. One night at his house, he excused himself to take a phone call outside. I thought he was calling Ivy."

Uh-oh. I flashed on the *honey* phone call Katie had overheard.

"While he was chatting, I gave in to my dark side. I snooped and found a number of future airplane tickets to Ohio."

"That doesn't sound unusual. Hank travels to meet his suppliers."

"But his suppliers aren't in Ohio. Not a one. I know because I asked. And these tickets" — she stabbed the air — "were scheduled every two weeks, like clockwork."

"He has children."

She nodded. "Two girls. At Vassar. That's in New York."

"An aging parent?"

"Both of his parents are deceased. However, his ex-wife lives in Ohio." She sucked back another sob. "How could he reunite with her when we're engaged?"

"You aren't officially engaged," I said judiciously.

"But we're going to be. We went shopping for the ring." She clasped my hand and held on tight. "I need you to come with me. As moral support. I want to question him."

"Pepper . . ."

"Please. He'll be at Great Threads. He always opens the shop by himself when he's in town. He says he likes the quietude of morning."

I wrested free of Pepper's grasp and hurried to Tina, who had rallied. Her tears were gone, her eyes clear and bright. She had been listening in and nodded *yes,* I could accompany Pepper. I promised we would talk about whatever had upset her when I returned. Tigger, like the good buddy he was, leaped onto the sales counter and nuzzled Tina under the chin.

Minutes later, Pepper and I arrived at Great Threads. Hank was standing inside at the sales counter. Pepper tapped on the glass door. Hank caught sight of us and his jaw fell open. He began to blink rapidly. Either we'd startled him or he knew he'd been caught out.

Recovering quickly, he smoothed his hair,

donned the tweed jacket he'd draped over a hard-backed chair by the shelves of shirts, and strode to the door. "Ladies, to what do I owe the pleasure?"

Pepper pressed passed him. "We need to talk."

"All of us?" he asked, eyeing me as I passed him.

Pepper whirled around and aimed a finger at him. "You and Darian." I remembered that searing look. The very first time I'd met her, Pepper had been royally ticked off at me. "When did it start? Tell me the truth."

Hank sputtered. "What on earth —"

"Don't pussyfoot with me, mister," Pepper commanded. "I saw the two of you kissing in your car. When did you hook up? Recently? Or has it been going on for a while? I have the right to know."

Hank closed the front door, locked it, and refocused on Pepper, his gaze dreary. "A few weeks ago. After a book club at the library."

"Why?" Pepper cried. "Wasn't I good enough?"

"It wasn't you, Pepper. Honestly. Darian" — he threw his hands wide — "needed a shoulder to cry on. Her husband has been secretly abusing her."

"Professor Drake? But he's so nice."

"Anger boils beneath the surface. He's dark and brooding. Darian was worried he'd hurt their teenaged son. I listened. I consoled. One thing led to another."

Pepper sucked back a sob. "You should have told me."

"I'm sorry." He reached for her.

She recoiled, wrapped her arms around her body, and edged away.

"Who is *honey,* Hank?" I asked softly.

He faced me, his forehead furrowed. "I'm not following."

I told him about the phone call Katie had overheard.

Pepper rejoined us. "Does *honey* live in *O-hi-o?*" She took her time pronouncing the state's three syllables. "I saw multiple airline tickets on your desk at the house."

Hank moaned.

"You go there a lot. You don't go for business," Pepper went on. "So who do you see? Your ex? Do you go there for booty calls?"

Turning as white as a sheet, he backed up and slumped into the chair that once held his jacket.

I whispered, "She's not an ex, is she, Hank? You're still married." Only now did I see the pale line on his left hand. He apparently removed his ring whenever he came back to Crystal Cove.

"You're still m-married?" Pepper stammered. "How long?"

"Thirty years."

Pepper swooned. I threw my arm around her and escorted her to a second chair. When she found her breath, she said, "You and I were talking about a December wedding. Did you plan on divorcing her before then, or was it all a lie?"

Hank didn't speak.

"Where does she think you go whenever you leave town?" I asked.

"To see my suppliers."

He was the personification of the traveling salesman joke.

Pepper pressed a hand to her chest. "Does she know about me . . . and I assume there are others besides Darian?"

He shook his head. "She's very trusting."

"So was I," Pepper mewled.

I said, "Hank, did Ivy Beale figure out your secret? Is that the reason the two of you didn't click on your date?"

Pepper gazed between us, clearly surprised that Hank and Ivy had dated and irritated that I hadn't looped her in.

"Yes, she discovered the truth." Hank rested his elbows on his knees and lowered his head. "She liked Pepper. She made me swear to leave town. She said if I did, she'd let it slide. I promised I would. I told her I needed ten days to finalize things here."

"But then she wound up dead," Pepper hissed. "How convenient."

Hank lumbered to his feet. "I didn't kill her."

"Your alibi is pretty dicey," I argued.

"No, it's not. I mean, yes, I lied about walking in the woods because I was" — he licked his lower lip — "with Darian. I couldn't say that at the time. I didn't want to ruin her reputation or give her husband cause to step up the abuse. Call her if you don't believe me, but please, for her sake, keep it confidential."

Pepper paced in front of the shelves of shirts. "I'm going to take the same stance as Ivy, Hank Hemmings. You need to leave town. Immediately. You need to put your business up for sale. And you need to cut Darian loose. If she's being abused, we have police officers that can address the situation without getting romantically involved."

Looking like he'd aged years in the past ten minutes, Hank agreed.

"And be true to your wife," she said as a parting snipe.

On the way back to Fisherman's Village, tears flowed down Pepper's cheeks. Repeatedly, she chastised herself for being a bad judge of men. Her tirade made me think of Ivy. Was it possible she hadn't been a good judge of men, either? Given that she'd eaten a cream puff dosed with a paralytic, I had to believe she'd known and trusted the person who had snuffed the life from her.

CHAPTER 28

Back at the shop, I was surprised to find only my aunt and Bailey tending to customers. No Tina. Apparently, she had gone home sick. I called to check on her. She promised she was okay. She claimed she had the sniffles. Despite protests, I told her I was ordering chicken soup from the Nook Café and having it delivered, and added that if she didn't answer her front door, I was coming over personally to spoon-feed her. She sighed and promised she'd rise to the challenge. Deciding she was young and capable of handling heartache for a night, I made the to-go order and then set thoughts of her aside.

Pepper, however, was a different matter. I stewed over her plight. Hadn't the poor woman faced enough sorrow in her lifetime? I called the precinct and asked for Cinnamon, but she wasn't in. Instead of leaving a voice mail message, I texted her. I wrote that I needed to talk to her. It was *urgent.* She didn't respond.

An hour passed. Two hours. No word from Cinnamon.

I slipped into the café and picked up egg salad sandwiches for my aunt, Bailey, and me. We took shifts eating. When I came back from lunch — I could only eat half; my appetite was quashed — I checked my cell phone. Still no response from Cinnamon.

For the next few hours, I chatted with customers, rang up sales, and straightened shelves.

After placing our last three copies of *The Art of Cooking with Lavender* alongside a new title, *Edible Flowers: From Garden to Palate,* and adding an array of silk lavender in a decoupage pot as decoration, I settled at the computer to review email orders. When I was done, I intended to track down Cinnamon one way or another.

As I always did, I hit Return to bring the screen to life. Out of nowhere, the computer bleated. Then the screen went wonky. Blocks of pink, blue, and black made the Word file that emerged look like a redacted spy document. What the heck?

"Bailey!" I shouted.

She hustled to the sales counter. "What's wrong?"

"You tell me." Like a gunslinger, I shot two fingers at the computer. The bleating was making my insides jittery. "Did I destroy the computer? What's going on?"

On the screen an animated skeleton came into view and uttered a promise to annihilate our computer.

At the same time, my aunt joined us. "Oh, my."

If it had been Halloween, I might have thought it was a prank. But it was spring. We were being hacked.

Bailey clicked a key and said, "Vera, hand me that notepad."

My aunt complied.

Bailey jotted a note but kept her focus trained on the computer and keyboard. The skeleton vanished, but the redacted-looking document did not. She tried to close it; it wouldn't obey. She made another memo on the pad then dragged the mouse arrow to the spot where she could quit the application. No words were visible.

"Bailey . . ." I began.

"*Shh.* I can do this," she assured me. "Breathe."

She wasn't talking to herself; she was talking to me. I did my best.

My aunt began rubbing her amulet. "We have backups, right?"

"Did it yesterday, not to worry," Bailey said, though perspiration beaded on her upper lip. She clicked on the computer's icon and dragged the mouse arrow down the column. She tapped on a blank space. "Gotcha," she said. As the computer started to shut down, she scribbled another series of notes. "I'll run the malware program and remove any vestiges of the virus and reboot. And then reboot and reboot and reboot."

Relieved that Bailey had it under control, my aunt said, "I need tea. Anyone want a cup?"

Neither Bailey nor I did.

"If you change your minds . . ." Aunt Vera strode to the stockroom and disappeared.

"Jenna" — Bailey beckoned me closer — "do you remember what you did before this happened? Which keys you tapped?"

"All I did was bring the screen to life."

"You weren't working on the Word document?"

"No. Maybe Tina was viewing it before she left for the day."

"Okay, relax. Go outside. Give me a little space. You're wound up after the ordeal with Pepper."

I was more wound up from not hearing from Pepper's daughter. What about *urgent* didn't Cinnamon understand?

As I edged from behind the sales counter, I glanced at Bailey's notes. Though they were Greek to me, they reminded me of the notes Tina had jotted about the cost of school. That image made me recall the notepads at Ivy's house. According to Cinnamon, Ivy's email had been hacked. Maybe she had suffered a computer snafu, too, and, like Bailey, had jotted notes to address the problem, except all of hers had started with a pair of initials and were followed by round numbers. Despite the fact that there were no dollar signs and no commas, could those have been cash amounts? Maybe Ivy had been worried about what the snafu might cost her.

"Go outside," Bailey repeated.

"I'm going." I stepped outside and drank in the fresh air, then stretched my arms overhead and bent to touch my toes. Tigger orbited my ankles and nuzzled my nose.

As I picked him up, a car door slammed. I whirled around. A woman got out of a car. Not Pepper. The *Closed* sign on her shop was still in place. I wondered whether I should check on her but decided against it. If she needed to wallow, I'd let her, like I would let Tina. Twenty-four-hour pity parties could be therapeutic. On the bright side, maybe Pepper was consulting with

Cinnamon, which would explain why I hadn't received a response from our illustrious chief of police.

My stomach growled. A half hour ago, Katie had brought in beautifully iced cookies shaped like flowers. I'd nibbled on one and had set it aside. Luckily, Rhett had invited me to an early dinner at Mum's the Word diner. I could use a hearty meal.

With Tigger in tow, I checked on Bailey, who was diligently trying to find the source of the problem. She told me she had it under control and ordered me to go home. She and my aunt would close up. I didn't argue. I sped to the cottage, dropped off Tigger, grabbed a sweater for the evening, and drove to the Pier.

Rhett was walking out of Bait and Switch as I arrived.

"Perfect timing," he said.

I wrapped my hand around the crook of his elbow, and we sauntered along the boardwalk, drinking in the restful sound of the surf and the excited chatter of people who'd come to have fun. Neither of us talked about our future. We would. At dinner.

As we neared the diner, I noticed a long line of people waiting to enter Theater on the Pier. The marquee boasted a new comedy written by a local playwright with a perfect title for the Spring Fling: *Flowers Make Me Sneeze.*

I nudged Rhett and said, "We should get tickets to see that."

"Good idea."

The *smack-smack* of feet pounding the boardwalk startled me. I pivoted to see who was running and in the nick of time dodged Yung Yi.

"Yung, you klutz," his wife, Suji, cried. She drew up short, gasping. "Jenna, are you all right?"

"I'm fine."

"Sorry, but we're late for the play." Suji held up two tickets. She was quite a beauty. Deep brown eyes. Perfectly formed lips. Unlike her husband, she didn't have a hint of an accent. She had been born and raised in San Francisco and preferred cookbooks featuring Italian food.

"You're right on time." I pointed. "The theater hasn't opened yet."

"True, but it's first-come, first-seated. We always have to sit at the rear because my sweet husband can't get his act together." She mock-frowned at him.

"I could not get our bassett hound to do his business in a timely matter. Sue me." Yung threw up his arms.

Suji laughed. "That dog has you wrapped around his little paw."

"And you are immune?"

Her cheeks tinged pink.

"Yung, how are you doing?" I asked.

"Why?" His brow furrowed.

"The other night. My fiancé and I" — I gestured to Rhett — "saw you with Oren Michaels chatting outside the Pelican Brief. Your poor hat," I said leadingly, making light of what he'd done to it. Knowing what Yung and Oren had discussed might solve all sorts of puzzles regarding Oren.

"What happened to your hat?" Suji asked.

"I threw it on the ground."

"You what?" She shook her head. "That hat is expensive. You know how tight things have been. We can't replace it if —"

"It is not damaged, sweetheart. It was all an act."

"Why were you acting?" Suji tilted her head.

"I was not acting. I was being dramatic. To goad Oren. Oh, look, the line is moving." Yung pecked her on the cheek and said, "Go inside. Find us a table. I will be right in."

Obediently, she joined the line, but before disappearing inside the theater, she glanced worriedly over her shoulder, which reminded me of the fretful way she'd reacted after her tarot reading with Aunt Vera the other day.

"If you must know," Yung said, "I was reaching out to Oren for advice. He is a friend. We used to be sailing buddies before I had to sell my boat." A smile pulled at his lips. "You know what they say about boats? The happiest day in your life is the day you buy your boat. The second happiest day is —"

"When you sell it," Rhett finished.

"Amen." Yung groaned. "What a money pit."

"Was Oren able to give you good advice?" I asked, seeing as he'd been dishing out a lot of it lately.

"He did." Yung lowered his voice. "I was being extorted. Someone sent me an email that said he knew what I did and that I needed to pay up or else. Oren suggested —"

"Was the email from someone named Goodguy?" I cut in.

"How did you know?"

"It's bogus."

Rhett eyed me curiously. I mouthed: *I'll explain.*

"But I did do something," Yung went on. "A month ago." He blinked rapidly. A flush of embarrassment ran up his neck. "It was an accident."

"What happened?" Rhett asked.

"I hit a young man on a bicycle in Santa Cruz. Late at night. I had been drinking, and my depth perception —" He waved a hand. "He swerved to the right and fell to the ground. I stopped to help him, but then he got up, cursed at me, and rode away. I . . ." He licked his lips. "I thought it was over and done. No harm, no foul, as you say. Until I received the email. The incident occurred at an intersection. There must have been street cameras."

"Was the blackmailer specific? Did he show you proof?" I asked.

"No."

"I'm telling you it's a scam. A shot in the dark." I repeated what Bailey had said about phishing cons and how blackmailers saturate the market with threats. "Don't pay."

"I cannot risk it. The bank" — Yung mewled — "is owned by a private family. Everyone has to sign an ethics clause when hired. If someone in human resources found out I had been involved in an accident when I'd been drinking, I would lose my job. You heard my wife. We are on a tight budget. I did not tell her about the shakedown. I did not want to lose face. So I confided in

Oren." He hesitated. "He was extorted, too. About two months ago. He paid the demand and never heard from the blackmailer again. He told me to do the same. I did not like hearing that. That is when I threw my hat on the ground."

"A reasonable gesture given the circumstance," Rhett said.

"Later that night, after more thought, I took Oren's advice."

I sighed. "You paid?"

He bobbed his head. "I worry every night that the blackmailer will contact me again, but so far he has not. I used a special fund, one I set aside for rainy days so my wife would not discover my disgrace."

Rhett placed a reassuring hand on Yung's shoulder. "If I were you, I'd tell your wife. You're a team. You make decisions together. She'll understand."

Yung nodded glumly. "She will be furious."

"And she'll get over it," I said, betting she'd already figured out what her husband had done, given her session with my aunt.

"Thank you," he said. "I appreciate your opinion. Good night."

After he slogged into the theater, Rhett and I went into Mum's the Word. A waitress seated us at one of the aqua-colored booths and within minutes took our order, the specialty beef stew as well as two sparkling waters.

When she left, I leaned forward, elbows on the table. "Time for me to confess. I got one of those emails, too." I held up a palm to prevent Rhett from interrupting. "I didn't pay it. I haven't done anything wrong as far as I know. The email wasn't specific as to my crime. Unlike Pepper's."

He blinked. "She received one, too?"

"Yes. A photo was attached to hers." I told him the rest. "I haven't informed Cinnamon, but not for lack of trying. I've left her a couple of voice messages; she hasn't responded. I didn't tell you because I put Bailey on the case. Granted, she hasn't been able to drum up any leads, so we don't know for certain if Pepper's and my emails are scams, but for now, Bailey's advice is to sit and wait."

"Sweetheart, that's not proactive. The police need to be informed."

"Is it possible . . . ?" I placed my hand on his as a notion came to me.

"What?"

"With this many Crystal Cove residents receiving emails, do you think someone we know could be the blackmailer? A local. Not just some random hacker in Timbuktu." I held up my palms. "Hear me out. I noticed something when I did the walk-through with Z.Z. at Ivy's." I told him how Jake Chapman, thanks to my father and aunt, had enlisted me for the job. "There were a couple of notepads with initials and numbers in the thousands beside them. What if the initials represented people being scammed and the numbers represented dollar amounts? One of the sets of initials was YY. Possibly Yung Yi."

"Are you suggesting Ivy was the extortionist?"

I nodded. "Except she was dead when I received mine and Pepper received hers."

"Maybe she sent them via an email scheduling program."

"Possibly." I raised a finger. "If Ivy was the blackmailer, maybe whoever killed her was one of her marks and took over where she left off."

"Who?"

"Oren recently bought a new truck and is investing in a boat. Hank is supporting a secret lifestyle with a wife in Ohio as well as a full-scale business in California and two or more girlfriends. And then there's Alastair Dukas, a former IT guy. He's out of a job and hunting for work, but maybe that's his cover. Lola says he tips big when he has lunch at the Pelican Brief. Working alongside Ivy, he could have had intimate knowledge of her scheme and now be rolling in dough."

"I love how your mind works." Rhett lifted my hand and kissed it. "Call Cinnamon."

I did. The call went to voice mail.

CHAPTER 29

"Good morning," my aunt said as I strolled into the shop the next morning. "You look pretty in pink. And festive."

I'd donned a pink-and-white-striped blouse, white jeans, and pink flip-flops, and I'd clipped a pink silk flower in my hair. Spring Fling was dictating my wardrobe.

"I hope you ate a good breakfast," my aunt went on. "We're going to be busy after church lets out today." She clapped her hands. "Follow me. How are your scissor skills?"

"What's going on?" I set Tigger on his kitty condo and stowed my purse behind the sales counter.

"Obviously you've forgotten. Today we're teaching young and old how to make crepe paper flowers. Everything's coming up roses," she trilled.

"You're in wonderful spirits. Did you have

a good date with Deputy Appleby last night?"

"They're all good."

Was she falling in love? So far, they'd kept their relationship casual but respectful.

"Bailey will be today's instructor." Aunt Vera motioned to my pal, who was already sitting at the children's table laying out crepe paper and chenille pipe cleaners in a variety of colors. "Each participant will get a small vase in which to plant their project," my aunt added.

Bailey had arranged a few dozen clear glass vases in varying shapes and sizes in the center of the table.

"Bailey told me she made over two hundred paper flowers for her junior high sock hop," my aunt continued, "so she's a pro."

"These will be a bit more upscale," Bailey assured me. "I've been watching all sorts of YouTube videos to hone my skills. Think of all the floral-themed cookbooks we'll sell afterward." Using a pipe cleaner as a pointer, she gestured toward the storage room. "By the way, did you see the adorable cookbook albums and recipe cards that came in?"

"I just walked in."

"Oh, right. Baby brain fog," she joked. "They're decorated with roses and azaleas and camellias. So pretty."

For the next hour, I sat beside her and trimmed crepe paper — some shredded to within an inch of the base, others cut into petal shapes. When I took a break to stretch my aching hands, I said, "Aunt Vera, have you heard from Tina?"

"As a matter of fact, she just called." My aunt was setting up for a morning tarot card reading. "She's on her way in."

That made me feel better. Hopefully she was on the mend. "How about from Pepper?" I asked.

"I haven't seen her."

"I'm going to check on her." Call me overly protective, but I simply wanted to know if she was on the mend, too.

As I walked out of the shop, a woman yelled, "Watch out, Jenna!"

Cinnamon, on rollerblades, dodged me, skidded to a stop in front of Beaders of Paradise, and whipped off her sunglasses. "Ha!" she crowed at her father, who trailed her. "Beat you!" Her cheeks were glowing and she seemed happy. No, *exuberant.* The last time I'd seen her smiling so broadly was at her wedding.

Noah, looking equally vigorous in leggings and snug T-shirt, drew to a halt and grinned, clearly enjoying spending time with his daughter. "By a nanosecond." He pushed his goggles up on his helmet. "I'm going into the café."

Cinnamon tried the door to the shop. Locked. "Jenna, where's my mother?"

"Not in."

"I can see that."

Noah said, "Want coffee?"

Cinnamon shook her head.

As he glided toward the restaurant, he pulled his cell phone from his pocket and wobble-walked inside on his skates while scanning the screen.

"Your mom had a tough day yesterday," I said, joining Cinnamon. "She went home for a personal day and hasn't made a re-appearance."

Her smile turned upside down. "Do you know what happened?"

"Yes."

"Why didn't you call me?" She took off her helmet and fluffed her hair.

"I did. I *have.* I even texted you."

"You never texted me."

"Yes, I did. And I wrote *urgent,*" I said, instantly regretting my snappish tone.

With a huff, she pulled her cell phone from her hip pocket, swiped the screen, and tapped her text icon. "Huh," she muttered. "There it is. It wasn't here earlier. Well, what's urgent?"

How much should I tell her? Neither Bailey nor I had worked out a solution to the blackmail issue yet, and I was reluctant to tell her about Pepper having visited Ivy before her death for fear of ruining her alibi. On the other hand, I'd made a promise to Rhett to fill Cinnamon in. On everything.

I decided to start with Pepper's breakup with Hank Hemmings. "Your mother discovered that Hank was not only cheating on her with Darian —"

"The librarian?"

"Uh-huh. By the way, Darian's husband is abusing her."

"You're kidding. He's so mild-mannered."

"Long story short, Hank became her confidant and one thing —"

"Led to another. Poor Mom. She was worried she'd lose him to another woman. I've tried to talk her into seeing a therapist to help her with her self-esteem, but she refuses."

The image of Pepper at a therapist's office made me laugh. Would she lie down? Sit up? Tell the doctor to *bleep* off? I said, "You might want to check on Darian. If she really is being abused —"

"Consider it done." Cinnamon twirled her hand. "Go on. You said *not only* in regard to

Hank. What else did he do?"

"He's married. His wife lives in Ohio."

"Oh, no. The lout."

I told her how Pepper had found travel documents at his place and had decided to investigate. "The realization broke your mother's heart."

"This is your fault," Cinnamon said.

"Mine?"

"Because of you, she thinks any citizen can do what the police do."

Though Cinnamon probably hadn't meant that as compliment, I took it as one, albeit backhanded.

"In Hank's defense," I said, "his tryst with Darian gives him a solid alibi for the night Ivy was killed."

"I never had him in my sights."

"Even after I told you Ivy might know a secret about him?"

"Everyone has a secret."

"Not like his. FYI, Ivy did discover it and threatened to expose him. She died before she could."

Cinnamon rolled her eyes. "Fine. I'll verify Mr. Hemmings's alibi. What else?"

I hesitated.

"Out with it, Jenna." She folded her arms across her chest but didn't tap her foot. It was probably too hard in skates.

"There are people in town getting stung by an email blackmail scam, including your mother and me." I elaborated.

"I agree. That stuff is usually bogus."

"I'm sure mine is, but your mother, um, did do something that could put her in deep water. She visited Ivy that afternoon."

"Are you certain?"

"She admitted it, and there was a photograph of her outside Ivy's embedded in her email." Quickly, I shared the theory that Ivy might have been the blackmailer and the killer might have taken over where she'd left off. I added that we hadn't opened the attachment, so we couldn't confirm that the photograph proved anything or had a time-stamp on it. "Your mother believes a person on a bicycle must have taken the photo. She doesn't know the person's identity."

"Okay" — Cinnamon flapped a hand — "I'll grant you that the optics aren't the best if Mom was seen there, but Ivy was her friend and she has a very credible alibi, provided by my father."

I worked my tongue around the inside of my mouth.

"Now what's eating you?" Cinnamon muttered under her breath.

I glanced over my shoulder. Noah was still inside the café. "What if your father provided an alibi for your mother in order to create one for himself?"

Cinnamon planted her fists on her hips. "Give me a break. He didn't know Ivy Beale. He's not a suspect in her murder."

"What if he lied about that? What if he did know her?" I shared the possibility that Ivy had been smuggling bonsais internationally. I added that at first I'd suspected Oren because he was buying a bigger, better boat, but what if Noah, being a horticulturist, had been her partner? "There was a bonsai on the floor beside her head. I don't believe it was part of the ritualistic way she'd been laid out."

"Jenna —"

"C'mon. Don't you see something odd about the timing of your father's return to town? Why now?"

"To get into the fish oil fertilizer business with Oren Michaels."

"How is that going?"

"Swimmingly," she joked, but there was uncertainty in her gaze. I would bet dollars to dimes that she hadn't pressed him on it. "I'll look into it. Happy?"

Noah skated up to us carrying a to-go cup. "Wow, Jenna, you're doing blockbuster business in the restaurant. There were a number of flower club parties, each over six people

371

strong. I handed out a few business cards. Hope that was okay. I told them sometimes I can get my hands on plants other nurseries can't." He took a sip of coffee.

Cinnamon cut me a sharp look. Apparently, her mind went to the same place mine had — the bonsais.

"What did I miss?" Noah asked. "How's your mom?"

"She's taking a personal day. Let's get going." Cinnamon pivoted.

"One sec." Noah pulled a key chain fitted with a utility knife from his back pocket. He popped open the three-in-one Allen wrench and knelt to adjust his rollerblades.

I said, "Cinnamon, before you go, may I ask a question?"

"Has my saying *no* ever stopped you?"

"Did you corroborate Crusibella's alibi?"

"The Overeaters Anonymous coach confirmed her appointment. Ms. Queensbury did not kill Ivy Beale."

I was relieved. I really did like Crusibella. "What about Alastair Dukas? Did you talk to him after my father texted you that his alibi was bogus?"

"Your father texted me, too?" She grimaced at her cell phone and shook it. "I didn't get that text. What's going on?"

"It might have to do with your cellular

provider. Let me fill you in. Alastair — Mr. Dukas — claimed he was doing inventory at Dreamcatcher the night Ivy was killed. Because Lola was involved in the book club's progressive dinner event, Dad took a three-loop tour along the boulevard. He never saw the lights on at the store."

"My, my. Haven't you been doing your due diligence?" Cinnamon taunted. "Would you like to join the police force and become official?"

"Would they let me wear flip-flops?" Call me crazy, but I enjoyed having the freedom to put on whatever I wanted.

Her father chuckled. "Got to love her spunk."

"Spunk." Cinnamon smirked. "Is that what it's called nowadays? I will follow up with Mr. Dukas, Jenna. Is there anything else?"

"One more thing. Well, three more, actually."

She moaned.

I told her about the shop's computer being hacked and the slashed bicycle tires. "The tires could be a prank, of course. Local teens having fun with the owner of the smallest house on the beach."

"It sounds like you've ticked someone off, young lady," Noah said.

Like the killer? I wondered.

Cinnamon said, "Jenna, you have to stand down. You are not equipped to handle a dangerous criminal."

That rankled me. I almost blurted that I'd taken karate and self-defense classes and I'd faced off with a few dangerous criminals in the past, but I bit my tongue because what I was not ready to do was deal with the ire of our chief of police. I saluted. "Yes, ma'am. Got any other suspects *you'd* like to tell *me* about?"

"As if."

CHAPTER 30

I strode into the shop, slipped into the stockroom, and called Pepper. She didn't answer her home phone or cell phone. I left a message on the cell saying I was concerned about her. Also, in the interest of full disclosure, I told her I'd spilled the beans to her daughter about her visit with Ivy on the afternoon of the murder. I assured her Cinnamon believed she was innocent; she'd said so to my face. Hopefully, that tidbit would put Pepper's mind at ease and she wouldn't be angry with me for talking out of turn. Whether Cinnamon would seriously consider her father a suspect in Ivy Beale's murder was up for debate.

As I ambled to the sales counter, I spotted Tina sitting with my aunt at the vintage table. Two tarot cards lay faceup on the tabletop. My aunt was poised to turn a third. Tina, looking young and innocent in a shirred white dress with minimal makeup and her hair twisted in a messy knot, appeared extremely focused. I didn't interrupt. The future she hoped to see in the cards obviously mattered.

I checked on Bailey, who was perched on a stool by the children's table, tongue wedged between her teeth like a little kid as she concentrated avidly on making enough materials for the crepe paper flower clinic. Sensing she didn't need my help, I orbited the shop, making sure all the books were in the right location and oriented in the proper direction. You wouldn't believe how many times customers slotted the books upside down.

Moments later, Crusibella and Z.Z. hurried into the shop, both carrying to-go bags from the Nook Café, neither dressed for church. I crossed to them because Crusibella was grinning from ear to ear.

"Don't you look happy," I said. "You must be relieved to know the police have exonerated you of Ivy's death. Your alibi held up."

"I'm thrilled about that, but that's not why I'm smiling." She swept strands of hair off her face. "Tell her, Z.Z."

"We might have a buyer for Crusibella's house."

"I didn't know you were selling," I said. "There's no realtor's sign in the front yard."

The two of them giggled like schoolgirls.

"It was a private deal," Z.Z. confided. "The buyer heard Crusibella needed money and might sell. She made an offer. We couldn't refuse."

More giggles.

"If the deal goes through," Crusibella said, "and with the extra cash my father is willing to invest, I'll have enough money to purchase Dreamcatcher."

"Wait. Whoa." I held up a hand. "Your father is alive?" I could've sworn my aunt told me Crusibella's parents had passed away years ago. I must have confused her history with someone else's.

Crusibella nodded. "I haven't spoken to him in years and out of the blue he called. Isn't it amazing?"

"Amazing." I glanced at my aunt, wondering if she'd had something to do with the reunion. She felt my gaze on her and offered a *Who, me?* look, and then continued with Tina's reading.

"My father told me he wants to get out of the stock market and invest in real estate." Crusibella fanned the air. "I don't care what the reason is, he's being supportive. That's a first. Like Ivy, I never had my parents' blessings growing up."

I thought of Noah and Cinnamon reconnecting and pictured Oren bonding with his father. Was the fact that Father's Day was weeks away causing all these men to come up to the mark?

"Tell me about Dreamcatcher," I said. "I thought the executor said the parents wanted out. They intended to sell the inventory and default on the lease."

"That was the case until Crusibella and I realized that if she bought all the inventory, we could negotiate separately with the building's owner about the lease, which we did. They agreed to a five-year option-to-purchase."

"Why we didn't think of it before is beyond me." Crusibella laughed. "Now I want a moment with Vera to see what my next legal step should be."

Aunt Vera relished advising her clients, but I often wondered if the pressure to provide consistently uplifting news might take its toll. As for giving advice about which legal steps to take, I hoped she'd instruct Crusibella to consult a lawyer.

Tina rose to her feet and hugged my aunt. "Thank you so much, Vera. That was exactly what I needed to hear." She smoothed the front of her dress and plumped the puffy sleeves.

Before she was able to move an inch from

the table, Crusibella and Z.Z. swooped onto the vacant chairs, nearly toppling Tina.

I steadied her and asked how she was doing.

Before she could answer, Alastair hurried into the shop and made a beeline for me. "Ms. Hart? Do you have a minute?"

Tina whispered that she was fine and we'd catch up soon.

Alastair straightened the collar of his polo shirt. "I'm sorry to barge in, but I hear you're hiring. I'd like to apply for the job."

"Where did you hear —"

"According to rumors, Tina is leaving."

I glanced at Tina and said, "Alastair, please have a seat at the children's table. Tina and I need to chat first." I waylaid my sweet clerk before she could reach the sales counter. "Is it true? You're quitting?"

She pressed her lips together. Her cheeks tinged pink.

"How did Alastair know?" I asked.

"My girlfriend must have blabbed to a few friends," Tina replied. "I meant to tell you first. Well, not *tell*. *Ask*. But . . ." She flailed a hand. "I had a chat with my father. I hadn't talked to him in a long time. I was always closer to my uncle, but you know . . ." Ever since Tina's aunt was murdered, she'd had a tough time communicating with her uncle. "Anyway, my father said I had to give culinary school a try before it was too late. Go full time. No distractions. He said he didn't follow his dreams and had always regretted it."

I really did need to check the calendar and remind myself we were not yet in June preparing for Father's Day. Otherwise, I was way behind on ordering relevant cookbooks.

"He offered to help with expenses," Tina went on. "He recommended I take a full load. No extra jobs. No dicey boyfriends. How could I refuse?" She spread her arms. "He wants to get married."

"Your father?"

"No, silly." She tittered. "My boyfriend. He proposed last night, but I told him what my father said. He was not pleased. Did I care? No, I did not. You want to know why? Because I heard through the grapevine that he went out on another date with that redhead. Did he think I wouldn't find out? Naughty, naughty." She scraped one finger against another in the *blame* gesture. "Too-ra-loo," she crooned like my aunt often did. "Oh, and guess what?"

"What?"

"Back to real life for a second." She tapped my forearm. "I put in for a grant to cover all my books and maybe even a few incidentals, and I think I'll get it because of need. Yay. Your aunt said during my reading that I'm on a financial upswing. Everything is going to get easier. She even hinted that there might be more than a grant in my future." She clapped her hands, her enthusiasm engaging. "Maybe that means I'll win the lottery. I bought a ticket. I'd like to go to France for an immersion program and eat éclairs, petit fours, and the five mother sauces."

"Sounds wonderful."

She gazed at me intently. "I hope you're not mad at me."

"I'm overjoyed for you. I love seeing young people achieve their dreams."

Listen to me. Young people. You'd think I was ancient.

"Consider this my two weeks notice," she said. "If you hire Alastair, I'll train him." She nodded in his direction. "He's quite dreamy looking, isn't he?"

"Eyes forward, missy," I said. "No boyfriends until after you graduate."

She mock-pouted. "Yes, boss."

I left her to tend the cash register and took an application form to Alastair, who was helping Bailey cut crepe paper. "Alastair . . ."

"Yes, ma'am." He shot to his feet and

pressed the wrinkles from the legs of his chinos.

"Fill this out," I said, impressed with his enthusiasm but leery of his status in Ivy's murder. "Have you had other offers of employment?"

"Crusibella isn't hiring. Miss Fairchild said she won't have an opening until Thanksgiving and that would be temporary."

"Well, take your time with the form. I'll need to call previous employers —" I balked. "That was insensitive of me. Please list employers prior to your current situation."

"Yes, ma'am."

The front door opened and Deputy Appleby strode in. Not in uniform. Dressed in a white shirt, blue slacks, white boater, and tennis shoes, he looked like he was prepared to take a walk.

Alastair stiffened. He took a step toward the deputy but held back when Appleby stopped next to my aunt and whispered in her ear. She suggested he get something to eat in the breezeway and held up her hand, fingers spread, meaning she would join him in five minutes. After she concluded her consultation with Crusibella and Z.Z.

I whispered to Alastair. "Do you want to

talk to the deputy?"

"No. I mean, yes. I mean" — he hitched a thumb — "I saw Chief Pritchett as she was skating away and yelled that I needed to speak with her, but she didn't stop. She probably didn't hear me."

Even though Cinnamon had said she would speak to Alastair, she was a woman on a mission to relax. Could I blame her for waiting until the end of the day to return to duty?

"Why did you want to talk to her?" I asked.

"Because I lied about my alibi the night Ivy died. I want to confess."

My pulse kicked up a notch. "Let me get the deputy for you."

I strode into the breezeway. "Deputy Appleby."

"Hey, Jenna." He'd eaten half of a muffin decorated with *flowerfetti* icing. "I never knew you could eat flowers."

"Katie's putting them in and on everything during Spring Fling. Got a second?"

"Sure." Appleby polished off his muffin and tossed the cupcake wrapper in the wastepaper basket to the right of the treats table.

I escorted him back to the shop. "You look quite dapper."

"I'm taking your aunt on a midday stroll. She wants to improve her health. I suggested we walk twenty to forty minutes every day."

"Excellent." I led him to Alastair. "Before you go on that stroll, Mr. Dukas has something to tell you. Go on, Alastair."

Alastair filled his cheeks with air and let out a quick breath. "Sir, I lied about my alibi on the night Ivy died. I wasn't doing inventory at Dreamcatcher."

"Deputy, my father will confirm that," I said. "He was touring the town and noticed the shop was closed and all the lights were off. He texted Cinnamon, but she never received the text."

"I didn't kill Ivy, sir," Alastair rushed to add. "You see, after she told me for the last time that she wasn't interested in me because I was too young, she fired me, and —"

"She fired you?" I blurted.

"Let me ask the questions, Jenna," Appleby said.

"You bet. Sorry to interrupt. Continue, Alastair."

"Yes, she fired me. She said it was hard having me around because she found me attractive, so she needed me out of her sight." As he swooped hair off his face and his biceps flexed, I could see why women of any age might find him distracting. "Anyway, that smarted, so I went on a bender."

"A bender," Appleby repeated.

"I got plowed, but, see, I don't drink. Ever." Alastair chopped one hand against the other. "Until that night, I'd never had a drink in my life."

"Because of your father," I stated.

Alastair nodded.

I said to Appleby, "His father was a drunk."

"Not was. *Is*. But not a mean one, just useless," Alastair said. "I, on the other hand, wanted to make something of myself. Live a life fulfilled."

Appleby said, "Got any proof?"

"An empty bottle of scotch."

"That won't substantiate your claim, son."

"I took selfies."

"Let me see." Appleby held out a hand.

"They aren't pretty. I'm puking." Alastair pulled his cell phone from his pocket and swiped the screen. He opened the camera icon and displayed the images to the deputy. "That's me in my bathroom. I took the photos to remind myself never to touch booze again. It's poison."

"For some," Appleby said. "Not for all."

"Look closely." Alastair stabbed one of the

pictures. "They're time-stamped. I can't doctor that."

Appleby nodded. "That pretty much covers the time period the coroner gave for time of death. Okay, young man, you may have been drunk, but you used your head and documented it. Good for you. I'll need you to forward those pictures to me." He handed Alastair a business card.

"Will do."

Appleby strolled to the front door to wait for my aunt to change into suitable walking clothes — her caftan was too cumbersome — and Alastair moved to the sales counter to transmit photographs.

Me? I didn't budge. I gazed around the shop, not registering faces as I tried to figure out who was still a suspect in Ivy's death. Hank had an alibi. Crusibella did, too. Pepper was in the clear, and now Alastair had removed his name from my list.

Unless I was missing something, only Oren Michaels and Noah Pritchett, given the coincidental timing of his arrival in town, were left.

Chapter 31

An hour later, as Bailey was giving her spiel to twenty attentive customers about how to neatly attach a petal to a floral stem, my father walked into the shop.

"Jenna," he called.

Worried that our customers might miss some of Bailey's instructions if he joined me, I hurried to him. "What's up?" Had his ears been burning? I'd been thinking about him ever since the Father's Day trend had started.

"I haven't been able to reach Cinnamon," he said. "She hasn't responded to my text, either."

"She's taking a personal day. Why are you so eager to touch base?"

"I wanted her to know that I'm meeting her father for brunch."

"Are you sure you've got the date right? She's rollerblading with him."

"Well, he agreed to meet, so maybe she

has a few other personal things to do" —
Dad waggled his eyebrows — "like spending time with her husband."

"Why are you meeting with Noah?"

Dad slipped his hands into his trouser
pockets. "I want to draw a bead on him.
Find out what his true intentions are and
learn more about this fish oil fertilizer deal."

"Did Lola put you up to this?"

He grinned. "I'll have you know I came
up with the plan myself."

I patted him on the shoulder. "Aren't you
a good surrogate father for Cinnamon,
always there in a pinch."

"I'm there for you, too."

"Yes, for me, as well. For all of us. You are
a rock."

My father's cheeks turned crimson. He
didn't take compliments easily. In his world,
everyone was expected to do his or her best.
"Do you want to join us?" he asked. "It
might make the meeting seem less hostile."

Did I ever. "Let me make sure everything
here is covered."

Tina promised me she could tend to the
few customers who were browsing books.
"And Gran's here," she added. "If I truly
need help, she's always willing to pitch in.
She knows the merchandise as well as we
do."

"Let's go." I gave Dad a nudge and followed him to the café.

As Noah had informed me earlier, the place was bustling. Nearly every table was filled with garden club members wearing floral-bedecked hats or floral-themed dresses. The hostess found us a table for four in the far corner. We sat and unfolded our napkins.

Dad said, "Customers seem to be enjoying the books you've placed on the bookcases."

I nodded. "So far, no major mishaps. No ruined books."

"You could donate any damaged copies to the library."

The mention of the library made me think of Darian. I hoped she would seek therapy and ultimately leave her husband. No woman should be abused.

Minutes after we received our menus, Noah strolled into the café. He'd changed into regular street clothes and a pair of loafers. He sat between my father and me and set his cell phone on the table. "Nice to see you again, Jenna." He swiped the phone's screen, checked email, and pushed the cell phone away. "Sorry, business."

We ordered quickly — a seafood omelet for me, lavender Belgian waffles for the men

— and then my father started in, slowly at first, softening him up by asking Noah about his wife and daughters.

After our meals were served, Dad asked more pointed questions. "Why come to Crystal Cove now?"

Noah grinned. "What better time to address a new business opportunity than in the spring?"

"How do you know Oren?"

"He and I connected online. I knew his father from when I lived here before."

My father frowned. "Why don't I believe you?"

Noah lifted his chin like a fighter daring my father to throw a punch.

"I've done a bit of research on fish oil fertilizer," Dad continued, ignoring the challenge. "There's plenty of the stuff around. Huge companies make it. What's your plan for manufacturing it?"

"It's not fully formed."

"How will you get enough from one fisherman to stock a thriving business? And do you have a sales plan in place?"

Noah's face went blank. He sputtered but said nothing, which confirmed what I'd surmised. He had made the business deal up on the fly.

The theory I'd come up with before

reared its ugly head. I said, "Noah, what do you know about bonsai trees?"

"They're short and easy to kill," he wisecracked.

"Did you know some are smuggled internationally?"

"Really? Fascinating. As I said, I've killed a few in my day. Never touch the things now. Too expensive."

My father took a sip of water and eyed me over the rim of the glass.

I winked at him. "Did you know Ivy Beale was a bonsai collector?"

"The woman who died?"

"Yes, she had dozens in her house."

"She must have had a green thumb." Noah's tone was even, his gaze neutral.

"I heard that a bonsai made from a Japanese thousand-year-old pine sold for over a million dollars."

"Wow, who'd have guessed?" Noah grew serious. He laced his hands together and lasered me with his gaze. "Is there a point to this banter, Jenna?"

Dad and I exchanged a look. He gestured for me to continue. At the same time our waitress arrived with our meals. She set my omelet down first.

After she left, Noah aimed his knife at me. "I think I get where you're going with this.

You want to know if I knew Ivy Beale and had a reason to kill her. No and no. I never met her. I really did go to the Pelican Brief to talk to Oren Michaels."

"Why?" My father stared hard at the knife. "Not for business. Oren would be talking up your deal if there were any truth to it."

Noah set the knife down. Chin lowered, he whispered, "Because I'm a victim of an extortion scam. A guy emailed me and said I did something bad and threatened that if I didn't pay up, he'd reveal it."

"So that's why you're always checking your cell phone," I said.

"Yes."

"Was it someone named Goodguy?"

"How do you —"

"I'm being extorted, too."

"What?" my father gasped. "Why didn't you tell me?"

"I think it's a crock, Dad. I didn't do anything bad. Did you, Noah?"

He heaved a sigh. "Sadly, yes. I borrowed some money from the till at work to pay for my daughter's medical bills. She's twenty-seven and didn't have insurance. She'd planned on getting it but hadn't gotten around to it. Then she had a female issue."

"A female issue?" my father repeated.

"Breast cancer. The doctor was worried

the cancer was aggressive. She needed an emergency lumpectomy. She couldn't wait to apply for insurance, and even if she did, given the current state of the market, the insurer probably wouldn't cover her preexisting condition. I told the doctor we'd pay cash. She worked with us on a deal, but I didn't have enough money, so I took" — he cleared his throat — "a small loan. Someone must have caught me on camera."

"Why didn't you ask your boss for an advance?" my father asked.

"That would have been the sane thing to do, but I wasn't in my right mind. I thought my daughter was dying. I —" Noah studied the silverware before raising his chin. "I intend to pay the money back in full. I'm waiting for my biannual bonus. Sales have been through the roof."

"So what did you do when you received the email from the extortionist?" Dad asked.

"I didn't have the money to pay. I was tapped out."

"So you reached out to Oren?"

"To his father. He insisted I talk to Oren."

"Why?" my father asked.

I said, "Because Oren was being scammed, too, as were a few of his friends. Oren paid up and the blackmailer backed off. He's been advising his friends to do the same."

"There are more?" My father's eyes widened.

"A number right here in town."

Noah gawped. "Honestly?"

"Yep." I gestured to him. "Go on. You talked to Oren —"

"Hold on. I'm getting to that." Noah raised his index finger. "Needless to say, I was furious. I wanted to nip it in the bud. As it turns out, my youngest daughter is quite computer-savvy. To keep up with her, I've taken a few online classes. With what little knowledge I had, I realized the extortionist's website, Scarletavenger.com, was a unique domain. Not Gmail or Yahoo or the like. So I did some research and found out it's owned by none other than" — he did a drumroll on the table — "Oren himself."

I gasped.

Noah bobbed his head. "There isn't a photograph of him on the site, and there's no personal info, but he put up pictures of that boat he plans to buy. I figured it out."

I mentally smacked my forehead. Pepper had remembered Goodguy's email domain as *vengeance dot something* not *avenger;* neither Bailey nor I had paid attention to it. Jake's *Joy of the Sea* was a beautiful red Avenger, top of its class. A *scarlet* Avenger.

"I came to town to have it out with the

guy, but I haven't been able to get him alone," Noah said. "So you see? I had nothing to do with Ivy Beale. Never met her. My *business* is with Oren." He tucked into his meal.

"How many more people is he extorting?" my father asked.

As I listed them, another notion came to me. "The notepads."

My father shook his head. "What are you talking about?"

I told him about the memos I'd seen at Ivy's house. "What if Ivy figured out what Oren was doing? What if she was chronicling his actions?"

"Why not contact the police?"

"Because she didn't have enough proof." I snapped my fingers. "Or maybe she did contact them, via email, but Oren, who was on to her, deleted the communication. Cinnamon said Ivy's email had been hacked."

"The police must have taken her computer," my father said. "They would have found evidence of that by now."

"Not if it went *poof!*" Noah flicked his fingers.

I swatted the tabletop. "Oh, gee! Why didn't I realize it before? Oren killed Ivy to keep his secret."

"Why would you think that?" Dad asked.

"He knew about the eyestones. What I mean is he knew that eyes were painted on them." I flashed on the brief conversation with Katie and me in the Nook Café kitchen. "But how could he know? The police haven't released the information, and none of the Mystery Mavens would have known, either, because the *eyes* were upside down. I was privy to the information later when Cinnamon clued me in. Oren had to be the one who'd painted them and put them that way. It all makes sense, from the cream puffs right down to the music that was playing when we found Ivy."

"What cream puffs? What music?"

I explained about the poison in the cream puffs. "And 'Love Theme from *Romeo and Juliet*' was playing at Ivy's house." I splayed my hands. "Don't you see? Oren put the music on specifically because he believed he and Ivy were ill-fated lovers. He didn't want her to die, but she had to."

Dad said, "Doesn't he have a solid alibi?"

I pushed my plate away. "Yes, a witness saw him moor his boat in the bay north of Crystal Cove. Maybe the witness is in on the scheme."

Noah whispered, "His father."

"Maybe." I pulled my cell phone from my

396

pocket and called Cinnamon. She didn't answer. I left a voice mail message and then texted her.

"I'm not leaving this to chance." Dad rose from the table without finishing his meal. "I'm going to the precinct. You" — he pinned me with a glare — "go back to work and wait for my call. And you —"

Noah locked his lips with an imaginary key.

CHAPTER 32

A short while later, while I was rearranging books on a display table and stewing over whether my father had connected with Cinnamon — she hadn't responded to my voice mail or text — I spied Pepper zipping into the parking lot on her e-bike. The sight made me think of Oren on the night he'd encountered Yung Yi. He'd been steadying his mountain bike — an e-bike, if I wasn't mistaken. I pictured the motorized gadget on the frame and recalled the sound of the motor kicking in when he'd engaged the pedals. What if Oren had stashed his bicycle near the bay north of Crystal Cove, and that was how he'd gone to and from Ivy's in less than a couple of hours? If I did the math, factoring in the time to sail a safe distance from the coast and the time to glide into the cove, traveling approximately twenty nautical miles an hour, then the physical distance between those two points might have been as little as fifteen or twenty miles. On a good day, I could ride fifteen miles an hour. How fast could an e-bike go?

Pocketing my cell phone so I wouldn't miss a call from Cinnamon or Dad, I said to my aunt, "Back in a few," and strode outside. "Pepper," I called. With her helmet on, she must not have heard me. She disappeared into her shop and closed the door.

The helmet. What if Oren had been the guy on the bike outside Ivy's when Pepper visited? Neighbors might be able to identify him.

"Hey, Jenna," a man said.

I whipped around and nearly choked when I saw Oren, his creel bag slung over his shoulder. He was heading for the archway between the Nook Café and Beaders of Paradise.

"A UPS truck is blocking the alley." He gestured to his truck, which he'd double-parked in a handicap zone. "Hope it's okay if I lug the fish this way to the kitchen."

My mind raced with a new possibility. Maybe I could keep him occupied in the café until the authorities showed up. "Sure. Why don't you take the shortcut through the café? Follow me."

"Nah, I smell pretty bad." Truthfully, he

smelled pretty much like he always did. Fishy.

"C'mon. It'll do our customers good to see how fresh our fish is."

Once inside, I gestured for him to lead the way. As he navigated the hall, I pulled my cell phone from my pocket and tapped in a quickie text to Cinnamon, not caring whether spellcheck fixed my typos.

"Katie, Katie, pretty lady," Oren sang as he sashayed into the kitchen. "I come bearing gifts."

Katie was at the dessert counter sifting confectioners' sugar onto a small cake.

"The alley is blocked," I said in explanation to her. "I told Oren to come this way."

"Whatever the boss says is okay with me." Katie finished the cake and set it in front of Bailey, who was seated at the chef's table.

"I wondered where you'd gone," I said to Bailey.

"I was starving and craved something savory." In addition to the dessert, an appetizer-sized portion of a salmon dish and another of a salad lay in front of her.

"Care to join?" Katie asked.

Seeing Bailey gave me another idea. "Say, Oren, have you eaten? Katie is always in need of taste testers for the day's special. It looks like Bailey has a three-course meal.

What's on the menu, chef?"

"Panko-encrusted salmon, daylily salad, and powdered —"

"Sorry. I can't. I'm running behind," Oren said. "And I don't want to get a ticket for parking in the handicap zone." He unzipped his canvas creel on a stainless steel counter and pulled out a large wrapped fish. "More croker. Fresh off the boat. As ordered."

"Yay." Katie inspected the fish. "It was so delicious the last time."

"Sure you won't stay for a quick bite, Oren?" I asked. "I could move your truck for you." *And hide the keys so you can't escape.*

Oren eyed me suspiciously. "What's going on, Jenna?"

"Going on?" My voice skated upward. Rats, so much for acting cool, calm, and collected.

Acting. Was it only a week ago Oren had come into the kitchen and cried about losing Ivy, the love of his life? He had been an actor in Los Angeles — a bit-part actor, but an actor all the same. He'd put one over on Katie and me.

"Why are you trying to detain me?" Oren asked.

Bailey glanced at me. So did Katie. The rest of the kitchen staff was too busy preparing meals to pay us any mind.

"Detain you? I want to feed you," I said, getting my tone under control. "You look a little thin. With Ivy's death, you've suffered quite a shock. Are you eating?"

"Uh-huh. Nice try." Oren zipped his creel and marched toward the double doors leading to the dining room. "I'm leaving now."

I grabbed a sauté pan and darted between him and the exit.

He snarled at me. "What do you think you know?"

"You killed Ivy."

Bailey gasped.

"You knew the eyestones were inverted," I went on. "Only the killer would have known that."

Oren made a U-turn and headed for the alley exit. I dashed in front of him with the sauté pan as my shield.

"You fed Ivy a cream puff laced with a paralytic so you could incapacitate her."

Grunting his annoyance, Oren seized a chef's knife from a knife block and aimed it at me. "Move."

"You know what your big mistake was, Oren? Blackmailing me. That made me dig deeper."

"It was him?" Bailey scrambled to her feet.

"Yep. He stole into my cottage to get my

402

email address off my computer."

Oren's silence confirmed my theory.

"When I didn't panic about the email and seek his advice like the others had, he slashed the tires of my bike to scare me."

"Get real," Oren said.

"Ivy found out you were blackmailing everyone, didn't she? She threatened to expose you. You might have hacked her computer and deleted her emails, but she left notes, Oren. There's physical evidence."

"Out of my way, Jenna," Oren ordered. "I don't want to hurt you."

"I'm not budging."

He lunged at me. I shrieked.

The staff froze.

Bailey didn't. She hurled an appetizer plate at Oren as if it were a Frisbee. I'd taught her how to throw a year ago. Before that, she'd had no arm. The plate caught him in the back of his head. He reeled toward Katie, who sprang into action. She swung the croker like a baseball bat. The fish connected with Oren's chest, and he stumbled in my direction.

I whacked his shoulder with the sauté pan.

Moaning, he crumpled to his knees and dropped the knife. One of the staff kicked it away. The others approached like an army, each carrying a kitchen utensil. The height-challenged pastry chef wielding the industrial-sized mixer looked ridiculous, but I wouldn't tell her. She was a hero in my eyes.

Looking dazed, Oren sat up and crossed his legs.

I crouched to meet him at eye level. "Tell me something. Why did you put the bonsai beside Ivy's head? Were you smuggling them?"

"Smuggling? No." A sad smile graced his lips. "Ivy was so happy that she'd learned how to prune them. Turning out miniature works of art gave her such pride and made her feel like she was really learning her trade. Her parents had never given her that kind of validation. I set the bonsai there" — he shrugged — "as an homage."

"I don't buy it, Oren. You put the eye-stones upside down. If you knew enough to use them, then you knew that if the eyes were inverted, the soul would be doomed to travel the River Styx for eternity."

"Inverting them was an oversight."

"So you're saying you really did love her?"

"With all my heart. Why do you think I put aventurine in her hands? I wanted her to love me as much as I loved her, but when she said she had to turn me in . . ." He moaned. "What can I say? I screwed up.

Uncovering secrets was her . . . *thing.* Like an itch she had to scratch. As for me, I'm into shortcuts. I couldn't let her stop me from making my fortune."

"How many others are you extorting?"

"Two to three hundred. I've lost count."

Whew! At three to five thousand a pop that added up to nearly a million dollars, not to mention it was a racket that could go unchecked for years.

The swinging door leading to the dining room pushed open. Cinnamon strode in, took in the scene, and instantly gripped the butt of her weapon. She glowered at me. Guess she wasn't going to award me Brownie points for assisting the police.

"Jenna, everyone, back up. Clear the area. Mr. Michaels, you are under arrest for the murder of —"

"Oo-o-oh." Bailey clutched her stomach. "Jenna, call Tito. The baby's coming!"

CHAPTER 33

Every member of the Mystery Mavens book club was in attendance at my father's house for Bailey's post-baby shower. Lola had decorated the living room with pink streamers and balloons, which totally clashed with the ocean-themed décor, but nobody seemed to mind. Katie had set a beautiful array of tea sandwiches, scones, muffins, and tea on the dining table. A platter of giraffe cookies decorated with pink-speckled icing sat on the coffee table. Gran had complimented me on the icing — yes, Katie was teaching me to ice; I had a long way to go before I would become an expert.

Bailey, who was sitting on the sofa next to me, held up the frilly pink dress Flora had given her, and cooed, "Ooh, it's so pretty."

"So is your baby girl." Flora passed the photographs of the baby to Z.Z. "Look at her gorgeous brown eyes."

Even though Baby Martinez had been

born a fairly decent weight, the doctor had wanted to observe her for another week. Preemies could have issues. So far, so good.

Z.Z. said, "Her smile could dazzle the world."

Bailey beamed. "I know, right?"

"Open another present," Lola suggested. "We've got to return to the hospital at some point today."

It had been touch-and-go for about two hours after I rushed Bailey to the hospital. Doctors had been worried about the umbilical cord wrapped around the baby's neck, but in the end, the oh-so-ingenious baby had extricated herself from danger, and she was born a mere two hours later. Bailey hadn't even had time to beg for drugs. Lola and my father had postponed their safari. Luckily, they'd purchased trip insurance. Lola hadn't left Bailey's side for more than an hour since the birth. Bailey was about ready to pull her hair out.

"Anyone for tea?" Dad pushed the tea trolley across the living room.

"I'd love a cup, Cary," Cinnamon said.

She had taken the day off and was sitting on one of the dining room chairs facing the sofa. Her husband, Bucky, was filling a plate with goodies at the dining table. After the shower, they were treating Pepper to dinner. Hank Hemmings had left town with his tail between his legs, but Pepper was still grieving. She had found a modicum of solace by helping Darian Drake find a good therapist. Nothing brought two women together like being hoodwinked by the same man. Cinnamon's father had gone home, too, although he and Cinnamon had made plans to meet up in a month. He wanted to introduce her to her half sisters. She was wary but excited.

"Open mine." Crusibella handed Bailey a package wrapped in gold paper and tied with a glittery silver bow.

"What's in it?" Bailey shook the package.

"A secret."

My guess was it was something from Dreamcatcher. Crusibella's house had sold in a day — all cash. An hour after the ink was dry, Z.Z. convinced the executor of Ivy's estate to sell every stitch of Dreamcatcher's inventory to Crusibella. When that deal was sealed, Z.Z. worked out the lease with an option-to-purchase with the shop's lessor. The shop had suffered no downtime. Even Alastair had stayed on board.

Bailey opened the package and gushed as she drew out a pink quartz picture frame. "It's gorgeous."

Crusibella said, "May your baby bring you

years of love and joy."

Bailey thanked her and then whispered to me, "Where's Tito?"

"In the guest room being grilled by Rhett, just like I grilled you." Since this was a co-ed party, we'd decided to have a simple party game of How Well Do You Know Each Other? I'd asked Bailey ten baby-themed questions. Rhett was asking Tito the same ones.

"He was so upset when he didn't get the scoop on Oren Michaels's arrest," Bailey said.

Oren had left the café peacefully with Cinnamon. She put him in jail; he was pending trial. Cinnamon hadn't been pleased that I'd cornered Oren in the café kitchen, but when she realized how many people were around and that I was in no danger of being harmed, she lightened up. She even thanked me for figuring out the niggling detail of the bonsai. That had baffled her as much as it had me.

Bailey winked at me. "I told Tito that, with a new baby, he might have to get used to missing a scoop or two if I go back to work. Do you know what he said?"

I shook my head.

"A reporter can write from anywhere, *mi amor.* How cool is that?"

I hugged her. "You snared a good one."

"So did you." She nodded toward Rhett, who strolled into the room and took a seat next to me.

Tito followed him and perched on the arm of the sofa beside Bailey. He laid his arm across her shoulders and gazed at her lovingly.

"Okay, Bailey, question number one." Rhett read from a three-by-five card. "When did Tito first know you were pregnant?"

Bailey stared at her husband while mulling over the answer.

Rhett whispered to me, "What did I miss?"

"Not much," I replied sotto voce. "A happy mama and her ecstatic friends *ooh*-ing and *aah*-ing."

Rhett cleared his throat and gazed at his watch. "Well, Bailey? Tick-tock."

"He knew when I told him," she answered.

"Wrong!" Rhett made a buzzing sound. "He knew the morning after you conceived."

"No way," she said.

"Way," Tito countered. "Everything about you changed. Your moods, your —" He twirled a finger at her.

She grabbed his hand. "Mind your manners. There are ladies present."

He chuckled.

"No more questions," Lola said. "Let's open the rest of the gifts."

Bailey obeyed. After each, she said thank you. When she was done, she sank back in the sofa. "I'm exhausted."

"One more," my aunt announced, waving an envelope overhead. Bailey moaned.

"It's not for you, dear." Aunt Vera offered the envelope to me. "This is for Jenna and Rhett."

"What is it?" I asked, taking the envelope from her. "A night's stay at Maison Rousseau in Napa?" We were driving to Napa after the party ended to look at the possible wedding venue.

My aunt scrunched her nose. "It's a tad more than that. Open it."

I pulled out an elegant folded silver card. On the front it read:

Two souls with but a single thought. Two hearts that beat as one.

I glanced at my aunt. "You already gave us an engagement gift."

"Think of this as a wedding gift. Read the rest." She pressed her lips together like the proverbial cat that had swallowed the canary.

I flipped open the card and a piece of

parchment paper fluttered out. I caught it before it hit the ground and scanned the words:

Crusibella Queensberry's house now belongs to the two of you. With all my love, Aunt Vera

Tears sprang to my eyes. "It's too much."

Rhett took the paper from me and read; his mouth dropped open. "Vera, no."

"Please," she begged. "It will bring me such joy. It's not on the beach, of course, and it doesn't have a complete view of the ocean, but it's within walking distance."

I glanced at my father. "Did you know?"

He grinned. "I might have dropped the hint."

I hugged him fiercely.

"She's also given Tina a year's tuition," he said. "She's been in a generous mood."

"Too-ra-loo," Aunt Vera crooned and rose to her feet. "If you've got it, share it. Now, off with you." She kissed my cheek. "Go to Napa and find a place where the two of you can say *I do.*"

RECIPES

SWEET

Chocolate Coffee Cupcakes
Chocolate Coffee Cupcakes,
Gluten-Free Version
Lemon Tea Cakes (à la the Sweet Pea)
Lemon Tea Cakes, Gluten-Free Version
Cinnamon Madeleines
Nutmeg Cookies
Nutmeg Cookies, Gluten-Free Version

SAVORY

Chicken Almond Tea Sandwiches
Chicken Tortilla Individual Ramekins
Cucumber Tea Sandwiches
Curried Egg Tea Sandwiches
Sun-Dried Tomato Basil Tea Sandwiches
Pear and Cheese Tea Sandwiches
Mascarpone Stilton Cheese Appetizer
Savory Cheddar Scone
Raita Appetizer
Whitefish Tea Sandwiches

CHOCOLATE COFFEE CUPCAKES

From Jenna:

Like my aunt, I love chocolate-and-coffee anything. Add in buttercream icing and sprinkles, even better. These cupcakes are not easy — you know I like easy — and they are time-intensive, but they are worth it. If you're worried about how many ingredients there are, do what Katie taught me to do: Divide the "wet" from the "dry" and think of them as two recipes that mix together. In this case, there's a third recipe — the eggs and sour cream.

(Yield: 1 dozen)

1/2 cup unsalted butter
3/4 cup brewed coffee (espresso is even
  better)
1/2 teaspoon vanilla

6 tablespoons dark chocolate cocoa
1 cup sugar
1 cup flour
3/4 teaspoon baking soda
1/2 teaspoon salt
1/3 cup sour cream
1 egg

Preheat oven to 350 degrees F. Line cupcake pan with cupcake liners.

In a medium saucepan, melt the butter. Add the coffee, vanilla, and cocoa powder. Set aside to cool.

In a medium bowl, whisk together the sugar, flour, baking soda, and salt. Set aside.

In another medium bowl, stir the sour cream and egg together. Slowly drizzle into the chocolate mixture and stir to combine.

Now, add the chocolate/egg mixture to the dry ingredients. Stir until there are no lumps.

Fill the cupcake liners about 2/3 full using a ladle or ice cream scoop. The texture is quite satiny and syrupy. Bake for 20–24 minutes or until a toothpick comes out clean. Cool on a wire rack. Do not frost until cooled completely.

Chocolate Coffee Buttercream Frosting
3/4 cup butter, softened
1 4-ounce package cream cheese, softened
1 16-ounce package confectioners' sugar
  (4 cups), more as needed
1/4 cup unsweetened cocoa powder
3 tablespoons brewed coffee (espresso is
  even better)
1/2 teaspoon salt
chocolate sprinkles, if desired

In a medium bowl, beat butter and cream cheese together. Slowly beat in confectioners' sugar, cocoa powder, coffee, and salt until smooth and spreadable. Add more sugar or coffee if necessary.

Spread on cupcakes and add sprinkles, if desired.

CHOCOLATE COFFEE CUPCAKES
GLUTEN-FREE VERSION

(Yield: 1 dozen)

1/2 cup unsalted butter
3/4 cup brewed coffee (espresso is even better)
1/2 teaspoon vanilla
1/4 cup plus 2 tablespoons dark chocolate cocoa
1 cup sugar
1 cup gluten-free flour (I use sweet rice flour)
3/4 teaspoon baking soda
1/2 teaspoon salt
1/2 teaspoon baking powder
1/2 teaspoon xanthan gum
1/3 cup sour cream
1 egg

Preheat oven to 350 degrees F. Line cupcake pan with cupcake liners.

In a medium saucepan, melt the butter. Add the coffee, vanilla, and cocoa powder. Set aside to cool.

In a medium bowl, whisk together the sugar, gluten-free flour, baking soda, salt, baking powder, and xanthan gum. Set aside.

In another medium bowl, stir the sour cream and egg together. Slowly drizzle into the chocolate mixture and stir to combine.

Now, add the chocolate/egg mixture to the dry ingredients. Stir until there are no lumps.

Fill the cupcake liners about 2/3 full using a ladle or ice cream scoop. The texture is satiny and syrupy. Bake for 20–24 minutes or until a toothpick comes out clean. Cool on a wire rack. Do not frost until cooled completely.

LEMON TEA CAKES

From Jenna:

As promised by Sweet Pea Bakery, the food truck that was serving high tea near Azure Park, I found this recipe on its website. It is moist and delicious and would make lovely gifts, wrapped in cellophane bags and ribbon. You can use small or mini loaf pans. If using the latter, be sure you reduce the baking time.

(Yield: 5–6 small loaf cakes or 10–12 mini loaf cakes)

For the cake:

2 cups granulated sugar
5 tablespoons lemon zest, approximately
   3–4 lemons
8 ounces unsalted butter, melted
4 large eggs, room temperature

3 cups all purpose flour
1/2 teaspoon baking powder
1/2 teaspoon baking soda
1 teaspoon kosher salt
1/4 cup lemon juice, no pulp, no seeds
3/4 cup buttermilk
1 teaspoon vanilla extract

For the syrup:

1/2 cup granulated sugar
1/2 cup lemon juice, no pulp, no seeds

For the frosting:

1-1/2 cups powdered sugar
3–4 tablespoons lemon juice, no pulp, no
  seeds

Preheat the oven to 350 degrees F. Spray
5–6 small loaf pans or 10–12 mini loaf pans
with nonstick oil.

Put the sugar and lemon zest in a bowl and
stir well to let the lemon oil mix with the
sugar.

Cream the butter and the lemon/sugar
mixture. Add the eggs and beat to combine.

In a small bowl, sift together the flour, baking powder, baking soda, and salt.

In another small bowl, combine 1/4 cup lemon juice, buttermilk, and vanilla.

Add half of the flour mixture to the eggs/lemon/sugar mixture, and then add half of the buttermilk mixture. Repeat and beat until smooth.

Divide the batter evenly between the pans, filling about 2/3 full.

Bake for 30–35 minutes or until a toothpick comes out clean. Reduce baking time if using mini loaf pans.

When the cakes are done, remove from oven and let cool for about 15–20 minutes before removing from pan.

Meanwhile, while the cake is cooling, make the syrup. In a small saucepan, combine the sugar and lemon juice and bring to a boil. Turn the heat to simmer and cook until the syrup thickens, about 5 minutes. Set aside to cool.

After turning the cakes out of their pans, set on a tray lined with parchment paper and poke holes in the bottom of the cakes using a skewer. Then drizzle half of the syrup over the holes. Turn the cakes over and drizzle the remaining syrup over the tops of the cakes. Smooth with the back of a spoon. Let cool.

While the cakes cool completely, make the frosting. In a small bowl, whisk together the powdered sugar and lemon juice to make a smooth but thin frosting. Add more lemon juice or water, if necessary. Pour the frosting over the tops of the cakes and let the frosting firm up. Serve immediately or cool in the refrigerator. By the way, these cakes do well in the freezer. Wrap tightly in plastic wrap and store in freezer bags.

LEMON TEA CAKES
GLUTEN-FREE VERSION

(Yield: 5–6 small loaf cakes or 10–12 mini loaf cakes)

For the cake:

2 cups granulated sugar
5 tablespoons lemon zest, approximately
   3–4 lemons
8 ounces unsalted butter, melted
4 large eggs, room temperature
3 cups gluten-free flour
1 teaspoon xanthan gum
1-1/2 teaspoons baking powder
1/2 teaspoon baking soda
1 teaspoon kosher salt
1/4 cup lemon juice, no pulp, no seeds
3/4 cup buttermilk
1 teaspoon vanilla extract

For the syrup:

1/2 cup granulated sugar
1/2 cup lemon juice, no pulp, no seeds

For the frosting:

1-1/2 cups powdered sugar
3–4 tablespoons lemon juice, no pulp, no
  seeds

Preheat the oven to 350 degrees F. Spray
5–6 small loaf pans or 10–12 mini loaf pans
with nonstick oil.

Put the sugar and lemon zest in a bowl and
stir well to let the lemon oil mix with the
sugar.

Cream the butter and the lemon/sugar
mixture. Add the eggs and beat to combine.

In a small bowl, stir together the gluten-free
flour, xanthan gum, baking powder, baking
soda, and salt. (Note the extra baking
powder for the gluten-free version of the
cake.)

In another small bowl, combine 1/4 cup
lemon juice, buttermilk, and vanilla.

Add half of the gluten-free mixture to the

eggs/lemon/sugar mixture, and then add half of the buttermilk mixture. Repeat and beat until smooth.

Divide the batter evenly between the pans, filling about 2/3 full.

Bake for 30–35 minutes or until a toothpick comes out clean. Reduce baking time for mini loaf cakes.

When the cakes are done, remove from the oven and let cool for about 15–20 minutes before removing from pan.

Meanwhile, while the cake is cooling, make the syrup. In a small saucepan, combine the sugar and lemon juice and bring to a boil. Turn the heat to simmer and cook until the syrup thickens, about 5 minutes. Set aside to cool.

After turning the cakes out of their pans, set on a tray lined with parchment paper and poke holes in the bottom of the cakes using a skewer. Then drizzle half of the syrup over the holes. Turn the cakes over and drizzle the remaining syrup over the tops of the cakes. Smooth with the back of a spoon. Let cool.

While the cakes cool completely, make the frosting. In a small bowl, whisk together the powdered sugar and lemon juice to make a smooth but thin frosting. Add more lemon juice or water, if necessary. Pour the frosting over the tops of the cakes and let the frosting firm up. Serve immediately or cool in the refrigerator. By the way, these cakes do well in the freezer. Wrap tightly in plastic wrap and store in freezer bags.

CINNAMON MADELEINES

From Katie:

These are one of my favorite cookies. Perfect for afternoon tea. They are so elegant because of their shape, and they're simple to make. The only delicate part is the glaze. Be light-handed.

(Yield: 12)

For the cookies:

1/4 cup unsalted butter
1 tablespoon good-quality honey
1 teaspoon pure vanilla extract
3/4 cup all-purpose flour
1 teaspoon baking powder
3/4 teaspoon ground cinnamon
1/4 teaspoon salt
1/4 cup granulated sugar
2 large eggs

For the glaze:

3/4 cup confectioners' sugar
2–3 teaspoons water
dash of cinnamon

Brush molds of a madeleine pan with butter; set aside.

Make the batter:

Melt butter in a small saucepan over low heat. Remove from heat and stir in honey and vanilla. Let cool 10 minutes.

In a small bowl, whisk the flour, baking powder, cinnamon, and salt; set aside.

Preheat oven to 325 degrees F, setting the rack in the center.

In a medium bowl, stir together sugar and eggs. Gently fold in the flour mixture until combined. Add the butter mixture and fold until combined. Cover the bowl with plastic wrap and refrigerate 30 minutes.

Spoon the batter into the prepared madeleine pan, filling each mold halfway. Tap the pan on the counter to eliminate air bubbles. If necessary, use moistened fingers to press the batter into the mold.

Bake until cookies have puffed and the edges are golden, 7–8 minutes.

Transfer the madeleine pan to a wire rack; let the cookies cool slightly. Unmold the cookies onto a rack, and let cool completely.

Make the glaze:

In a small bowl, stir together sugar, water and cinnamon until the glaze is smooth and thick. Add more water if necessary. Using a small pastry brush, paint the ridged side of each cookie with the glaze. Let set 15 minutes.

Cookies can be stored in a single layer in an airtight container up to 3 days.

NUTMEG COOKIES

From Jenna:

I cajoled this recipe out of the baker at Latte Luck Café and am so glad I did. These are perfect for any time but especially good as a holiday gift. They also freeze well. By the way, I prepared two different baking sheets — one that was buttered, one that was lined with parchment paper. The one that was buttered created a darker, crisper cookie.

(Yield: 24-36 cookies)

1 stick butter, softened
1/2 cup sugar plus 1-1/2 tablespoons sugar
2 egg yolks
1 cup flour, sifted
1 teaspoon cream of tartar
1 teaspoon nutmeg, more if desired

In a medium bowl, cream together butter,

sugar, and egg yolks. Add sifted flour, cream of tartar, and nutmeg. Mix together.

Drop by spoonfuls on cookie sheet, 8 to a cookie sheet. They will spread.

Bake at 375 degrees, 10–12 minutes maximum. Should be lightly brown around edges when removed from oven.

Let cool 1 minute, then remove from tray and set on paper towels to cool. These get very crisp.

NUTMEG COOKIES
GLUTEN-FREE VERSION

(Yield: 24-36 cookies)

1 stick butter, softened
1/2 cup sugar plus 1-1/2 tablespoons sugar
2 egg yolks
1/2 cup sweet rice flour
1/2 cup tapioca starch
1 teaspoon cream of tartar
1 teaspoon nutmeg, more if desired
1/4 teaspoon xanthan gum

In a medium bowl, cream together butter, sugar, and egg yolks. Add gluten-free flours, cream of tartar, nutmeg, and xanthan gum. Mix together.

Drop by spoonfuls on cookie sheet, 8 to a cookie sheet. They will spread.

Bake at 375 degrees, 10–12 minutes maximum. Should be lightly brown around edges when removed from oven.

Let cool 1 minute, then remove from tray and set on paper towels to cool. These get very crisp.

~ SAVORY ~

CHICKEN ALMOND TEA SANDWICHES

From Katie:

I love tea sandwiches. They're so easy to make and extremely satisfying to eat. They are a perfect balance to the sweet treats served at high tea. For this recipe, you will need to poach the chicken because you want this chicken to be as tender as possible. Don't worry, it's not a time-consuming thing to do.

(Makes 4 full sandwiches or 16 tea sandwiches)

1 cup chicken stock
1 cup water
1 teaspoon coarse pepper
1 bay leaf
8 ounces chicken breast
1 stalk celery, chopped finely

2 tablespoons sliced almonds
1/4 cup sour cream
2 tablespoons mayonnaise
1 teaspoon lemon juice
2 tablespoons finely chopped parsley
salt and pepper, to taste
1 ounce butter, softened
8 slices white or wheat bread

In a small saucepan, combine the stock, water, pepper, bay leaf, and chicken, and bring the liquid to a boil. Reduce the heat and simmer for about 15 minutes or until the chicken is cooked through. You might want to turn the chicken once or twice. Remove the chicken from the liquid. You may dispose of the liquid. When cool enough, chop the chicken finely.

In a medium bowl, combine the chicken, celery, almonds, sour cream, mayonnaise, lemon juice, and parsley. Season with salt and pepper to taste.

Spread butter over the bread slices thinly. Top half of the slices with the chicken mixture and then top with remaining bread. Cut the crusts off the bread. Then cut each sandwich into shapes — 3 rectangles or 4 triangles are best. Keep covered with plastic wrap until ready to serve.

CHICKEN TORTILLA
INDIVIDUAL RAMEKINS

From Katie:

*My mother used to make this recipe in a 9 ×
13 pan and serve for brunch as well as dinner. I thought individual ramekins would be a
nice touch for a book club party. They're so
easy to serve. Just so you know, there are
disposable ramekins to make this even easier
with the cleanup. And, yes, sometimes even I
use canned goods.*

(Serves 8–12)

1 pound skinless boneless chicken breasts
   or thighs, baked ahead, chopped (about 2
   cups)
1 chopped onion (about 1 cup)
2 4-ounce cans green chiles, diced
1 12-ounce can cream of chicken soup,

condensed

1 12-ounce can cream of mushroom soup, condensed

1 cup milk

12 corn tortillas, sliced

2 cups shredded cheddar cheese, more if desired

Precook the chicken breasts or thighs. I like to wrap them in foil and bake at 300 degrees F for 30 minutes. Remove from oven. Cool and cut into small bites. Leave the oven on.

In a large bowl, combine the onion, green chiles, cream of chicken soup, cream of mushroom soup, milk, and chicken.

In individual oven-safe ramekin dishes, layer the following as you would lasagna:

Sauce with chicken
Tortillas lengthwise and widthwise
Sauce with chicken
Tortillas lengthwise and widthwise
Sauce

Cover with shredded cheddar cheese.

Bake at 300 degrees F for 35–45 minutes and cheese is crispy. Let cool about 20 minutes before serving.

If you'd like to make this as a casserole, layer in a 9 × 13 pan and bake at 300 degrees F for 1 hour. Let cool 20 minutes before serving.

CUCUMBER TEA SANDWICHES

From Katie:

For cucumber tea sandwiches, here are a few little tips, exactly as I stated in my demonstration at the shop: The English cucumbers don't have as many seeds and possess a pleasant, crisp flavor. Do remember to cut them thinly. Some people like to remove the skins. I would if the skin is waxy, but usually I like to leave the skins on. Personally, I like the crunch. And lastly, don't use too much cream cheese. You don't want to overwhelm the flavor of the cucumber.

(Makes 16 sandwiches)

8 slices white bread
4 tablespoons cream cheese
2 English cucumbers, sliced thinly
   (if desired, remove peel)

1/2 teaspoon sea salt
1/4 teaspoon ground black pepper

Lay the white bread on a cutting board. Spread each slice with 1/2 tablespoon cream cheese. Layer the cucumbers on top of four slices of bread with cream cheese. The cucumber may overlap since they are so thin. Sprinkle with salt and pepper. Top each with the other slice of bread.

Carefully remove the crusts and then cut each sandwich diagonally into four triangles.

Remember to keep the sandwiches covered with a damp towel or plastic wrap until ready to serve. Otherwise, they will dry out.

CURRIED EGG TEA SANDWICHES

From Jenna:

I love Indian spices, particularly the flavor of curry. Adding curry to this delicate sandwich adds just the right amount of zing. Katie taught me how to make the perfect hard-boiled egg. She heats up the water to boiling and, using tongs, sets each egg into the water. She leaves it boiling (on medium heat) and cooks the eggs for 10 minutes. Then she removes the eggs with tongs and sets them in a bowl to cool. Voilà. Done. The shell comes right off without a mess. The yolk is a perfect yellow color.

(Makes 4 full sandwiches of 16 triangles)

6 hard-boiled eggs, chopped coarsely
1/3 cup mayonnaise
2 teaspoons curry powder, more if desired

salt and pepper to taste (for a nice variation, use white pepper)
8 slices white bread
2 cups shredded iceberg lettuce

In a medium bowl, mash the eggs, mayonnaise, and curry powder together. Season
with salt and pepper to taste.

Spread the egg mixture over half of the
bread slices. Top with a small amount of
lettuce on each sandwich and then the
remaining bread slices. Cut the crusts from
the bread. Cut each sandwich into four
triangles.

SUN-DRIED TOMATO BASIL TEA SANDWICHES

From Katie:

Herb butters can be fun. They can be a part of an elegant menu, or they can be an easy way to give an ordinary dinner a little zest. By the way, they keep extraordinarily well. You can use all sorts of fresh herbs like rosemary, parsley, and tarragon. They will keep in the refrigerator for up to two months and in the freezer — yes, the freezer — for up to six months. Because of the garlic in this recipe, cover tightly in your refrigerator.

(Makes 12 full sandwiches or 24–48 triangles)

4 ounces softened cream cheese
1/3 cup finely chopped sun-dried tomatoes
   in oil, drained

2 tablespoons shredded cheddar cheese
2 tablespoons shredded Parmesan cheese
Dash of salt and pepper
1/2 cup of basil butter, softened (recipe
  below)
12 slices bread (you may choose the flavor)

In a large bowl, mix the cream cheese, sun-dried tomatoes, cheddar cheese, Parmesan cheese, and a dash of salt and pepper.

Spread the basil butter onto six of the bread slices. Top with the cheese and tomato mixture. Place the remaining slices of bread on top. Carefully cut off crusts and cut into desired shapes.

Basil Butter
(Yield: 1/2 cup +)

1/4 cup basil leaves
3 cloves garlic
1 tablespoon lemon juice
1 teaspoon salt
pinch of sugar
1/2 cup butter, softened

In a food processor, grind the basil and garlic. Add the lemon juice, salt, and sugar. Pulse to mix. Add the butter into the food processor and blend until smooth.

PEAR AND CHEESE TEA SANDWICHES

From Jenna:

The combination of goat cheese and pears really appeals to me. I would imagine you could use any cheese you'd like. Blue cheese might be nice. Now, there are times I really like nuts and times I don't, so again, you decide. With or without? They do add a nice crunch.

(Makes 8 sandwiches or 16–32 triangles)

4 ounces of crumbled goat cheese, softened to room temperature
2 red Bartlett or Bosc pears, core and seeds removed, diced
1/2 cup watercress, chopped
1/4 cup pecans, chopped (or nuts of your choice, if desired)

4 tablespoons honey
16 slices of white bread

In a small bowl, mix the goat cheese and pears. Add the watercress, pecans (or nuts of your choice) and honey. Spread the mixture on 8 slices of bread. Top the sandwiches with the remaining slices of bread. Carefully remove crusts and cut the sandwiches into desired shapes.

If you're not a goat cheese fan, try blue cheese.

MASCARPONE STILTON CHEESE APPETIZER

From Pepper:

I don't honestly know what to say about this recipe. Everyone seems to like it. It's colorful and savory, and mascarpone is simply the easiest cheese in the world to mold. Put on music while you're cooking and sing along. It makes the chore more fun.

(Serves 12–16)

2 tablespoons honey
1 pound mascarpone cheese (room temperature is key)
8 ounces Stilton cheese, crumbled
1/2 cup pecan pieces, or any nut you choose
1/2 cup Craisins (cranberry raisins)

In a large bowl, stir the honey into the mascarpone.

In a very small bowl-shaped dish (cereal bowl size), spray the sides with cooking oil. Line the bowl with plastic wrap covering all sides. Be sure to push the plastic wrap flat. Spray again with cooking spray or baste lightly with oil. Spread the sides and bottom of the wrap with the mascarpone mixture, about 1/4 inch thick.

Cut Stilton into slices about 1/4 inch thick and line the mascarpone mixture with slices. Then layer the mascarpone and the Stilton, one after the other, until you reach the top. Final layer should be mascarpone. Tightly seal with plastic wrap.

Refrigerate for a few hours until the mascarpone is firm. To serve, remove the plastic wrap, tip the bowl onto a serving plate, and remove the plastic wrap liner. Press crushed pecans or any nut you choose on the sides. Decorate with Craisins.

Serve with your favorite crackers.

SAVORY CHEDDAR SCONES

From Katie:

These little scones are so easy to make. The white pepper gives them a real punch. They're a perfect addition to any tea or breakfast. If you don't have buttermilk on hand, you can create it by mixing 2/3 cup milk (less one tablespoon) plus 1 tablespoon vinegar. Let that mixture stand for about five minutes before using.

(Makes 8)

2-1/2 cups flour
2 tablespoons granulated sugar
1 tablespoon baking powder
1 teaspoon salt
1/4 teaspoon white pepper
1/2 cup butter, cut into small pieces
3 large eggs (2 for the recipe, one for the

egg wash)

2/3 cup buttermilk

2/3 cup sharp cheddar cheese, grated

1/4 cup chopped chives

Preheat oven to 375 degrees F. Prepare a baking sheet with parchment paper.

In a large bowl or food processor, whisk together the flour, sugar, baking powder, salt, and white pepper. Cut in the butter. The mixture should be the texture of coarse cornmeal.

In a small bowl, whisk 2 eggs with the buttermilk. Add to the flour mixture and stir (or pulse) until just combined.

Stir (or pulse) in the cheddar and chives.

Turn the dough — it will be sticky — onto a well-floured board. Knead gently. Divide the dough and roll each into a circle about 3/4 inch thick. Set the scones on the prepared baking sheet, and cut each circle into 4 triangles. You might have to moisten your knife between cuts.

In a small bowl, whisk the remaining egg. Brush the egg on top of the scones.

Bake the scones for 20 minutes until golden.
Remove from oven and serve warm.

Raita Appetizer

From Jenna:

Aunt Vera gave this recipe to me. It is so tasty and so easy that, yes, even I can make it. Honestly, I'm becoming a pretty good cook. Working alongside Rhett has given me tremendous confidence. I can't wait to see what the future may bring.

(Serves 6–8)

1/2 cucumber, grated or finely chopped (I prefer using English cucumbers)
1 5-ounce container plain Greek yogurt
1 large handful mint leaves = about 1/4 cup chopped
pinch of salt
2 tablespoons green chiles, finely chopped
pita triangles

Remove the core of seeds from the cucumber. Then grate or finely chop. Wrap the grated or finely chopped cucumber in a paper towel and squeeze out any excess water.

In a small bowl, mix together the cucumber, yogurt, mint leaves, salt, and green chiles.

Put mixture into a pretty bowl and serve chilled as an appetizer with pita triangles.

WHITEFISH TEA SANDWICHES

From Lola:

My restaurant is known for making hearty meals as well as fish and chips and fish taco sandwiches. But when I dine, I like to eat lightly. This sandwich fits the bill. As I told Jenna, it would be a great addition to an all-white wedding menu. For a high tea, it would be simply elegant.

1 pound smoked whitefish fillet
1/2 cup mayonnaise, plus more for garnish
2 tablespoons freshly squeezed lemon juice,
   1 whole lemon
pinch freshly ground white pepper
3/4 cup celery, finely diced
24 thin slices white sandwich bread

In a food processor, mix fish, mayonnaise, lemon juice, and white pepper until smooth.

Turn the mixture into a bowl and stir in half of the celery. Cover and refrigerate.

Just before serving, make the sandwiches. Lay out the bread and top 12 slices with 1/4 cup of the salad. Place a slice of bread on top of the salad. Trim the crusts and cut into triangles. If desired, press remaining diced celery against the ends of the sandwiches. To hold it in place, use extra mayonnaise.

Set the sandwiches on a tray and cover with plastic wrap until ready to serve.

ABOUT THE AUTHOR

Daryl Wood Gerber is the Agatha Award–winning, nationally bestselling author of the French Bistro Mysteries, featuring a bistro owner in Napa Valley, as well as the Cookbook Nook Mysteries, featuring an admitted foodie and owner of a cookbook store in Crystal Cove, California. Under the pen name Avery Aames, Daryl writes the Cheese Shop Mysteries, featuring a cheese shop owner in Providence, Ohio.

As a girl, Daryl considered becoming a writer, but she was dissuaded by a seventh-grade teacher. It wasn't until she was in her twenties that she had the temerity to try her hand at writing again . . . for TV and screen. Why? Because she was an actress in Hollywood. A fun tidbit for mystery buffs: Daryl co-starred on *Murder, She Wrote* as well as other TV shows. As a writer, she created the format for the popular sitcom *Out of This World.* When she moved across the country with her husband, she returned to writing what she loved to read: mysteries and thrillers.

Daryl is originally from the Bay Area and graduated from Stanford University. She loves to cook, read, golf, swim, and garden. She also likes adventure and has been known to jump out of a perfectly good airplane. Here are a few of Daryl's lifelong mottos: perseverance will out; believe you can; never give up. She hopes they will become yours, as well.

To learn more about Daryl and her books, visit her website at DarylWoodGerber.com.

The employees of Thorndike Press hope you have enjoyed this Large Print book. All our Thorndike, Wheeler, and Kennebec Large Print titles are designed for easy reading, and all our books are made to last. Other Thorndike Press Large Print books are available at your library, through selected bookstores, or directly from us.

For information about titles, please call:
(800) 223-1244

or visit our website at:
gale.com/thorndike

To share your comments, please write:
Publisher
Thorndike Press
10 Water St., Suite 310
Waterville, ME 04901

CPSIA information can be obtained
at www.ICGtesting.com
Printed in the USA
BVHW072140190821
614825BV00004B/5